Breakfast
in Bed

Breakfast in Bed

ROCHELLE ALERS

KENSINGTON PUBLISHING CORP.
www.kensingtonbooks.com

DAFINA BOOKS are published by

Kensington Publishing Corp.
119 West 40th Street
New York, NY 10018

All Kensington Titles, Imprints, and Distributed Lines are available at special quantity discounts for bulk purchases for sales promotions, premiums, fund-raising, and educational or institutional use. Special book excerpts or customized printings can also be created to fit specific needs. For details, write or phone the office of the Kensington special sales manager: Kensington Publishing Corp., 119 West 40th Street, New York, NY 10018, attn: Special Sales Department, Phone: 1-800-221-2647.

Dafina and the Dafina logo Reg. U.S. Pat. & TM Off.

ISBN-13: 978-1-4967-2573-8
ISBN-10: 1-4967-2573-5
First Kensington Trade Paperback Edition: September 2017
First Kensington Mass Market Edition: October 2020

ISBN-13: 978-1-4967-0773-8 (ebook)
ISBN-10: 1-4967-0773-8 (ebook)

10 9 8 7 6 5 4 3 2 1

Printed in the United States of America

"Come, eat my food and drink the wine I have mixed.
Leave your simple ways and you will live; walk in
the way of insight."
—Proverbs 9:5-6

Chapter 1

Sprawled on a chintz-covered recliner in the sitting area in one of DuPont House's suites, Tonya Martin crossed her bare feet at the ankles, while her friends claimed matching chairs with cushioned footstools. She had spent the past half hour talking to them when she should have retired for bed.

Earlier that morning, Tonya, Jasmine Washington, and Nydia Santiago had flown into the Louis Armstrong New Orleans International Airport and then crowded into a taxi for the drive to the Garden District. They had come to New Orleans for Hannah DuPont-Lowell's wedding to college professor St. John McNair. Boarding the same aircraft with her friends helped Tonya to overcome some of her anxiety about flying. Her fear had come from a return flight to the States from France during which the jet's landing gear failed and the pilot was forced to make an emergency landing at New York's JFK airport. Several hundred passengers and crew used the chute to exit the aircraft, and Tonya wound up with a severely sprained ankle that kept her off her feet for several weeks.

Fortunately, the mid-October weather was much more tolerable than it had been during her first visit to the Big Easy. Then the late-June record-high New Orleans temperatures and humidity had sapped all of her energy. At that time Hannah outlined her intent to transform her historic ancestral home into an inn and convert the two guesthouses on the estate into a café and supper club. The corporate attorney wanted Tonya to invest in the venture, while offering her a twenty-five percent share in the new business as the executive chef.

"I still can't believe you're going to move down here."

Tonya stared at Nydia for several seconds, and then a hint of a smile tilted the corners of her generous mouth. When she worked as assistant chef for Wakefield Hamilton, a private international investment bank, she was familiar with all personnel on sight or by name, but it was not until she and dozens of other employees were unexpectedly let go, with generous severance packages, after the bank merged with another institution and she, Jasmine, the assistant director of personnel, and accountant Nydia spent several hours at Hannah's high-rise apartment that the four bonded over omelets and brunch cocktails. They had talked for hours about what they wanted for their futures, and once Tonya revealed she was going to wait until after Labor Day to look for another position, the others also agreed to do the same.

"I also can't believe it," Tonya said. "In less than four months I'll become a Louisianan and I'll eventually run my own restaurant for the first time in my life."

Nydia ran her fingers through the wealth of thick, black, shiny curls falling over her forehead as a smile crinkled the skin around her large hazel eyes. "I believe everyone should work for themselves at least once on their lives."

Jasmine nodded. The former interior designer turned human resource specialist attempted to lift her arched eyebrows. The masque on her face was drying and beginning to crack, which meant it was time for her to remove it. "I hear you, Nydia. I do miss running my own shop."

Twin dimples appeared in Tonya's cheeks as she pursed her lips. "What's stopping you?" she asked Jasmine. "Even if you don't want to go back to interior decorating, you can take Hannah up on her offer to help her run the inn."

Jasmine twisted several strands of hair around her forefinger. "It sounds tempting, but I'm not ready to leave New York. Everyone and everything I have is there. And as my parents' only child, I want to be there for them, even though they are still active. They belong to a bowling league and are very involved in their church."

"Are they retired?" Nydia asked.

"Yes. My father was a high school principal, and my mother a trauma nurse."

Tonya crossed her arms under her breasts. "Would they be opposed to moving down here with you?"

A beat passed before Jasmine said, "I don't know. They would have to sell their house, while I would have to find a buyer for my condo."

Nydia made a sucking sound with her tongue and teeth. "I've seen your condo and trust me, my friend, you wouldn't have a problem unloading it. I've saved enough money for a down payment, but there's no way I'm going to purchase property when my boyfriend can't come up with at least half."

Tonya frowned. "I thought you'd stopped seeing him."

A slight blush darkened Nydia's gold-brown complexion. "We still talk."

Tonya's frown deepened. "Are you talking or sleeping together?"

Nydia managed to look contrite. "Both."

Jasmine narrowed her eyes. "Didn't you promise us you would get rid of the bum? Don't be like me, *mija*. I know as a woman you have physical needs, but you can't let that cloud your judgment when it comes to letting a man use you, even if it's only for sex. He will keep coming back, talking out the side of his mouth, because he knows you better than you know yourself."

"Why do you sound like such a man hater, Jasmine?" Nydia asked.

Jasmine recoiled as if she had been jabbed with a sharp object. "Is that what you think? That I'm a man hater because of my lying, cheating-ass ex-husband?"

"What else could it be?" Nydia countered.

Tonya knew it was time to intervene before the two women said something they would later regret. Their friendship was still too new and much too fragile to withstand a barrage of verbal insults. "Calm down, Nydia. Jasmine is trying to look out for you because she doesn't want you to go through what she experienced with a man she loved and trusted. I know nothing about your boyfriend other than what you've told us, but if you were my daughter I'd tell you what I said the last time we were here. Get rid of him and block his number. You'll never be able move on until you do. I'm going to ask you one question, and then this topic of conversation is over. Do you love him enough to want to spend the rest of your life with him?"

The seconds stretched into a long silence, and then Nydia said, "I don't think so."

"If that's the case, then kick his sorry ass to the curb," Jasmine whispered.

Raising her arms above her head, Nydia exhaled an audible breath. "Maybe I need to get out and find someone else."

Jasmine shook her head. "I wouldn't recommend that. Take some time to find out who you are, what you really want in life *and* in a man; otherwise you'll end up in the same situation just because you don't want to be alone."

Tonya nodded. "Jasmine's right."

Nydia appeared deep in thought. "Tonya, how long have you been divorced?"

"Sixteen years. Samara was five when I left my husband. I just couldn't take his wanting to control my life."

"How long were you married?" Nydia asked her.

"Fourteen years. I'd just completed my second year in college when I discovered I was pregnant. Samuel and I married right away because his father never married his mother, and he always resented that. I was four months along when I lost the baby. I went back to college at night and worked at a day care center during the day, while all Samuel talked about was trying for another baby. I wanted to finish college, but that didn't happen when I got pregnant again. I miscarried again. He blamed me for not taking care of myself, and for trying to do too much.

"We compromised when I dropped out of school and became a housewife. We moved out of our one-bedroom apartment in the Bronx to Brooklyn and rented an apartment in his aunt and uncle's brownstone. He was a subway motorman and earning enough so I could afford to stay home. I was twenty-eight when I got pregnant again. The doctor put me on complete bed rest, and nine months later I gave birth to my daughter. That's when everything changed. Samuel became even more possessive and controlling. He had his aunt and uncle watching me constantly, and I had to report to him when I left and where I was going. After a while I decided I'd had enough."

With wide eyes, Jasmine stared at her. "He let you leave?"

A wry smile twisted Tonya's mouth. "It wasn't about his *letting* me. I waited until he'd left for work, then called my brother and told him to come to my apartment. I'd packed all of Samara's clothes, and just enough for myself, and my brother drove me to my parents' house in Queens."

Nydia leaned forward. "Did he come after you?"

"No. He was afraid of my brother, who belonged to a gang dealing drugs and had no problem shooting folks who got in their way. My brother hadn't come alone. He brought his boys. One had a sawed-off shotgun and the other one carried an automatic." She bit back a smile when seeing expressions of shock and horror on Nydia and Jasmine's faces.

"What happened to your brother?" Jasmine asked.

She felt a cold shiver snake its way up her back when she recalled having to identify her brother's body. "He OD'd on drugs." A beat passed. "Fast-forward. My mother worked nights, and when it came time for Samara to go to school, my mother looked after her while I finished college." Tonya closed her eyes as she struggled to keep her emotions in check. "The hardest thing I ever had to do was leave my daughter when I moved to Providence, Rhode Island, to attend Johnson and Wales College of Culinary Arts. Initially, I'd enrolled in the two-year program leading to the associate in science degree. Then when I realized I wanted to run my own business, I knew I would have to get a BS in business studies."

Jasmine pressed her palms together. "Well, Miss Lady, the sacrifice has been well worth it, because you're on your way to opening a restaurant. And Samara doesn't appear to be negatively affected by what you had to go through to secure her future."

Tonya had to agree with Jasmine. She and Samara had talked about Tonya having to leave her with her grandparents for extended periods of time, and her daughter always managed to assuage her guilt by saying she did what she had to do to save them both. Her daughter had grown up with a mother and two grandparents who had given her everything she needed for a happy childhood: love and protection.

Nydia shifted into a more comfortable position. "I still feel bad about telling Hannah that we would sleep with St. John after she'd broken up with him."

"It worked, didn't it?" Jasmine said, laughing.

"Yes, it did," Tonya agreed. "If we hadn't hit her over the head with the tough love, then we wouldn't be here to witness her marrying one of the finest brothers in New Orleans." St. John had proposed marriage and then admitted that he had been unfaithful to his wife, and that was when Hannah broke it off with him, because of her own late husband's infidelity.

"We still don't know why he cheated on his wife, but Hannah has to be okay with it, because in two days she'll no longer be DuPont-Lowell, but Hannah McNair," Jasmine said. "I'm really jealous of her because she's going to marry a man who started out as her best friend."

"Remember," Tonya reminded Jasmine, "it took her more than forty years to realize she'd always been in love with him."

Resting the back of her hand to her forehead, Nydia pantomimed swooning. "It's just like in the romance novels. She found her happily ever after with a man with a hero's name. If only I can get my boyfriend to act more like a hero."

Tonya slipped off the recliner. "Enough talk about heroes, heroines, and romance novels. Will y'all please leave my room so I can get some sleep? I don't need to stand up as Hannah's maid of honor with bags under my eyes." What she really wanted to say is that she was tired of Nydia complaining about her no-account boyfriend. What the beautiful accountant had not realized was that she could have the pick of any man from any racial or ethnic group, who would treat her with more respect than the man now using her for his own selfish motives.

She understood young love, because she had been there and done that, but what she refused to understand was stupidity, expressly if it was staring her in the face. But, then denial was almost as difficult to admit as blame was to accept. "Remember, Nydia, what I told you about possibly renting my apartment. I have the option of renewing my lease for one or two years. I know you don't need two bedrooms, but why don't you come by and look at it and see for yourself. Perhaps you can use the smaller bedroom for a home office."

Nydia nodded. "Jazz and I aren't leaving until Sunday night, and I know you're not going back home until Wednesday. I'll call you Thursday, and we can set up a time to get together."

Tonya had decided to delay her return to New York because she still needed to go over things with Hannah, who had mentioned she and St. John weren't taking a honeymoon until the end of the fall semester. Then they planned to fly to the South Pacific and tour several islands. "If you decide to take it, then I'll renew it under my name and inform the management office that I'll be doing a lot of traveling and my niece will be staying in the apartment with me."

"Okay, Titi Tonya," Nydia teased, grinning.

Jasmine grimaced, and the masque looked like tiny shards of broken glass. "What are you going to do with your furniture if and when you finally give up your apartment?"

"I'm going to ship everything to Atlanta for storage. My daughter plans to rent an apartment or house once she graduates, and not having to buy furniture will save her a lot of money."

"Lucky girl," Jasmine intoned.

Tonya had saved and sacrificed taking vacations in order to pay her daughter's tuition and room and board so that Samara wouldn't be burdened with student loans once she graduated. She told Samara that she had done her part in underwriting the cost of her undergraduate education, and she was on her own for any advanced degrees she wanted to pursue.

Waiting until the two left her room and closed the door, Tonya turned off the lamp on the bedside table, slipped into bed, pulled the sheet and lightweight blanket up over her shoulders. Fortunately, she did not have man problems, and it was probably the reason she continued to date Darius Williams. Whenever he called asking to see her, he never exhibited any hostility when she said she needed to spend time alone. The one time he mentioned marriage, Tonya was emphatic when she told him she didn't want to marry again; she enjoyed her single status and the freedom of living her life by her own set of rules.

And if she married Darius, she knew she would not be able to pick up and move to New Orleans, because her husband never would agree to leave his family-owned auto body repair shop. Getting laid off and Hannah asking her to invest in the future of the DuPont Inn had come at the right time in her life.

Tonya realized she was not so much anti-marriage as she was overly cautious when it came to the type of man she wanted in her life, because it wasn't until years after she married her high school sweetheart that she saw another side to his personality. It was subtle at first, but Samuel Alexander turned from a jovial, laid-back, affectionate man into a suspicious, controlling monster. It became a battle of wills—she wanting to go to cooking school, while he wanted her home with their young daughter. Even when she suggested her parents were willing to look after Samara until she completed her studies, he would fly into a rage, accusing her of being a bad mother.

Six months after her divorce was finalized, she enrolled in Johnson and Wales University College of Culinary Arts with the intent to eventually own and operate her own restaurant. She worked hard, studied even harder to graduate, and it paid off when she secured her first position as a sous chef at an Upper East Side restaurant boasting an elite clientele ranging from A-list movie stars to captains of industry and international businessmen.

Tonya had been employed for a year when the IRS placed a lien on the restaurant because the owner failed to pay millions in back taxes, and she found herself looking for employment elsewhere. Wishing to diversify her skills, she left her young daughter in the care of her parents once again, and this time she flew to Europe and Asia to take a series of cooking courses. Tonya found her niche in France when she traveled throughout the country perfecting regional dishes. Cooking had become an addiction—one she never wanted to give up.

Now she planned to invest in a new venture, which would afford her total autonomy and a share in the profits of the DuPont Inn. It also meant she would have to relocate, but that did not pose much of a problem, because there wasn't anything binding her to New York. Her daughter, who had begun her senior year at Spelman College, elected to live off campus in an apartment with a roommate, while hinting she had planned to make Atlanta her permanent home once she pursued graduate studies at Georgia State University.

Transitioning from living in New York to New Orleans was certain to go smoothly for Tonya. Her parents had settled into a gated retirement community in Florida, and the timing was right because her apartment lease was due to expire at the end of January. Hannah suggested she live in one of the guesthouses until renovations to the main house were completed. Then she would move into one of the first floor bedroom suites.

Earlier in the year she had celebrated a milestone birthday, and at fifty she decided it was time to change her life. She cut her shoulder-length dreadlocks, joined a sports club to work out, took yoga lessons, and scheduled a standing monthly appointment for a facial and full-body massage. The result was a twenty-five-pound weight loss; not only did she look younger, but also felt better than she had in years. The week before, she had cut her hair again—this time into a short, curly style that showed off her face to its best advantage and was perfect for the warmer Louisiana climate.

She sighed softly. In two days she would be a bridesmaid when her friend married a man whom she had not known she loved when both were in high school. It had taken Hannah forty years to openly express to St. John that she had always loved him, and just seeing the way they looked at each other, Tonya knew they were meant for each other.

Although Tonya professed not to want to marry again, she was realistic enough to know there were some forces she was unable to predict or control. Her breathing deepened, and after a while all thoughts of men and marriage faded as she finally fell asleep.

Chapter 2

Tonya stared at her reflection in the mirror and smiled. It had been a long time since she'd had her face made up by a professional. The esthetician did an incredible job of accentuating her eyes with smoky shadows and several coats of mascara. The orange lipstick matched her gown and complemented the orange undertones in her brown complexion.

Hannah had secretly made appointments for her cousins, LeAnn and Paige DuPont, and her bridal attendants to undergo a complete beauty makeover. Teams of hairstylists, makeup artists, and masseurs had descended on DuPont at exactly ten o'clock that morning and supplied their services in second story bedroom suites.

When Hannah made plans for her wedding, she insisted it would be small and intimate, declaring she wanted none of the pomp and pageantry of her first wedding, to the son of an influential Baton Rouge family. She and St. John agreed to limit the number of guests to fewer than fifty, which included family, close friends, and his colleagues. Hannah joked that if she had not chosen her former coworkers to stand in as her attendants, the Toussaints and Baptistes would've outnumbered the DuPonts ten to one. The afternoon ceremony was scheduled to take place at four o'clock in the estate's garden, followed with a cocktail hour, and then a sit-down dinner promptly at six in the mansion's ballroom.

Tonya's beauty regimen began with the expert ministrations of the masseur lulling her into a state of utter and complete relaxation. After a light lunch of a green salad, sliced melon, and fruit-flavored sparkling water, the stylist had cut her hair in a becoming style before directing her to the adjoining bathroom to shower and wash her hair with a thick avocado-based shampoo, followed by a Moroccan argan oil leave-in conditioner.

The esthetician completed her makeup by midafternoon, and once the stylist brushed her hair into a sophisticated style, Tonya could not stop staring at her image in the mirror. The talented woman had tapered the sides and back, and brushed lightly graying curls off her face. All of her life Tonya had attempted to tame her curly hair with chemical relaxers, flatirons, and large rollers, followed by sitting under a hair dryer, but the strands seemed to have a mind of their own, and they either curled tightly in the rain or frizzed in high humidity. Exasperated, she decided not to cut her hair; instead she wore twists, which she washed and re-twisted every weekend. Once they were shoulder-length, she fashioned them into a bun at the nape of her neck.

The stylist brushed a few wayward strands into place. "Do you like it?"

Tonya turned and smiled at the stylist, who had spiky black hair and light-blue eyes and a pale complexion that indicated she was not a sun worshipper. "I love it."

Callie smiled. "You have wonderful wash-and-wear hair. If you keep it this length, then you shouldn't have a problem managing it." She reached into the pocket of her smock and handed Tonya a business card. "Try to come by the salon every four to six weeks for a trim."

Tonya stared at the card and noted the address. The salon was located in the Lower Garden District. "Do I have to call to make an appointment?"

"Our shop is always crazy busy, so call me on my cell. The number is on the back of the card. Let me know when you want to come in, and I'll program you into the computer."

"I will. And thank you."

Waiting until Callie walked out, Tonya slipped the orange silk duchesse satin gown off the padded hanger and stepped into it. She eased it up over her hips and adjusted the spaghetti straps over her shoulders. When Hannah mentioned she was having a fall wedding and wanted orange as a dominant color, Tonya, Nydia, and Jasmine met at a Madison Avenue bridal boutique and after several hours selected dresses in the same color, which flattered their complexions. They had chosen slip-style gowns with narrow straps crisscrossing bared backs.

Tonya selected a high-waisted A-line design with a low neckline, Nydia a wrap style with a bow accentuating her narrow waist, and Jasmine had chosen a gown with a squared neckline, drop waist, and fitted bodice with a

French lace overlay and beading. After adjusting her gown, Tonya slipped her bare feet into a pair of silk-covered, four-inch pumps in variegated shades of yellows, reds, oranges, and browns.

Peering closely into the mirror, Tonya studied her face. She had been blessed with skin that was as close to perfect as any woman would want. It was neither too dry nor too oily, and it lacked discolorations. The makeup artist had blended foundations and powder until they were an exact match for a complexion she likened to henna. It was not often she wore makeup, given her profession, but there was something about the eyeshadow, russet-hued blush on her cheekbones, and the terra cotta color on her lips that made her feel ultra-feminine. And it had been much too long since she had felt that way. The last time was when she spent the year in Europe. Men, regardless of their ages, shamelessly flirted with her. Some were bold enough to approach her, saying they liked her face or hair, and others her voluptuous body. Even with the weight loss she still thought of her figure as curvaceous.

Three taps on the bedroom door garnered her attention. Turning on her heel, she walked over and opened it. Coiffed and resplendent in her gown, Jasmine flashed a Cheshire cat grin. "Wow! You look stunning."

"It's the makeup."

Jasmine swept into the suite with the aplomb of a runway model. Her black, silky hair was brushed off her face and secured with crystal hairpins behind her right ear. Charcoal-gray shadow on her lids accentuated her almond-shaped eyes, while the gown's burnt-orange color complemented the tawny undertones in her khaki-brown complexion.

"It's more than makeup, Tonya. I don't know why you

downplay your looks, but you're definitely the total package. No one would ever believe you're fifty."

She wanted to tell Jasmine that she had worked hard to get into shape, and worked even harder to stay in shape. Tonya knew one of the first things she needed to do after moving to New Orleans was find a health club where she could work out. Although she and Jasmine were the same height and weight—five-five, one hundred thirty pounds—the younger woman had retained the slimness of someone half her age.

She opened her mouth to inform Jasmine that fifty was nothing more than a number, when Nydia and Hannah entered the suite. Smiling, Hannah held her arms out at her sides. The tall, green-eyed, natural blonde was stunning in a platinum gown with a flowing skirt and empire-waist of beaded silk crepe and georgette. Orange blossoms were pinned into the elegant chignon on the nape of her long neck.

"How do I look?"

"Beautiful," Nydia crooned. "St. John is a lucky man."

Resting her right hand over her throat, Hannah closed her eyes for several seconds. "I'm a lucky woman," she countered. "I still can't believe that I'm going to marry a man I've loved from afar all my life. And it never would've happened if it hadn't been for you guys. You're the sisters I've always wanted."

Nydia blinked back tears. "Stop it, Hannah, before I start crying and can't stop. And let me warn you that I don't cry pretty."

Tonya approached Hannah and grasped her hands, her gaze fixed on the dazzling cushion-cut emerald surrounded with brilliant blue-white diamonds on her right hand. "Please don't get teary, Hannah. Not today. I've always said I didn't want to marry again, but if I found someone like your St. John, I'd marry him faster than a cat could flick its tail."

Jasmine moved closer. "I thought you said you'd never marry again."

Tonya gave her a long, penetrating stare. "I said I *didn't want to marry again*, not that I'd never. You're the one who said you never wanted to get married again."

Lowering her eyes, Jasmine stared at the toes of her pumps, which matched those of the other attendants. "You're right."

Nydia joined the others, reaching for Jasmine's and Hannah's hands. The others followed suit as they formed a circle. "I want to give thanks for my friends who always keep it real."

"Amen," the other three chorused.

"Mom, everyone's waiting for you."

Tonya stared at Wyatt Lowell standing in the hallway outside the suite. Hannah had asked her son to give her away in marriage. When he had arrived at DuPont House for the rehearsal and the dinner that followed, she noticed many of the women in attendance staring at him. Tall, dark-haired, and deeply tanned, the pilot, wearing a tailored tuxedo, looked as if he'd just stepped off the pages of *GQ*. Hannah had spoken proudly of her son, who'd graduated from the U.S. Air Force Academy and become a test pilot. After fulfilling his commitment to the military, he went on to fly commercial jets for a major airline carrier.

Tonya noticed he was extremely attentive to his attractive stay-at-home wife and two young sons, wondering if he felt guilty about having to leave his family for extended periods of time when he was reassigned to international routes on which he flew to many Asian countries.

Hannah inhaled, and then slowly let out her breath. "I'm ready."

Lifting the hem of Hannah's skirt, Tonya, Jasmine, and Nydia followed Hannah and Wyatt along the hallway to the rear of the house. They descended the staircase to a door opening out onto the path leading to the meticulously maintained garden.

The weather had decided to cooperate. Although warm, the humidity wasn't oppressive, and there was a hint of a breeze blowing in off the waterways surrounding the city. Hannah had insisted on simplicity, refusing to wear a veil or carry a bouquet of flowers. The only allowance for flowers were the ones in her hair and the orange blossom boutonnieres worn by St. John; Daniel McNair, St. John's father and best man; his cousin Eustace Toussaint; and brother-in-law Kenneth Vernon.

Two large white tents were set up in the garden; chairs covered in white organza and tied with orange satin ribbons were set up theater-style under one, and round tables with folding chairs and several long tables with chafing dishes under another, while dozens of burning citronella candles kept insects away. The mouthwatering aromas wafting in the air reminded Tonya that she needed more than a green salad and melon for her to sustain her energy.

She still could not wrap her head around the fact that within three months she would move from New York to put down roots in a suburb of New Orleans. She would leave behind the sound of car horns and the incessant wailing from emergency vehicles around the clock. And instead of crowding into a subway car like sardines in a tin can to reach her job, she would walk less than a hundred feet to guesthouses that would be configured into a café for a buffet breakfast for the inn's guests and a supper club for the general public.

At exactly four o'clock, the wedding planner ushered everyone into their places as the string quartet playing concertos segued into the Anita Baker classic hit "Just Because." The song was also one of Tonya's favorites. She was moved by the heartfelt lyrics—"*I love you because you're you*"—and it was obvious to Tonya just looking at Hannah and St. John, they truly did love each other because of who they were.

There had been a time when she believed she and Samuel were going to spend their entire lives together, but unfortunately it was not to be. If only he had allowed her to follow her dream, she knew they still would be married. The most difficult decision she had had to make was depriving Samara of growing up with her father, because Samuel had not grown up with his. She agreed to allow Samuel visitation, but after two years he stopped coming to see his daughter. He had married again and become the father of twin boys. For him, Samara was out of sight and out of mind.

A videographer and photographer took their positions and captured every action and image for posterity. Tonya smiled at St. John's father as he offered her his arm. The former New Orleans police officer looked incredibly elegant in formal wear. The skin around his light-brown eyes crinkled when he returned her smile with a gentle one of his own. When she met Daniel McNair for the first time, she never would have guessed that he had recently celebrated his eightieth birthday.

They processed slowly down the flagstone path, which was strewn with white rose petals, stopping several feet from the pergola of climbing white roses where the black-robed officiant waited to begin the ceremony. Her smile grew wider when she saw Daniel exchange a fist-bump with St. John as father and son stood next to each other. Jasmine followed, escorted by Eustace, and then Nydia with Kenneth.

The garden at DuPont House was the perfect setting for an afternoon autumn wedding. There was no deck, patio, porch, or terrace separating the house from the garden, and the flagstone path reminded Tonya of a carpet leading into a fairy tale–like, year-round Garden of Eden, with trees, mosses, grasses, and colorful flowers seemingly growing in wild abandon.

The day before, she lingered in the garden before the rehearsal and admired the variegated grasses, climbing ivy and roses, succulents, and arbor of fruit trees. Tucked away in an area where seeded ornamental grasses grew to a height of two feet were all-weather benches and chairs positioned just feet from a man-made waterfall filled with koi. Having the garden so close to the guesthouses would be convenient once she planted a vegetable and herb garden. As a chef, she knew freshly picked fruit, vegetables, and herbs were certain to enhance the flavors of any dish.

The quartet playing the familiar strains of the "*Wedding March*" shattered her musings. Tonya could not pull her eyes away from St. John's face when Wyatt led Hannah down the path, and he stood with his father. Nothing on him moved, not even his eyes. And it was not for the first time she felt that Hannah had been given a second chance at love with a man with whom she would spend the rest of her life. Hannah and St. John were the perfect pair. Both were tall, slender, and extremely attractive.

The first time Hannah introduced her to St. John, Tonya was taken aback by his good looks, intelligence, and sophistication. Rays of sunlight filtering through the ancient oak trees shrouded in Spanish moss illuminated St. John's deeply tanned tawny face and cropped silver hair. His neatly barbered mustache and goatee added character to his lean face. It was only when the minister asked who was giving the bride away in marriage that a hint of a smile tilted the corners of his mouth at the same time he extended his left hand to Hannah.

Even though Hannah had insisted on simplicity, there still was an atmosphere in the garden that reflected an ethereal elegance. All the groomsmen wore tuxedos, dress shirts with wing collars, and orange silk bowties, while St. John added an orange satin vest under his tuxedo jacket. Tonya felt moisture pricking the backs of her eyelids when Wyatt placed his mother's hand in St. John's outstretched one, the younger man kissing her hair.

At the rehearsal dinner Wyatt's ten-year-old son had asked Hannah that if she was their grandmother, then was St. John their grandfather? It had been Wyatt who told them yes, he was, because his father had died before his first son's second birthday. Both boys appeared overjoyed they now had two grandmothers and two grandfathers.

Time seemed to stand still as Hannah and St. John exchanged vows, followed by an exchange of bands. When the minister gave St. John permission to kiss his wife, those in attendance applauded and whistled as he kissed her and lifted her off her feet. Her face was nearly the color of the orange blossoms in her husband's boutonniere as they traversed the path amid a shower of flower petals. Tonya followed the newly married couple, her left hand cradled in the bend of Daniel's elbow.

Time seemed to go by in slow motion for Tonya as she posed for photographs with the wedding party, the bride and groom's parents, and family members before she and the other bridesmaids headed into the tent where the cocktail hour was winding down. She managed to nibble on bite-size morsels of cocktail corn cakes with spicy mango salsa, buckwheat blinis with sour cream and caviar, and deviled eggs with red caviar, while washing them down with a glass of bubbly rosé champagne. It was enough to stave off hunger until dinner. Lifting the hem of her gown, she filed into the house with the rest of the wedding party and into the ballroom where tables were set up banquet-style.

Light from a quartet of chandeliers shimmered off collections of heirloom table settings of bone-white china, delicate crystal stemware, and gleaming silver engraved with a bold D in Edwardian script. Tonya tried imagining women from a bygone era who once graced this same ballroom in one of the grandest houses in the Garden District, coquettish women peering over their lacy fans at fastidiously dressed suitors seeking to woo them as wives or mistresses. Hannah had related tales about the historic house, filled with priceless antiques, that had become the residence to generations of DuPonts, beginning with Etienne DuPont who left France for Haiti in the eighteenth century. He then traveled to the Louisiana Territory with his mixed-race mistress and their children to begin a legacy that continued to the present day.

Hannah had contracted with two catering companies for the cocktail hour and dinner. Guests were offered a choice of the traditional steak, chicken, and fish plates or the southern Louisiana regional Creole and Cajun dishes. Eustace, owner of the family's restaurant Chez Toussaints, exchanged his tuxedo jacket for a chef's coat and hat. He joked that he had the distinctive honor of being St. John's groomsman *and* the caterer for his cousin's wedding.

A member of the waitstaff directed Tonya to her seat at a table where she was flanked by two men. The man on her left introduced himself as Paul Lee, St. John's colleague. The exquisitely attired man on her right made her acquaintance as Cameron Singleton, the bride's investment banker. Hannah, who did not want a table for the bridal party, had instructed the planner to seat complete strangers next to each other. It allowed everyone to become acquainted with one another, while she and St. John were seated facing each other at opposite ends of the table.

"How long have you known Hannah?" Cameron Singleton asked Tonya.

She gave Cameron a sidelong glance. Everything about his deportment was a reminder of the wealthy Wakefield Hamilton clients seeking to invest their vast fortunes in American companies. They arrived in chauffeured-driven cars wearing haute couture and were greeted in their native tongues by multilingual employees and then escorted to the executive dining room for meals rivaling White House state dinners.

Cameron's clean-shaven, tanned face and classically handsome features radiated good health, while flecks of gray shimmered like gold in his thick, fashionably styled light-brown hair. It was when she met his steel-blue eyes that she felt slightly uncomfortable. It was as if there was no warmth behind the penetrating orbs.

"It's been about five years. We worked together in New York."

"Are you also an attorney?" he asked.

Smiling, Tonya shook her head. "No. I'm a chef."

Cameron's eyebrows lifted a fraction. "So, you're the one who will run the restaurant once Hannah converts this house into an inn?"

Her smile faded quickly. "You know about that?"

He smiled for the first time, the gesture softening his features and lighting up his luminous eyes as he inclined his head. "Yes. My family's firm has managed the DuPont fortune for at least eighty-five years. She came to me earlier this summer to solicit my advice about liquidating some of her investments to ensure the viability of the inn."

A hint of a smile played at the corners of Tonya's mouth. "So, you're the one who suggested she get investors."

Cameron's smile grew wider. "Guilty as charged."

"I'm glad you suggested it, because if you hadn't, then I doubt whether I'd ever plan to move down here." Their conversation was preempted when a waiter asked for their dining selections. Tonya chose traditional New Orleans dishes, while Cameron opted for prime rib.

"When are you moving?" he asked.

"I'm projecting early next year." She didn't tell Cameron she still had to discuss the legalese in the contract

Hannah had drawn up before presenting it to her own attorney for his perusal, and once approved she would then authorize her bank to electronically transfer the agreed-upon amount to Hannah's bank account.

"What about your friends?"

She noticed Cameron was staring directly at Jasmine, who was engrossed in conversation with a man who appeared obviously enthralled with her. Tonya knew by the direction of Cameron's attention that he too was interested in the interior designer turned human resource specialist.

"I don't know. You'd have to ask Hannah about Jasmine and Nydia."

Cameron blinked slowly at the same time a sardonic smile flitted over his firm mouth. "Oh, I will."

Tonya was slightly taken aback at his response, and within seconds she knew instinctually that if Cameron wanted something, then it was his intent to go after it. But she wanted to warn the seemingly arrogant moneyman that Jasmine was not one to fall for the charm he appeared to turn on and off with such precision that it had probably had taken him years to perfect. She transferred her attention to Paul, leaving Cameron to stare longingly at Jasmine.

Glasses were filled with sparkling water and different wines as the waitstaff moved silently and efficiently about the tables. The disc jockey, who had set up his equipment earlier that afternoon, decided on a playlist of Broadway show tunes. He adjusted the volume so the diners did not have to shout to one another.

Tonya had to admit the caterers had outdone themselves with selections ranging from prime rib, grilled lamb chops, and salmon, Cornish hens, flounder stuffed with crabmeat, and blackened tuna. The accompanying sides included red beans and rice, broiled asparagus parmigiana, dirty rice, baked black-eyed peas, and Creole eggplant gratin. Although she had eaten dishes from all over the world, Tonya discovered she had fallen in love with New Orleans cooking.

She had sampled gumbo and red beans and rice in different Creole-themed New York City restaurants, but they could not compare to what Eustace prepared, and if she planned to open a restaurant, then she knew she had to perfect the local cuisine in order to compete with the many other establishments in the city. Hannah had tentatively projected opening the DuPont Inn in time for Mardi Gras. The smaller guesthouse would be renovated into a café to provide a buffet breakfast for inn guests, while the projected date for the supper club's grand opening was scheduled for later that summer. By that time she knew she would be more than ready to offer international as well as familiar dishes.

Dinner was leisurely and interrupted several times with toasts to the bride and groom, who both stood up to acknowledge everyone. The mood changed, becoming livelier as the DJ switched his playlist to more upbeat tunes, while the waitstaff set up a number of round tables, each with seating for six for the reception. The invitation indicated dancing would follow dessert and coffee. Tonya knew she had eaten too much and prayed she would not encounter a wardrobe malfunction in which her breasts escaped the revealing décolletage. A silent voice had told her when she first tried on the gown that she was flirting with danger, but she ignored it because it made her feel feminine *and* sexy.

As soon as coffee was served, she sought out Eustace

in the kitchen that never ceased to overwhelm her with its size and functionality. When first introduced to the cook, Tonya thought she could have been looking at her twin brother, because they had the same reddish-brown complexion and dimpled cheeks. Father of three, grandfather of seven, standing several inches above six feet, Eustace had years ago forfeited the opportunity to play college football to join his father running Chez Toussaints.

Eustace crossed massive arms over his broad chest and smiled at Tonya. "Are you here to grade us like they do with restaurants in New York City?" he teased.

She smiled. "If I had to give you a grade, then it certainly would be an A, along with a Zagat rating. I just want you to know that you've outdone yourself tonight."

Eustace inclined his head. "Thank you, madam chef. How long are you going to be in town?"

"I'll be here until Wednesday afternoon."

"Why don't you come by the restaurant tomorrow and I'll show you some Toussaint secrets for some of our best-selling dishes."

Tonya went completely still. Cooks and chefs were notorious for not revealing the ingredients that went into their more popular dishes. "Okay," she said when she finally recovered her voice.

"I'm catering another party tomorrow afternoon, so I'll have my brother come by and pick you up—say around seven. I hope that's not too early for you."

"Of course not," she replied, much too quickly. If one of the most renowned cooks in the city was willing to reveal his family's secrets and wanted her there at midnight, then she would be ready and willing to agree to any time. "Thank you, Eustace."

He waved a large hand. "There's no need to thank me. If my cousin's wife is going to open a restaurant, then the chef that's going to run the restaurant can't embarrass the family."

Tonya nodded. It was apparent Eustace regarded Hannah as family now that she was married to St. John.

She returned to the ballroom. The banquet tables had been cleared, and the guests claimed seats at the round tables as bartenders were taking drink orders. Tonya had just claimed a chair at a table with St. John's sister, brother-in-law, and their children when the DJ announced the bride and groom were going to share their first dance as husband and wife. St. John had shed his jacket, while Hannah had changed her shoes. Tonya was as surprised as everyone when they assumed dance positions for the tango.

A roar of approval went up in the ballroom as they literally floated across the floor like professional dancers to Adele's "Sweetest Devotion." Hannah boasted that she had become St. John's dance partner over the summer. *They are perfect together*. The thought had entered Tonya's head unbidden. It had only taken seconds for her to acknowledge that Hannah had it all: a magnificent home, a brilliant, handsome new husband, and a new career as an innkeeper.

She exhaled an audible sigh and smiled. Never again would she be called into an office and told it was to become her last day. And knowing she would own and operate her own restaurant strengthened Tonya's resolve to make her own dream a reality.

Chapter 3

Gage Toussaint exhaled a groan at the same time he slowed the SUV to just under the city's speed limit. He was past tired. In fact, he was exhausted and had stopped short of cursing out his brother after Eustace left a voice mail message asking him to pick up Tonya Martin at DuPont House Sunday morning at seven in the blasted a.m.

Not only had he been up early Saturday morning helping Eustace prepare dishes for his cousin's wedding to Hannah DuPont, but he also played several sets later that night. He had left the restaurant and then rushed to Jazzes to rehearse several new numbers with the house band for a surprise birthday celebration that was to be held at the club. If the guest of honor had not been an old friend and an elected official, Gage would have looked for another horn player to take his place. After rehearsing, he had just enough time to return to his apartment, shower, and change before returning to the jazz club to set up for the party.

Gage felt old, completely drained, although at forty-six he would not have thought of himself as old. However, he knew for certain he had to decide whether he wanted to be a full-time chef, full-time musician, and/or high school music instructor, because he found it more and more difficult to combine two careers. If he joined Chez Toussaints full-time, then that meant he had to be at the restaurant at six in the morning to prepare for the lunchtime customers and fulfill ever increasing catering orders. That was nearly impossible when there were nights he did not leave Jazzes until just before dawn. Although he loved cooking, it still was not his passion. Music was.

He continued driving along a wide avenue lined on both sides with large, imposing homes with magnificent gardens that had given the neighborhood its name: the Garden District. DuPont House was a plantation-style house built in the late eighteenth century by free people of color when Louisiana was still a territory. Gage turned off through the open gates, maneuvered up the winding drive to the antebellum mansion, and stopped. He shut off the engine.

The figure of a woman rose from the shadows from where she sat on the porch. Gage had not realized he'd been holding his breath until she came closer. Galvanized into action, he got out. The first thing he noticed was her dimpled smile. Unconsciously a smile parted his lips as he mounted the stairs, his gaze fixed on her beautiful face. It was impossible for him to pinpoint her age because he did not see a single line or wrinkle in a face without a hint of makeup. The women who worked at Jazzes and some female patrons wore so much makeup he doubted whether he would recognize them without it. Everything about Tonya was refreshing, from her stylishly cut, short, lightly graying hair and bare face to her white camp blouse, navy-blue cropped slacks, and navy deck shoes.

He extended his hand. "I'm Gage Toussaint. My brother asked me to pick you up and take you to the restaurant."

She stared at his hand for several seconds before offering her own. "Tonya Martin. I hope your coming here so early didn't inconvenience you."

"Of course not," Gage said, much too quickly.

He had gotten home from the club at four, picked up the voice mail, and then set his smart phone to wake him at six. He lay sprawled on the recliner in the living room rather than go to bed because he did not want to oversleep. After a cold shower and a cup of strong, hot black coffee, he felt alert enough to drive.

Tonya reached for the leather tote on the rocker. "I'm ready whenever you are."

Cradling her elbow, Gage led her off the porch to the Audi, the subtle scent of her perfume wafting to his nostrils. He leaned in as she slid onto the passenger seat, wondering what it was about the woman his brother wanted to bring to Chez Toussaints that made him feel slightly off balance when he knew nothing about her other than her name.

He noticed she didn't wear any rings, but that was not an indication whether she was married or single. One thing he knew for certain was she had not grown up in the South. Within seconds of introducing herself, he recognized a Northern inflection in her voice. Gage took his seat behind the wheel and then secured his seatbelt. He punched the start-engine button, shifted into gear, and headed for Tremé.

Tonya glanced at Gage's profile in an attempt to see the resemblance between him and Eustace, but there was nothing in the younger man's appearance to indicate they were even remotely related. When Eustace said he would have his brother pick her up and bring her to his restaurant, she never would have expected him to be the man she recalled playing trumpet with the band at the jazz club she had visited during her first trip to New Orleans.

Nydia and Jasmine had remarked on his good looks, while she had merely stared, finding him breathtakingly attractive. Seeing Gage on stage was very different from sitting a few feet away from him. Large gray-green eyes framed by long black lashes, a palomino-gold complexion, and delicate features, cleft chin, and cropped straight black hair with flecks of gray made him drop-dead gorgeous. And to add to the total package was a rich baritone voice with a distinctive Southern drawl.

"When Eustace told me he would have his brother pick me up, I never would've thought it would be you," she said after a comfortable silence.

His right hand resting on the gearshift while he steered expertly with his left when he turned a corner, Gage smiled. "Why would you say that?"

"You don't resemble each other."

Gage smiled. "We're brothers from different mothers. Eustace's mother died when he was still an infant. Pop waited almost ten years before marrying again. And what do you mean you didn't think it would be me?"

Tonya stared at his profile, then moved downward, her gaze lingering on the tiny musical notes tattooed on his right forearm. She was not overly fond of tattoos and men wearing earrings but found the ink and the tiny hoops in his pierced lobes fitting for a musician. "I saw you playing at Jazzes."

Taking his eyes off the road, he gave her a quick glance. "When was that?"

"It was late June, when my friends and I came down to hang out with Hannah."

"How long were you here?"

She paused, counting the days. "We'd planned to stay two weeks, but it got so hot that we just stayed a week. I met Eustace for the first time when I volunteered to help him at your family's reunion."

Gage's eyebrows lifted. "So you're the cook he talked about."

Tonya's mouth tightened in frustration. She lost track of the number of times people referred her as a cook when she had worked and sacrificed so much to become a professional chef. "I'm not a cook."

Gage looked at her again. "What are you?"

"I'm a chef."

"Are you kidding?"

She shook her head. "No. I'm a graduate of Johnson and Wales."

A beat passed. "Aren't you the chef who will be cooking for Hannah once she opens her inn?"

Tonya knew it was premature to openly acknowledge she would take over the cooking duties for the café and supper club. She and Hannah still had to go over the contractual agreement making her an investor in the DuPont Inn. Then she had to discuss the details with her attorney. Once he assured her that it would be a worthwhile business arrangement, she'd sign.

"You've heard about that?"

Gage nodded. "Everyone's talking about the DuPont House becoming the DuPont Inn."

"Is the talk positive or negative?"

"It's mostly positive."

"What have you heard that's negative?"

"That the DuPonts are cash-poor. And they've decided to convert DuPont House from a private residence to a business to raise enough money so they won't have to sell it."

"Is that what you believe?" Tonya asked him. She knew for certain that Hannah was far from being cash-poor, because she admitted her late naval career-officer husband, although he'd cheated on her, had made provisions that resulted in her becoming a wealthy widow.

Gage shook his head. "I don't have an opinion one way or the other, but I like the idea that folks will have another place to stay during Mardi Gras when many hotels and motels are filled to capacity with out-of-towners. During that time some locals rent out rooms in their homes to make a little extra money."

"Is that what you do?"

Stopping for a red light, he gave her an incredulous stare. "No. I don't like strangers sleeping in my place."

"Is that your decision or your wife's?"

Gage's expression changed, becoming one of amusement. "You're not very subtle in wanting to know if I'm married."

Tonya recoiled as if someone had slapped her across the face; she found him incredibly arrogant. Did he actually believe because of his good looks she would be interested in him? That he was so used to women coming on to him that he grouped her with the others?

"I couldn't care less about your marital status, because whether you're married or single has no bearing on my life."

"Are you married?"

"No."

A Cheshire cat smile spread over his features. "Well, that makes two of us. I was married briefly, but it didn't work out. What about you, Tonya? Did you ever take the plunge?"

Her former annoyance vanished as Gage went up several points on her approval scale. One thing she admired in a person was directness. Apparently there was no beating around the bush for him. "Yes. But like you, it didn't work out. The best thing to come out of my marriage is my daughter."

"How old is she?"

"Twenty-one. She's now in her senior year at Spelman."

"You don't look old enough to have a twenty-one-year-old."

"Is that a subtle way of asking my age?" Tonya teased.

The light changed, and the SUV shot forward when Gage stepped on the gas. "No. There are two things I've learned to never ask a woman, and that is her age *or* her weight, because one or two have brought holy hell down on me."

Tonya smiled. "I had just turned twenty-nine when I had Samara. Now you do the math."

"You're fifty!"

Tonya managed not to laugh when his jaw dropped. "Yes."

"Damn, woman! You look good."

Pinpoints of heat flooded her face. "Thank you. What's the expression? 'Good black don't crack.'"

"It's more than good black. It's good genes *and* healthy living."

"You're right about that," she agreed. "I try to work out several times a week. If I move here I'm going to have to find a sports club, because the food down here is like crack. One bite and you're instantly addicted."

Throwing back his head, Gage laughed, the low, rich sound reverberating inside the vehicle. "I suppose it would be to someone not used to eating it. I've grown up eating Creole and Cajun dishes all my life, so there are times when I don't want to see or eat it."

Tonya wanted to tell Gage that it was obvious that he did not overeat because of his slim physique. "What do you eat instead?"

"I'll prepare a coq au vin, or if I want something light it will be salmon salade niçoise."

Slumping back against the leather seat, Tonya realized Gage had mentioned preparing a traditional Provençal salad from Nice, which is traditionally made with tuna. "You're a chef." The query was a statement.

"Guilty as charged."

"You're a chef and a musician?"

Gage nodded. "I'm part-time chef and part-time musician. I help Eustace whenever he has a catering event, and I'm committed to playing with Jazzes' house band on the weekends. I wanted to make it to St. John's wedding, but unfortunately I had a prior engagement at the club."

"Are you going to assist Eustace today, because he told me he has to cater a party later this afternoon?"

"No. The party is too small. A book club alternates

holding monthly Sunday afternoon meetings at a different member's homes, and a few months ago they had Eustace cater the event for the first time. They started out with only ten members, and now they're up to eighteen. Cooking for eighteen is like child's play when compared to more than fifty. That's why I don't understand why my brother would ask you to assist him today unless he wants to give his kids a break after last night's wedding reception."

Tonya stared out the windshield at the passing landscape. They had left the Lower French Quarter and entered Tremé. "He's offered to show me how to prepare some of Chez Toussaints' more popular dishes." Gage came to a complete stop in the middle of the street; the motion was so abrupt that if she had not been wearing a seat belt, there was no doubt she would have hit the dashboard. "What are you trying to do? Give me whiplash?"

Gage managed to appear contrite. "Sorry about that. Did I hear you correctly when you said Eustace is going to give you *our* family's secret recipes?"

Tonya hid her annoyance behind a polite smile. "He didn't say he was going to give me anything."

"Show or give. It's all the same," he countered angrily.

There was one thing Tonya was not going to do with Gage—and that was argue with him. That he could do with his brother. "I suggest you talk it over with your brother," she said.

"You can bet I will," Gage said under his breath. Two minutes later he maneuvered into the parking lot behind the freestanding building housing Chez Toussaints.

Tonya did not know what she expected the restaurant to look like, but it was not the one-story, clapboard structure sorely in need of a new coat of paint. However, it did sport a new roof and windows, and that indicated some recent improvements to the building. Gage did not shut off the engine before he came around the Audi to help her out. There were two white vans in the parking lot with the name of the restaurant painted on the sides.

"Aren't you coming in with me?" she asked when he unlocked the restaurant's back door and held it open for her. They were standing in an area with floor-to-ceiling shelves stocked with jars of canned fruits and vegetables and a number of tin containers labeled flour, rice, grits, and differing types of sugar. A walk-in refrigerator-freezer and a trio of freezer chests took up two walls in the artificially air-cooled space.

Gage massaged the back of his neck. "No. I'm going home to get some sleep. Eustace will call me when it's time to take you back to DuPont House."

Suddenly it dawned on Tonya that Gage had come to get her when he probably had not had much, or any, sleep after working at Jazzes. "You don't have to do that. I'll call DuPont House and either LeAnn or Paige can bring me back." She had taken an instant liking to Hannah's cousins, who had regaled them with stories about their involvement with the civil rights movement in the late sixties and early seventies. They told of marches and sit-ins where they risked being clubbed by police or bitten by their dogs. They also had lost count of the number of times they were hauled off to jail for unlawful assembly.

"Don't bother them. All I need is a few hours, and I'll be good as new."

"But . . ." Her words trailed off when he turned on his heel and walked out.

"Est-ce que tu, Gage?"

Tonya recognized Eustace's deep voice. She had no-

ticed during the Toussaint-Baptiste family reunion that
many of them spoke to one another either in French or
Haitian Creole. "No, it's not Gage," she called out as she
made her way into the restaurant's kitchen.

Eustace stood at the preparation table chopping green
onions, bobbing his head in time to the music flowing
through speakers from the radio on a shelf. Again, she
was taken aback by the lack of space in the kitchen, from
which came some of the most delicious dishes she had
ever eaten. The entire restaurant, with a wood-burning
brick oven, was a little larger than the beachfront bunga-
low where she vacationed as a child with her parents and
grandparents.

He smiled, dimples winking at her from rounded cheeks.
"Good morning. You got here just in time for me to show
you how to make boudin balls. There are some aprons on
a table over in the corner."

Tonya washed her hands in a deep stainless-steel sink,
drying them on a towel stacked next to the aprons. She
approached Eustace, watching intently as he removed a
pot from an industrial stove and poured the mixture through
a strainer, reserving the liquid and meat separately. "What's
on the menu?"

"Boudin balls with a rémoulade sauce. Fried chicken
wings, red beans and rice, seafood pasta salad, jalapeño-
cheese cornbread, and bourbon whiskey bread pudding."

"Should I assume no one will be counting calories?"

Eustace chuckled, the sound rumbling in his deep,
wide chest. "Not today. The book club ladies claim they're
allowed one cheat day each month, and today is that day.
They eat, drink, and then they talk about books." He
turned a meat mixture onto a cutting board. "Please give
this a fine chop."

Tonya slipped on a pair of disposable gloves before selecting one of the knives in a knife block. "Do they order the same dishes every month?"

"It varies, but they have to have their wings and red beans and rice."

She made quick work chopping the meat mixture. "This smells wonderful."

Eustace nodded. "I prefer making my own mixture to buying ready-made boudin sausage. If you let pork shoulder, chicken liver, garlic, onion, poblano and jalapeño peppers, salt, celery, and chili powder marinate overnight before letting them simmer for a couple of hours, it'll enhance all the flavors. After you chop the meat, add cooked white rice and freshly chopped parsley and green onion until the mixture has a pastelike consistency. After that cover the bowl with plastic wrap and chill it in the refrigerator for at least two hours or more. I'll be right back. I have to get something from the other fridge."

Tonya mixed the ingredients Eustace had set aside on the table. The aroma coming from the bowl was intoxicating, and she looked forward to sampling at least one boudin ball once they were fried to golden perfection.

"When frying the boudin balls, do you use regular bread crumbs or panko?" she asked after he returned from the storeroom carrying a large aluminum bowl filled with chicken wings.

"I make my own bread crumbs. I always add a little cayenne to give them an extra kick for the boudin balls. I cube stale French bread, put them in the oven to dry it out, and then grind them in the blender. You'll find three labeled jars in the fridge: plain, cayenne, and the third with grated cheese."

"Where do you buy your fresh herbs?"

"I order them from the vegetable market. You folks up North call them green grocers, but I refer to them as *halle de légumes*." Eustace exhaled an audible groan. "I must be having a senior moment. I forgot to ask you about Gage."

"What about him?"

"Did he growl at you because I asked him to pick you up?"

"Not at all. In fact, he was rather pleasant."

Eustace grunted. "That's a first," he drawled. "Usually my brother is like a bad-tempered bear coming out of hibernation if I ask him to help me after he's played a gig."

"He said he was going home to get some sleep."

"I keep telling him he has to decide what he wants. Either he's going to be a chef or a musician. It can't be both."

Tonya pretended interest in stirring the mixture, adding the reserved cooking liquid a ladleful at a time until it had a pastelike consistency, rather than agree or disagree with Eustace. She knew catering parties and running a kitchen were not only time-consuming but often overwhelming, and afterward she usually fell asleep within minutes of her head touching the pillow. She removed a length of plastic wrap from an industrial-size box and covered the bowl.

"How many wings are you making?" Tonya asked.

"About five pounds. I always cut off the tips and save them for chicken stock." Eustace picked up a meat cleaver. "I don't mind frying chicken, but for some reason I hate frying wings."

"Why don't you cook them in the oven?" Tonya suggested. "To save time I usually season them, line a baking pan with foil and coat it with cooking spray. Arrange the wings skin side up in a single layer and bake them about forty minutes or until they're no longer pink. After that I drain off the fat, put the wings in a bowl and toss them with sauce. Then I rearrange them back in the pan and bake about five minutes or more until glazed."

Eustace appeared deep in thought. "You may have something there. Do they come out crispy?"

She nodded. "Yes. Do you have any sriracha sauce on hand?"

"I have every hot sauce known to man in the store-room. Why?"

"Let me make a few with a creamy sriracha sauce and you can judge for yourself if you want to offer them to your clients."

"Okay, chef, you're on. You do your thing while I whip up some breakfast for us. I can't see us making all this food while our bellies are growling."

Tonya lost track of time as she prepped the wings while Eustace grilled fresh shrimp for one of her favorite dishes: shrimp and grits. The aroma of freshly brewed coffee filled the kitchen and reminded her why breakfast was her favorite meal of the day. Coffee, crisp bacon, fried eggs over easy, and buttery biscuits was her one-day-a-week guilty pleasure.

She discovered, despite the proportions of the kitchen, it was as well stocked as the one at the bank. Eustace had a variety of pepper sauces ranging from mild to hot enough to bring tears to one's eyes. There were also shelves with jars of seasonings labeled in French, and she assumed these were the ingredients that were family secrets. Tonya had just placed the pan with the wings in the oven when Eustace invited her to sit and eat.

"How often do you eat like this?" she asked him as

they sat opposite each other at a table in the restaurant; the whole restaurant's seating capacity was no more than thirty.

He peered at her over the rim of his coffee mug. "Much too often. I have a forty-year high school reunion next year, and I've promised my wife that I'm going on a diet. I know the only time that's going to happen is if I get the hell out the kitchen."

"Who will take over from you?"

Eustace dabbed the corners of his mouth with a napkin. "I'd like for Gage to run the restaurant, but somehow I don't see that happening. It's going to be a lot of responsibility for my girls, because they have husbands and kids to look after. We used to open every day for lunch and dinner, but that's before we started catering. Now we open Monday through Friday from eleven to two for lunch."

"What about the weekends?" Tonya asked in between forkfuls of cheesy grits.

"That's when we cater parties. And if we don't have anything on the calendar, then we kick back and relax."

"Once I move down here I'm willing to help out. It's probably going to be a couple of months before the guest-houses are converted into eating establishments, so in the meantime I can hone my skills working here."

Eustace blinked slowly. "Are you sure that's what you want to do?"

"I'm very sure. If I'm going to prepare New Orleans dishes, then why not learn from the best?"

"I'm a cook, not a chef, Tonya."

"And I'm not a cook, but a chef, Eustace," she countered. "Right now you're the teacher and I'm the apprentice. If I begin as your sous chef, then maybe your daughters can take some time off to be with their families."

Crossing his arms over his chest, he gave her a long, penetrating stare. "We'll begin with you working in the kitchen one week for the lunch crowd so you can get an idea of how we operate. After that, you can help with catering. I'm sure Gage will appreciate the extra help."

Tonya knew Eustace was being optimistic, because she had learned from past experience that chefs were territorial when it came to their kitchens. Pushing back her chair, she stood up, Eustace rising with her. "I'm going to check on the wings."

Fifteen minutes later Tonya watched Eustace as he took a bite of a wing slathered in sriracha sauce and sprinkled with green onions. "Do I pass the test?"

"Damn, woman. These are insane! What did you do to cut down on the heat?"

"I mixed the sauce with mayo and lime juice."

"Nice!" he drawled with a wide grin. "What other varieties do you make?"

"I'm partial to a citrus pepper rub, a bourbon-espresso barbecue sauce, and my personal favorite is a Thai peanut sauce. But I'm always careful with the peanut sauce because some folks have peanut allergies."

"You have your first assignment. Prepare them all. I'll make certain to label the tray with the wings with the peanut sauce."

Eustace tuned the satellite radio to a station featuring Motown classic hits. Tonya lost herself in the music as she sang along with Marvin Gaye, Stevie Wonder, the Four Tops, the Temptations, and Gladys Knight and the

Pips. She concocted the various sauces for the wings while Eustace put up a pot of red beans and gathered the ingredients for his seafood pasta. She and Eustace worked well together, she assisting him shucking fresh oysters, peeling and deveining shrimp, and chopping green onion and shallots, halving the time it would have taken him to prepare the dish alone.

He uncorked a bottle of dry white wine, filling two glasses and handing one to her. "Whenever I cook with wine, I always have a glass."

Smiling, Tonya touched her glass to his. *"Voici un merveilleux professeur."*

"Je vous remercie."

"You won't think he's a wonderful teacher when he begins yelling at you."

Tonya turned to find Gage standing only a few feet away, smirking at her. He had come into the kitchen without making a sound. He had exchanged his t-shirt, jeans, and running shoes for a white golf shirt, khakis, and cognac-hued loafers. She glanced up at the wall clock. Where had the morning gone? It was almost one o'clock.

"What if I yell back at him?" she teased in French.

Eustace glared at his brother. "Don't start none, there won't be none," he warned.

Gage held up both hands. "It's all good, big brother. What can I do to help?"

"We've made everything but the bread pudding."

"I'll make it," Gage volunteered. He glanced over at the trays of wings. "I know you didn't make these."

Eustace shook his head. "Tonya did. There's a plate over there with a few samples."

Gage washed his hands, slipped on an apron, and headed for the plate with the wings. He picked up one, biting into it and chewing it slowly. "Sh-it-it!" The expletive came out in three syllables. "This is the best Thai wing I've ever had."

Eustace angled his head at the same time he crossed his arms over his chest. "Watch your language, Gage. Have you forgotten there's a lady present?"

Gage winked at Tonya. "Sorry, ma'am."

She grimaced. Kids referred to her as *ma'am*. Not men who were closer to her own age. "Apology accepted."

"Try the sriracha ones," Eustace urged.

Tonya met Gage's eyes as he sampled each of the wings, and she knew instinctively they would be a big hit with the book club ladies. And they were healthier because they were baked, not fried. Seeing the brothers together made her aware that although they did not resemble each other their body language was similar. Gage had the advantage of being at least two inches taller, while Eustace probably outweighed him by at least thirty or possibly forty or more pounds.

Gage washed his hands again, wiping them on the towel he'd tucked under the apron ties. "It looks as if you have a little competition, big brother."

Nodding his head slowly, Eustace flashed a knowing grin. "I don't mind competition if it enhances Chez Toussaints' reputation."

Gage approached Tonya and rested a hand on her shoulder. "Be careful that Eustace won't try and steal you away from Hannah."

Tilting her chin, Tonya stared up at the man who stood a little close for comfort as she inhaled the intoxicating scent of his cologne. "That will never happen," she said when he dropped his hand. "I've committed to running the café and supper club for the DuPont Inn." Gage gave her a startled look with this pronouncement. His expression indicated he hadn't been apprised of the extent of Hannah's business plans.

"Hannah's also opening a supper club?"

"Yes."

"When did she decide this?" Gage asked.

"I don't know," Tonya replied. "You'd have to ask her."

A slight frown appeared between his luminous eyes. "When St. John told me about Hannah converting the house into an inn he only mentioned that she would operate it like a B and B."

Now that the proverbial cat was out of the bag, Tonya saw no further need to act as if the establishments attached to the DuPont Inn were top secrets. "I would never relocate only to serve breakfast, because she could get anyone down here to do that. She's given me the opportunity to run my own restaurant, and that's something I've wanted to do since graduating culinary school."

Gage lifted his eyebrows a fraction at the same time he exhaled an audible sigh. "Good luck with that, chef."

Tonya glared at Gage. Instead of congratulating her, he had wished her luck. Why couldn't he be happy or encourage her? Was he envious, or had he believed she would not be able to make a go running her own business? She shook off his cryptic remark like a dog after a bath. There was no way she was going to let anyone— men in particular—steal her joy. It was the reason she ended her marriage to a man she'd loved enough to marry.

"As soon as you're finished making the bread pudding, I'd like you to take me back to DuPont House." Her words were dripping with sarcasm, but Tonya was past placating anyone who openly verbalized their negativity.

It had taken a while, but she made it a practice not to associate with toxic people.

Eustace cleared his throat, shattering the uncomfortable silence and the stare-down between Tonya and his brother. "Gage, why don't you take Tonya back now? Thanks to her, I'm a couple of hours ahead of schedule."

"I can wait," she said. "I'd like to see how you make your bread pudding." Tonya didn't tell him that if his version of the poor person's dessert was exceptional, then it would be something she would definitely include on her dessert menu.

Eustace gave her a half smile. "Are you sure?"

Tonya returned his smile with a warm one of her own. "I'm very sure."

She was not about to let Gage's negativity dampen her enthusiasm to learn the secrets behind his brother's signature dishes. If he sought to discourage her, then he was in for the shock of his life.

Chapter 4

Gage knew by Tonya's clipped tone that she did not like his response. Maybe he should have warned her that since there were so many restaurants in New Orleans, unless she offered dishes that were truly exceptional, her establishment might not survive.

"I'll show you how to make the bread pudding."

Tonya glanced over at Eustace, who nodded his acquiescence. "Okay."

Eustace took off his apron. "If that's the case, then I'm going home and put my feet up for a couple of hours. These big dogs are quick to remind me how long I've been standing."

Gage stared at his brother under lowered lids. "That's because you do too much. You were up all day yesterday cooking for St. John's wedding, and now you're back here this morning cooking for the book club. I told you before, it's time you let go the reins and let your girls take over the day-to-day business, while you just concentrate on filling catering orders."

"And who's going to help me with the catering?"

"I will," Gage volunteered.

Compressing his lips, dimples deepening in his rounded cheeks, Eustace appeared deep in thought. "Maybe I'll start coming in four days a week instead of five so they can get used to running everything. Then after a couple of months it will be three days, and then two. After that I'll relinquish all responsibility for Chez Toussaints to them."

Gage nodded. "That sounds like a plan. Now, go home and make love with your wife for a change while Tonya and I finish up here. I'll drop Tonya off at DuPont House, and then come back and deliver the food to the book club ladies."

Eustace shot Tonya an uncomfortable look before he turned and walked out of the kitchen. Waiting until he was out of earshot, she asked Gage, "Did you have to embarrass him like that?"

Opening the refrigerator, Gage removed a large plastic container filled with pieces of torn French bread and placed it on the prep table. "He isn't as embarrassed as he is conscience-stricken. Just the other day my sister-in-law came to me in tears. She believes Eustace is having an affair because she cannot remember the last time they were intimate. I reassured Janine that if my brother is having an affair, then it's with Chez Toussaints. He comes in at dawn Monday through Friday and doesn't leave until late afternoon. And if he has to cater a party, then it's much later. He's probably so tired when he gets home that he just collapses. I can't even get him to take a night off on the weekend to come to Jazzes to unwind."

"How old is Eustace?"

"He's fifty-seven."

"Isn't that a little young for him to retire?" Tonya asked Gage, as he reached for a jar of cinnamon and bottle of pure vanilla extract off an overhead shelf.

"It is. But, remember, he would only be semi-retired, because he still will be catering."

"I'll get the eggs, butter, and sugar," she volunteered, opening the refrigerator and taking out the ingredients for a basic bread pudding recipe. "What's the secret in making Chez Toussaints' bread pudding?"

"We bake our own French bread for the bread pudding."

Tonya blinked slowly. "Why bake it when you can buy it?"

Gage stood next to Tonya, realizing for the first time that she was much shorter than she appeared. He was six-three, and the top of her head came only to his shoulder. Maybe it was her slimness that made him think she was taller. She wasn't skinny, far from it; although her body was slender, it was still curvy. In fact, he liked everything about her, because he preferred women who were comfortable with their bodies.

He had dated women who refused to let him touch their hair because they feared it would loosen their extensions. Then there were those who would not permit him to squeeze their breasts because of implants. The last woman he dated but refused to sleep with would only splash water on her face, for she feared losing the lashes glued to her lids, and she complained that her acrylic nails had become an obstacle when buttoning or unbuttoning her clothes. He wanted to be with a woman who did not have a laundry list of dos and don'ts. What happened to women who learned to love who they were without altering their appearances? It had gotten to a point that when a man went to bed, he woke up with a woman he barely recognized in the morning.

"New Orleans–style French bread is a uniquely light loaf made with yeasts you can only buy in specialty shops. The oven in the far corner is the one we use expressly for baking breads for this dessert. We do buy the rest."

"How long have you been making your own bread?" Tonya asked.

Gage measured the equivalent of a loaf of torn bread into a large aluminum bowl. "My dad started making it when he married my mother. She continues the tradition handed down from the French who came to Louisiana from Acadia."

"Your mother is Cajun." The query was a statement.

"That she is."

"Does she speak Cajun French?"

Gage smiled. "Yes. I speak traditional French, Cajun French, and Haitian Creole. It's been a family tradition that goes back more than a century that everyone in the family speaks more than one language. I know it's somewhat rude, but when we don't want folks to know what we're talking about, we immediately shift from English to a dialect."

"I realized that when I helped Eustace at your family reunion. I understood most of the French, but not the Creole. I'm lucky to get by with whatever French I picked up in France."

He gave her a sidelong glance. "You lived in France?"

Tonya nodded. "I spent nearly a year there perfecting regional dishes. I also took cooking courses in China, Southeast Asia, and the Mediterranean."

"With that much experience, why aren't you working for a restaurant serving international cuisine?"

"I did." Tonya explained how she, Hannah, and dozens of others were downsized when the Manhattan-based investment bank they had worked for merged with an out-of-state bank.

"So, learning to prepare southern Louisiana dishes is your last frontier?" he teased, smiling.

She returned his smile with a dimpled one of her own. "I'd like to think so. Where did you do your training?"

"France. I'd just graduated Julliard when I decided to go to Paris on holiday. What I intended to be two months stretched into a little more than two years. I was fortunate enough to train under one of the best chefs in Europe."

"You went from the Big Easy to the Big Apple, and then onto the City of Lights."

Gage laughed softly. "And now I'm back to stay, while you're leaving the Apple for the Easy. Even though New York is the city that never sleeps, New Orleans is the birthplace of the cocktail, along with a celebrated reputation for food, music, and drink."

"Is it true what they say about *laissez les bon temps rouler?*"

"*Oui, Madame.* I didn't realize how much I'd missed my home until I came back."

"Why did you come back?" Tonya asked.

A beat passed. "My father was diagnosed with a very aggressive form of pancreatic cancer. I wasn't back more than three months before he passed away. That's when I had to step up and help Eustace."

Tonya braced an elbow on the table and cradled her chin on the heel of her hand. "How old were you when you came back?"

"I'd just turned twenty-three. I graduated high school at sixteen and college at twenty."

"Your parents didn't have a problem with you living in a foreign country at that age?"

Gage shrugged his shoulders. "There wasn't much they could do when I'd left home at sixteen to study in New York. I'd saved enough money from playing gigs during my last two years at college that I didn't have to ask them to subsidize the trip."

"What made you decide to live in Paris instead of coming back to the States?"

"A week before I was scheduled to return to the States I met three expatriate musicians who invited me to move into their flat once I'd joined their band. Meanwhile I got a job at a Michelin-starred restaurant, and after a while I worked my way up from dishwasher to sous chef and eventually assistant chef."

"Were you still playing with the band?"

Gage nodded. "Once the restaurant closed for the night, I went directly to the bar where I played sets until dawn. I didn't get a lot of sleep, but at that time I was able to get by on less than five hours of sleep."

Tonya met his eyes when he gave her a long, penetrating stare. "Should I assume you're still not getting much sleep?"

He smiled, and attractive lines fanned out around his brilliant eyes with the expression. "I'm good during the week. It's the weekends that are challenging."

Her eyebrows lifted questioningly. "You don't work during the week?" she asked. She watched him intently as he measured the ingredients for the bread pudding, and then he slipped on a pair of disposable gloves to blend the mixture with his fingers.

"I do have a day job. After I returned to the States I went back to college to get a master's degree in education. Right now I'm teaching music at a local high school."

"Does it have a marching band?"

"Yes. Why?"

She lowered her arm. "What I miss most not going to a Southern college are the marching bands."

Gage smiled. "There's nothing better than Friday night football, cheerleading, and marching bands."

"Do you direct the marching band?"

"No. I'm an artist in residence. The grant's objective is for me to start up a jazz band for high school students who plan to pursue a career in music."

"You're lucky."

"Why would you say that?" he asked.

"Because so many schools have cut their music and art programs while your school has a marching and jazz band."

"That's because music is so much an intricate part of this city's history. I know a number of musicians who fund-raise to support our schools' music programs." Gage filled the greased pockets of two muffin tins and spooned the pudding into the pockets, filling each just barely to the top.

"What do you use to make the sauce?" she asked, changing the topic of conversation.

"I use unsalted butter, sugar, orange juice, eggs, and bourbon. You can substitute rum or brandy for the whiskey, or if you want a nonalcoholic sauce, then use vanilla extract, although most vanilla does contain alcohol. By the way, have you eaten?" he asked her.

"Yes. Your brother made breakfast for me earlier this morning."

"Did you have beignets?"

"No."

"Breakfast isn't breakfast unless you have a beignet. Do you know how to make them?"

"Yes!"

Tonya's smile was dazzling. When she'd first come to New Orleans and had beignets and café au lait for breakfast, she knew she had to learn to make the fried, puffy, golden brown dough dusted with confectioners' sugar. It took her two tries before they were doughy and with enough air inside so they wouldn't sink to the bottom of the fryer.

"Maybe one of these days you'll make them for me."

Her smile slowly faded. "That probably won't be for a while."

He halted placing the tins on baking pans. "What do you mean by a while?"

"I don't plan to move down here until next year."

He went completely still. "Next year?"

"Yes. I still have to tie up a few things in New York." Her explanation appeared to satisfy Gage; he covered the pans with plastic wrap and put them in the refrigerator. "Aren't you going to bake them now?" she asked.

"No. I'll put them in the oven after I take you home. The ladies don't meet until four."

Tonya removed her apron, dropped it in a canvas bin with soiled linen, and picked up her tote off the stool. She followed Gage out of the restaurant to the parking lot. He opened the passenger-side door to the SUV for her and waited until she was seated before rounding the vehicle to sit behind the wheel.

Gage slipped on a pair of sunglasses, started the engine, and then executed a smooth U-turn, and that is when Tonya noticed his hands for the first time. They were somewhat delicate for a man his size, the fingers long and beautifully formed. "How many instruments do you play?"

"I can play every instrument in the orchestra. I haven't mastered the harp, so I don't count that one."

She smiled. "You must like music."

"I love it."

"More than cooking?"

There came a moment of silence before Gage said, "No. Right now they're even." He gave her a quick glance. "Did you always want to be a chef?"

"Yes. As a child I spent summers with my grandparents in Daytona Beach, Florida, and my grandmother prayed I'd grow up to become a better cook than my mother. It wasn't that my mother is a bad cook, but her dishes are very bland because my dad has a sensitive stomach. Grandma said it's hard to season food after you cook it."

Gage nodded, smiling. "She's right. So, your grandmamma taught you to cook?"

Tonya told him about sitting on the porch helping her grandma snap the ends off greens, and peeling white potatoes, which would eventually be added to smoked ham hocks after the skin was removed. "Nowadays folks wanting to eat healthier use smoked turkey instead of ham."

"What do you plan to serve at your supper club?"

"I'm leaning toward tapas."

Gage gave her a quick glance. "In other words, you'll serve appetizers rather an entrées."

"Yes, only because I plan to offer a fusion cuisine. Of course there will be quite a few popular appetizers, along with sushi, Asian, French, Spanish, and Mediterranean dishes."

"Don't you think that's a little daunting?"

Tonya stared out the windshield as she chose her words carefully. Did he actually believe she would attempt to run a restaurant without having a concrete plan in place? "No. Once I train my staff, it shouldn't be daunting." She wasn't a man hater, but Tonya had come to realize that it was men who openly expressed doubt whenever she mentioned running her own restaurant, while most women encouraged her to go for it.

"Good luck with that," Gage said under his breath.

The drive ended in complete silence, and when he maneuvered up to the front of DuPont House, Tonya didn't wait for Gage to come around and assist her. "Thanks for the ride." She didn't bother to give him a backward glance as she walked up the steps to the porch. She opened and closed the door and exhaled an audible breath.

There was something about his tone when wishing her luck that reminded Tonya of her ex-husband whenever he had attempted to discourage her from returning to college. After a while she learned to ignore his subtle digs, and in the end she promised herself not to let the naysayers or doubters affect her decision to determine her future.

She walked through the entryway to the parlor to find Jasmine sitting on a loveseat reading a magazine. The muted television was tuned to the New Orleans Saints' game. Her head popped up. "Nydia and I were talking about sending out Nawlins' finest to find you."

Tonya flopped down on an armchair. "I went to Chez Toussaints so Eustace could show me how he makes some of his dishes." She paused. "Where's everyone?"

Jasmine closed the magazine. "LeAnn and Paige went to the Saints' football game, and Nydia's taking a nap. She claims she's exhausted."

"That's because once the dancing began she never sat down," Tonya reminded Jasmine.

"Word," Jasmine drawled. "I can remember a time when my weekends would begin on Thursdays and not end until Sunday morning."

Partying had never been an option for Tonya. "It was different with me. I met Samuel while I was still in high school, and because he was raised in a church where dancing and drinking were frowned upon, we didn't go out."

"What did you guys do for fun?"

A melancholy frown flitted over her features. "Now that I look back, I realize we never had much fun. We'd get together with family members for Sunday dinner or on holidays, but that was the extent of our so-called fun." She waved her hand. "I don't want to talk about the past."

Jasmine nodded. "Okay. I need for you to give me your opinion about someone."

Tonya's curiosity is piqued. "Is it a he or a she?"

"It's Cameron Singleton."

"What about him?" she asked, when she wanted to tell her friend that the man hadn't been able to keep his eyes off her during the reception.

"He asked to take me out."

Tonya settled back into the chair; her impassive expression did not reveal what she was feeling. It appeared that whatever Cameron wanted, he was willing to go after. "And what did you tell him?"

Jasmine lowered her eyes. "I told him that wasn't possible because I was leaving today to go back to New York."

"And what did he say?"

"He claims he comes to New York every May to hang out with his college buddies, and if I'm available then, he would like to take me out."

"And what did *you* say?" She had asked Jasmine yet another question.

"I told him I didn't know where I would be or what I would be doing seven months from now, so I couldn't give him an answer."

Tonya shook her head in exasperation. "Did you at least give the man your number?"

"Yes."

"Well, well, well. You did something right."

Vertical lines appeared between Jasmine's eyes. "Why would you say that?"

"He's only asking for one date. You preach to Nydia about seeing someone other than her trifling boyfriend, and meanwhile you need to take your own advice. You've been divorced for nearly two years, and it's time you started dating again."

"I'm not ready for a relationship," Jasmine argued softly.

"No one said anything about a relationship, Jazz. Go out with different men, and just have a good time. That's the only way you're going to get over that slug you married."

"Is that what happened to you, Tonya? You didn't get over your ex until you hooked up with Darius?"

"I'd gone out with several men before I met Darius. They were co-workers, and I'd promised myself that I would never get *that* involved with a co-worker, because if we broke up then I would have to see them every day."

"So, what did you do when you dated them?"

"We would take turns cooking for each other, or when we were off we would go on drives out to Long Island or Upstate New York to eat in little out-of-the-way restaurants to sample the dishes on their menus. I dated one guy who was into old black-and-white movies, and we'd spend hours watching them. In other words, we became good friends."

"What makes Darius different from the others?"

Tonya crossed her feet at the ankles. "I'm allowed to be who I am. Whenever I tell him I can't see him because either I'm too tired, or I have to work a party, he doesn't give me grief or attitude. In other words, I have the freedom to live my life however I want."

Jasmine closed her eyes for several seconds. "Have you told him you're planning to move down here?"

Tonya shook her head. "Not yet. I'll tell him once I get back. Hannah and I still have to go over a few things in our contract."

"Does he ever talk about marriage?"

A hint of a smile lifted the corners of Tonya's mouth. "No."

"Not ever?"

"Maybe once. When we first met, I told him I was divorced, and he told me he wasn't husband material."

"What did he mean, he wasn't husband material?" Jasmine asked.

"I never asked."

Jasmine pulled her lip between her teeth as she appeared deep in thought. "What kind of vibes did you get from Cameron?"

Tonya decided to tell her what she'd witnessed. "That he's a man who goes after what he wants."

An expression of uncertainty flitted over Jasmine's features. "I hope you're not talking about me."

"No, I'm not," Tonya lied smoothly. She didn't want to frighten her friend into rejecting a man who appeared interested in her. Five months ago she hadn't known anything about Jasmine's personal life; however, the day she, Hannah, Jasmine, and Nydia were downsized with dozens of other employees had become one that had changed their lives forever. Former employees of the investment bank, they were now friends and soon-to-be business partners.

"I know you have a problem with trust because of your ex," Tonya continued, "but there has to come a time when you let go of the past. Look at Hannah. If she hadn't gotten over her late husband's infidelity, she never would've married St. John. Some men cheat. That's just what they do, Jazz, and you need to understand that they're probably in a minority, or the institution of marriage would never survive."

"How did we go from my going out on a date with Cameron to marrying him?"

"You're the one who mentioned marriage. All I'm saying is go out with the man. What do you have to lose?"

The seconds ticked, and then Jasmine said, "I'll think about it."

You do that, Tonya thought. There were times when she felt more like a counselor and an older sister when dealing with Nydia and Jasmine. Perhaps it was because she and Hannah were in their fifties and had adult children that they shared a similar outlook on life. "Well, not for nothing, you have seven months to think about it," she said after a comfortable silence.

"I don't know whether I told you, but I have an interview on Tuesday for a position with an agency that prepares single women with children to transition from living in shelters into permanent housing."

Tonya was slightly taken aback with Jasmine's disclosure. "I thought you were going to go back into the interior decorating business."

"I'd thought about it, but then I changed my mind, because it would mean starting over. Remember, I lost all my clients once I sold my business after the divorce."

"Have you given any more thought to investing in the inn with me and Hannah?"

Jasmine's eyebrows lifted slightly at the same time a smile trembled over her lips. "I've been giving it some thought, but . . ." Her words trailed off.

"But you don't want to leave your folks," she said, finishing her statement. Jasmine nodded. Tonya understood her friend's reluctance to move more than a thousand miles away from her parents. She had become an empty nester and at the same time her parents moved to a Florida retirement community in Daytona Beach; however, she made it a practice several times a year to drive to Atlanta and pick up Samara to visit with her daughter's grandparents.

"Thirteen hundred miles between New York and New Orleans is just too much in the event of an emergency," Jasmine said.

"Have they talked about leaving New York?"

Jasmine paused. "I know Daddy was talking about moving back to North Carolina, but he says it's just talk."

"Perhaps he'll change his mind one of these days," Tonya predicted.

"Who's going to change their mind?" Nydia asked as she walked into the parlor and flopped down on the loveseat next to Jasmine.

"My father," Jasmine answered.

Tonya stared at Nydia's puffy eyes. "It's really not nice to say, but you look a hot mess."

Nydia closed her eyes. "I know. I think I had too much champagne."

"You think? How much did you have?" Jasmine asked.

Nydia's lids fluttered. "I stopped counting after the fifth glass."

"Damn!" Tonya said under her breath. "You're an accountant, but it appears that you have a problem with adding."

Nydia moaned softly. "Please don't remind me of that." She moaned again. "It feels as if someone is playing congas in my head."

Jasmine placed the back of her hand to Nydia's forehead. "You don't have a temperature, so you're probably hungover."

"I'm never drinking champagne again," she said, grimacing. "But I have to admit Hannah and St. John really know how to throw a party."

Tonya nodded in agreement. Everything about Hannah and St. John's wedding, cocktail hour, and reception was nothing short of perfection—all of which made her look forward to relocating with the excitement of a child opening presents on Christmas morning. Working in restaurants, or assisting the head chef at the bank, paled in comparison to opening her own establishment, and she looked forward to the challenge of taste-testing recipes that would eventually end up on the supper club's menu, while hiring and training a kitchen staff and musicians to play live music on weekends would prove less challenging. After all, New Orleans was filled with musicians looking for work as a permanent house band.

Nydia pushed to her feet. "I'm going to get some coffee. Would anyone else like a cup?"

"Not me," Tonya said.

"I'll pass, too," Jasmine added.

Once Nydia returned to the parlor, the three women talked at length about Hannah's plan to turn her ancestral home into a business. Jasmine continued to voice her opposition to investing in the venture because she did not want to relocate, while Nydia continued to be ambivalent about leaving her boyfriend.

Hours later, Tonya stood on the porch watching the taxi as it drove away with her friends for their return flight to New York. She would follow them in two days, and once she put her affairs in order she would return to New Orleans—this time to begin the next phase of her life.

Chapter 5

Tonya climbed down off the stepladder and walked over to the bedside table to answer the telephone. She had spent most of the morning going through closets and selecting unused and outdated clothes and accessories she planned to donate to a neighborhood charity. She glanced at the display; the call was from her attorney's office.

"Hello."

"May I please speak to Ms. Martin?"

"This is she."

"Ms. Martin, this is Ms. Stewart from Davis, Keen, and Harris. Mr. Keen has given his approval for your agreement with Mrs. McNair. You'll get an email confirming this, along with the attached agreement. Do you have any questions?"

Tonya sat down on the side of her bed as her heart pounded a runaway rhythm. "No, I don't."

There came a pause from the other end of the connection. "Congratulations, Ms. Martin, on your new venture."

"Thank you so much."

She placed the receiver in the handset and fell back across the bed. It had taken her and Hannah several days to discuss the terms of the partnership agreement before she was willing to commit to invest in the DuPont Inn. Tonya wasn't able to compete with Hannah when it came to the legalese; however, the business courses she had taken in college had given her an advantage as they revised the contract that would make her a part owner. Once approved by her attorney, Tonya would electronically transfer the agreed-upon amount from her bank to Hannah's.

She picked up her cell phone and tapped the messages icon.

Tonya: It's official. I'm now an innkeeper.

Within seconds, she got a reply from her daughter.

Samara: Congratulations! We'll celebrate when we get together. Late for class. I'll call you later.

Every Thanksgiving she drove to Atlanta to pick up her daughter before traveling south to Florida, where they shared the holiday with her parents. Now that she was going to move to Louisiana, the drive would take hours instead of days.

Tonya slipped off the bed and made her way to the smaller bedroom her daughter had decorated like a studio apartment. An off-white sofa covered with Haitian cotton converted into a full-size bed, and a desktop computer and printer sat on a computer table. Bookcases packed with books and magazines spanned one wall, while another was decorated with framed movie posters and photos of Samara's favorite movie and recording artists.

She sat down at the desk, booted up the computer, and then switched on the printer. As soon as she typed in her password to access the Internet, she saw the message from her attorney's office. Tonya downloaded the cover letter and document, electronically signed and dated the agreement, and forwarded the signed document to Hannah for her signature before printing it.

When she had broached the subject of Nydia subletting the apartment, Tonya realized she had been somewhat premature, but now with the signed agreement she hoped her former co-worker would move in. Nydia had promised to come over later that afternoon to decide whether she wanted to sublet it for the following year. Rent for two bedrooms in the renovated East Harlem walk-up was high, but not as prohibitive when compared to other neighborhoods on the Upper West Side and East Side of Manhattan.

Tonya made two phone calls: one to her parents and the other to Darius. Her mother was overjoyed that they would be able to see each other more than two and occasionally three times a year. And instead of Tonya making the drive to Florida, the elder Martins planned to put New Orleans on their travel itinerary. After their retirement, her parents had sold their home in a New York City suburb, relocated to Daytona Beach, and moved into Ronald Martin's ancestral home. However, the aging structure needed major repairs. He updated the three-bedroom house, sold it to a young couple, and then moved into an upscale fifty-five-and-over gated retirement community with on-site amenities that included a nine-hole golf course, swimming pools, tennis courts, resident medical personnel, and an in-house chef.

The call to Darius went unanswered, and Tonya left a voice mail message for him to call her. It was time she let the man she had been seeing for more than a year know that she planned to relocate. She exhaled an audible sigh and felt as if she had been released from an invisible prison. The instant she was told that her position as an assistant chef at Wakefield Hamilton had been eliminated, her mind had gone into a tumult.

Although she was given a generous severance package, that still did not belay her anxiety about her future. And despite her experience, Tonya loathed having to update her résumé and contact former co-workers about available positions.

It was only after Hannah invited her, Nydia, and Jasmine to join her at her Manhattan high-rise apartment for an early brunch that a strange calmness came over Tonya, as she was reminded that she was a highly skilled chef and her life was totally unencumbered. She had mailed off a check for Samara's last year at Spelman College, she was debt-free, and the money she received in the severance package was enough for her to maintain her current lifestyle for more than a year.

Hannah inviting her, Jasmine, and Nydia to her apartment changed everything: her association with the other women, and now her future. Once Tonya had revealed she planned to take the summer off before looking for another position, Hannah invited her to come to New Orleans, and after some urging Nydia and Jasmine agreed to accompany Tonya and her daughter. It was during her first visit to New Orleans that Hannah asked her about investing in her business venture of converting DuPont

House to DuPont Inn. She made Tonya an offer she found hard to refuse. If she invested in the inn, then she would maintain a twenty-five percent ownership in the business, along with operating an onsite café exclusively for inn guests and a supper club for the general public.

Hannah talked about a tentative opening date of next February, but her decision to install an elevator in the two-story house pushed back the opening until late summer or early fall. Tonya did not mind the delay, because it would give her more than enough time to acquaint herself with the local cuisine and interview, hire, and train her kitchen and waitstaff.

She left the bedroom and headed for the kitchen. She had promised Nydia she would prepare dinner for her. She decided to prepare several Caribbean-inspired dishes: Cuban black bean soup, rice and pigeon peas, and chicken in a garlic sauce.

Tonya had just finished setting the table in the dining area when the intercom chimed through the apartment. She walked down a narrow hallway to the front door and tapped the button on the intercom panel. Nydia's image appeared on the small monitor. She tapped another button, disengaging the lock on the downstairs door. One of the many perks in renting an apartment in the renovated building was security. Closed-circuit cameras were integrated within the intercom system and allowed tenants to see who was ringing their bell.

Tonya opened the door to her apartment and waited for Nydia to walk up four flights. A knowing smile parted her lips when she saw her friend momentarily stop midway up the staircase before continuing. "Shame on you," she chided. "You're too young to be winded."

Nydia exhaled an audible breath as she slowly made

her way to the landing. "I'm not used to walking stairs. I can't believe you do this every day."

She opened the door wider. "Sometimes I do it several times a day. Come in and sit down before you collapse."

Nydia blew out another breath as she slipped her arms out of the straps of her leather backpack. She placed the backpack on the floor, hung her jacket on a wall rack, and kicked off her shoes and left them on a thick mat by an umbrella stand. "I see why you're so slim," she remarked as she walked the length of the hallway to the living/dining area. "Four flights aside, I must admit that you live on a wonderful block."

Tonya smiled. Trees lining both sides of the street shaded brownstones and several townhouses and two four-story apartment buildings "Walking stairs helps me to keep in shape."

Nydia glanced at her over her shoulder. "How much weight did you lose?"

"Twenty-five pounds. The year before I turned fifty I decided it was time to stop talking about going on a diet and actually do it. But it wasn't easy when you cook for a living."

Nydia sniffed the air. "Something smells good. In fact, it smells like something my mother would make."

"It's chicken in a garlic sauce."

"Do you cook every day?"

"I try not to. Whenever I cook I usually make enough to last for at least two days. By the third day I want something different." Tonya pointed to a chair in the living room's seating grouping. "Please sit down. Can I get you something to drink?"

*   *   *

Nydia sat on an armchair with animal print cushions. The furnishings in the living/dining area reminded her of the interior of an African hunting lodge. A zebra-print rug covered the glossy parquet floor; the off-white sofa and matching loveseat cradled throw pillows covered in colorful animal prints.

"I'll just have water, please."

Sinking lower in the chair, Nydia closed her eyes for several seconds. If she moved into Tonya's apartment, then everything would change for her. She was currently renting a furnished studio apartment in a private house in the Bronx where the landlady monitored everyone coming and going. A few times the woman complained that she did not want Nydia having men spend the night at her apartment. And she countered that she did not have a trail of men coming to see her, just one man and he was her boyfriend. But lately she had not thought of him as her boyfriend, because she could not depend on him to take care of himself. He lived with his sister and was unable to save money, which meant she would be responsible for paying all their bills. Her father had preached repeatedly that a man should always pull his own weight and not depend on a woman to take care of him.

Tonya returned and handed her a glass of water. "After you finish your water, I'll show you the rest of the place."

She took a long swallow, and then placed the water on a glass coaster resting on the kente cloth runner spanning the length of the mahogany coffee table. "I'm ready now."

Nydia followed Tonya through the living room and dining area and down a hall. She peered into a bathroom with a claw-foot tub, shower stall, pedestal sink, and commode. The colors of seafoam-green and pale yellow, along with potted plants on the window ledge, gave the space a tropical appearance. The shelf below a low table held a collection of towels in tropical colors of pink, green, yellow, and pale blue. Candles in the corresponding colors crowded the top of the table.

The bedroom was only feet from the bathroom. She stared at an iron off-white queen-size bed, double dresser, and matching bedside tables. Nydia smiled. The entire room was decorated in white with varying shades of blue ranging from cornflower to robin's egg, from the pale walls with a border embossed with tiny blue flower buds to the blue-and-white-striped linens and quilt.

"I love it."

Tonya nodded. "As you notice, I'm somewhat of a minimalist. I really don't like clutter, even though there is enough space for a bench at the foot of the bed and a corner chair."

"There are times when less is more."

"You'll probably like Samara's room, because she's even more of a minimalist than her mother."

When Nydia walked into Samara's bedroom, she knew exactly what Tonya was talking about. "This is the perfect office."

"The sofa converts into a bed."

"I'll use it as a sofa rather than a bed because I don't intend to have company."

Tonya gave her a sidelong glance. "What about your boyfriend?"

"I'm really done with him. After we had that conversation the day before Hannah's wedding, I knew I was fooling myself hoping, wishing, and praying that Danny would change into someone I wanted him to be. And I don't want to go into a situation where I have to fight with him about money." She paused. "I love your apartment and the neighborhood, so I'm ready to move in whenever you give me the word."

"Don't you want to know what the rent is?"

Nydia shook her head. "I don't care how much it is. I still have the money from my severance, and I have more saved. Right now I'm doing the books for a guy who owns a restaurant in City Island and here in East Harlem."

"How did you get the job?"

"My cousin works for him, and he put in a good word for me after his boss's accountant passed away. Not only am I doing his books, but I'll also prepare his employees' tax documents."

Tonya flashed a dimpled smile. "Good for you. Now, how does it feel to work for yourself?"

Nydia scrunched up her pert nose. "It feels real good, because I can make my own hours. I go to each restaurant once or twice a week to pick up the receipts and time-cards. Then I go back to deliver payroll checks. Now that I look back, I believe Wakefield Hamilton did us a favor when they laid us off."

"I know they did," Tonya said in agreement, "because now it's official. I'm going into business with Hannah."

"Congratulations. I know you've been talking about running your own restaurant, and now that's possible."

"It's not going to happen for a while, but at least I know it's going to become a reality before the end of next year."

Nydia's eyelids fluttered wildly. "Are you saying you're not going to move in January?"

Tonya rested an arm over Nydia's shoulders. "I'm still moving. I've paid the rent through the end of January, so the increase won't go into effect until February's rent."

She removed her arm, walked to the desk, picked up a letter, and then handed it to Nydia. "Here's what I'm currently paying. The other two figures are what I'd pay if I were to renew for one or two years."

Nydia quickly did the computations in her head. Renewing for one year would almost triple what she was currently paying for her current apartment, but then she would have so much more for her money. And she could also write off a home office expense for the smaller bedroom. "Renew it for one year, and I'll give you a bank check for the entire year."

"You don't have to do that."

"Yes, I do," she argued softly. "I'd feel more confident knowing that it is one expense I don't have to concern myself with."

Tonya nodded. "I pay my rent online, so the first of every month I'll send in the payment. Before you leave I'm going to introduce you to the building superintendent as my niece, so he won't call the police when he sees you using keys to get into my apartment. If after a year you still want to live here, then I'll have management put your name on the lease and the apartment will be yours. There's talk of the building going co-op, so if you're a current tenant then you'll have the advantage of first preference when it comes to purchasing the unit."

Nydia angled her head. Tonya had always wanted to run her own restaurant, while she always wanted to own property. "That's something I'll consider when the time comes."

"Are you ready to eat and raise a toast to seal our deal?"

She hugged Tonya, while struggling not to get too emotional. It was the first time she would be in complete control of her life and her future. She had lived at home while attending college, and it wasn't until she passed the CPA examination and secured the position at the investment bank that she was able to pay off her student loans. After that, she moved out of her parents' apartment and into the three-family house. The rent for the studio wasn't prohibitive, which had allowed her to save most of her salary. She had sacrificed by not going on vacation because her goal was to own property.

"Thanks, Titi Tonya."

"There's no need to thank me."

Nydia blinked back tears. "You don't know how my life will change once I move here."

Tonya nodded. "I have an idea that it will be very good for you."

"I have a favor to ask you, but if you don't want to do it, then I'll understand."

Tonya's brow furrowed. "What is it?"

"Would you mind if I move in earlier than January? Right now I'm paying my landlord month to month, and the woman is truly a witch. She clocks my every move, and I suspect she goes through my things when I'm not there."

"You don't have to tell me about folks clocking you, because I went through the same thing when I lived with my ex-husband's aunt and uncle. You can move in anytime you want. It'll be nice having someone to cook for other than myself."

"And I'll show you how to make some of the Puerto Rican dishes I picked up from my relatives who live on the island."

"I just happened to make a few dishes you would be familiar with. But you're going to have let me know if I get a passing grade with the rice and peas. When you made them when we were in New Orleans, I knew I had to try and make it myself."

Nydia leaned back and crossed her arms over her chest. "If you can make good *arroz con gandules,* then you're a badass."

"We'll find out, won't we?" Tonya teased.

"Let me wash my hands, and then I'll join you."

Nydia walked into the bathroom and closed the door. She bit down on her hand to keep from screaming with joy. She had not lied to Tonya when she told her she was through with the man to whom she had given too many chances. Even if she had not secured a position in which she could utilize her education and skills, she was still grateful to be earning some money. After washing and drying her hands, she joined Tonya in the kitchen. Once the chef lifted the lid on the pot of rice and pigeon peas, she knew Tonya had hit the jackpot. The mouthwatering aromas wafting from the pot reminded her of Christmas when her extended family gathered together to celebrate the holiday where *arroz con gandules*, *pernil*, and *pasteles* were always on the menu.

"My *abuela* used to say once a woman could cook, then she was ready for marriage."

Tonya made a sucking sound with her tongue and teeth. "Yeah, right. Been there, done that. Now it's your turn."

"I don't see that happening for a while," Nydia stated. "I'm going to listen to Jasmine's advice and take the time to find out who I am and what I want. And right now that's not a man."

Tonya opened the refrigerator and took out a bottle of

chilled white wine. She handed Nydia a corkscrew. "You can open the wine while I put the first course on the table."

Later, Tonya was sitting in bed reading the novel she wanted to finish to find out who had killed the beauty queen when her cell phone rang. It was Darius returning her call. She picked it up before it rang again. "Hello."

"Hey, Tee. I just got your voice mail message."

"I called you because I need to tell you something."

"What is it?"

"I want to tell you in person."

A sigh came through the earpiece. "I can't come tonight, because I'm bone tired and I'm about to go to bed."

"Then it can wait until we see each other."

"Come on, Tonya. Let's not play games. Tell me now or forget it."

There was something in Darius's voice that indicated something was bothering him, and because she never wanted to be his analyst, she decided not to ask. "I'm moving to New Orleans."

"When did you decide this?"

Tonya closed the book. "I told you when I came back from New Orleans this summer that I was thinking of moving down there."

"Thinking, Tonya! Thinking is a lot different from actually making a decision."

She counted slowly to ten. "You're right. And I've made a decision to move to New Orleans, because there's nothing keeping me here."

"What about me?"

"What about you, Darius?"

"Don't I mean anything to you?"

"Yes. You're my friend." She wanted to tell him he would never be more than a friend because she could not see herself living with or being married to him. There were occasions when he would stop talking altogether, and Tonya would be forced to tell him to leave.

"I'm your friend because you won't allow me to be more than that."

Tonya bit back the acerbic words on the tip of her tongue. "You knew when we started seeing each other that I didn't want a commitment."

"That's probably because you were sleeping with someone else whenever you told me you couldn't see me."

"Good night and good-bye." She ended the call. Tonya did not want to believe Darius had accused her of cheating on him. She stared at the phone in her hand. Seconds later she blocked his number. He wasn't able to get into her building unless she let him in, and luckily he didn't have the number to her landline.

"Never again," she whispered.

Tonya now knew for certain she had made the right decision to start over in a new state, where she could control her own destiny. She would become Eustace's apprentice, and once she opened the supper club, she planned to incorporate what she had learned from him with the dishes she had perfected while working at other restaurants.

She opened the book again, and when she finally closed it she was shocked by the ending. The beauty queen's murder wasn't a murder but a suicide. All the clues pointed to her lover, who had refused to leave his wealthy wife to marry her. Tonya placed the book on the bedside table, turned off the lamp, and pulled up the sheet and blanket over her shoulders.

Nydia had given her an A-plus on dinner, while she promised to teach her how to make *pasteles*—tamales filled with pork, chickpeas, yucca, olives, capers, and other spices—*mofongo, alcapurría*, and *coquito*.

Sleep was elusive as Tonya found her mind filled with all that had happened earlier that day. She would become an innkeeper, Nydia planned to move in November first, and she had lost a lover. *It's all for the best*, her inner voice reminded her. Once she believed in her instincts, she was able to fall asleep and not wake up again until ribbons of sunlight slipped between the slats of the window blinds.

She lay in bed, staring up at the ceiling. It was a brand new day and the beginning of a new life for her. And in another three months she would leave her home state to put down roots in another one. She had told Darius there was nothing in New York to keep her there. Her parents were in Florida, and her daughter planned to live in Georgia. Moving to New Orleans meant she would be closer to her loved ones.

Sitting up and swinging her legs over the side of the bed, Tonya headed for the bathroom humming her favorite song: "O Happy Day."

Chapter 6

Three months later

Tonya turned down the street leading to DuPont House and then maneuvered through the open gates and along the winding path that led to the mansion generations of DuPonts had called home. She had driven from Daytona Beach to New Orleans after spending a week with her parents and managed to make the six-hundred-mile trip in less than nine hours. She had just removed her luggage from the SUV's cargo compartment at the same time Hannah walked out onto the porch. The former corporate attorney was still tanned from three weeks of honeymooning in the South Pacific. Once she returned to the States, Hannah had downloaded dozens of photographs of her and her husband island-hopping from Bora Bora to Fiji and Tahiti. Tonya was looking forward to seeing them.

Tonya had not shared Thanksgiving with her daughter and parents, because Samara had opted to spend time with several classmates living in the Atlanta area. And when she told Samara she would see her for Christmas, again she was surprised when her daughter said she had secured a position tutoring because she wanted to save money for her graduate studies. Tonya was tempted to tell her daughter that she would be willing to subsidize her, but stopped herself just in time. After all, she wanted the college senior to become an independent, responsible adult willing to work and sacrifice for whatever she wanted or needed.

Hands resting at her waist, Hannah flashed a wide grin. "Let me take you to the guesthouse where you can rest yourself. You must be exhausted from all that driving."

Tonya grimaced when encountering stiffness in her back after sitting for hours behind the wheel of her newly purchased Honda Pilot. It had been years since she had owned a car. Public transportation had become her mode of getting around, but living and working in Manhattan was different from living and working in New Orleans— a city that would take her time to learn to navigate.

"All I want is a cool drink, a warm shower, and a bed."

Hannah hugged Tonya. "When you called to tell me you were driving straight through, I brought over something for you to eat. It's in the fridge. You just have to heat it in the microwave. Speaking of food, you don't have to do any shopping for a while. The kitchen cabinets are stocked and so is the freezer. And if there is anything you need, then just raid the pantry in the main house."

She returned the hug, and then pulled back to look at the tall, green-eyed natural blonde. "Thank you. Marriage agrees with you," she teased, smiling.

Hannah returned her smile. "That's because being married to St. John agrees with me. I never thought I could be as happy and contented as I am now."

"Good for you."

"Come with me," she said, picking up the large quilted weekender and leading the way along a flagstone path around the house to where two guesthouses stood several hundred yards from each other. "We'll talk once you've had something to drink and eat. I would've invited you to come to the house in Marigny, but St. John has been hosting off-campus meetings with those in his department to discuss a few courses they either want to add or drop, and because of their different schedules, it's almost impossible to meet on campus."

Tonya watched as Hannah unlocked the door and stood to one side for her to enter. During her last visit she had surveyed the structure of less than one thousand feet of living space where she would live until the restoration and renovations to the main house were completed. There was a parlor, dining area, eat-in kitchen, two bedrooms, and a bathroom with a separate shower stall. The guesthouse had been updated over the years. A stacked washer-dryer was concealed behind the doors of a utility closet, which eliminated the need to use the laundry room in the main house. The wood floors gleamed with a coat of wax, and the familiar scent of lemon lingered in the air. Hannah told her the cleaning company had worked diligently to get the guesthouse ready before her arrival.

"How are the renovations coming?"

"Not fast enough, but I've decided not to stress out over it, because the approval for installing the elevator is still pending. Meanwhile, work will begin on the upstairs suites next week, now that all the furniture has been removed."

"Where did you put the furniture?" DuPont House was filled with priceless antiques dating back several centuries.

"An adjuster from the insurance company catalogued them before they were crated and taken to a warehouse. I delayed emptying the suites on the first floor because my cousins don't want to move in with me and St. John until the last possible moment. They claim they don't want to encroach on the newlyweds."

"They're right," Tonya said in agreement. "That's why I suggested moving in here. Not only do you need your privacy, but also time to get accustomed to living with each other. By the way, how are your cousins enjoying their retirement?"

Shaking her head, Hannah rolled her eyes upward. "I rarely get to see them. If they're not attending a home or away Saints' game, then they're cruising with a group of retired teachers who refer to themselves as the Wild Bunch. They're gone so much that Smokey now lives with me and St. John."

"Didn't they just come back from a four-month cruise?"

Hannah nodded. "Right now they're embarking on either weeklong or four-day cruises to the eastern or western Caribbean. They've been talking about taking the *Queen Elizabeth 2* world voyage next year. The ship leaves New York early January and doesn't return until mid-May."

It was Tonya's turn to shake her head. "I like the ocean, but I'd rather sit on a beach and watch it rather than live on it for months."

"I'm with you. Where do you want me to put this bag?"

Tonya flopped down on a chintz-covered loveseat and kicked off her running shoes. "Just leave it by the door. I'll empty it later."

Hannah folded her body down to a matching armchair and crossed her feet at the ankles. "The boxes you shipped are stacked in the smaller bedroom. I left remote devices to open the gates and another one to open the garage on the kitchen countertop. You'll also find an extra set of keys for this place and the main house. Now that I'm living in Marigny, there's room in the garage for your vehicle. I noticed you have New York plates on your SUV. Is it a rental or a lease?"

"Neither. It was my Christmas gift to me." Within minutes of test-driving the Honda Pilot, Tonya fell in love with the spacious sport utility vehicle. "Once I moved to Manhattan I got rid of my car, because I didn't want to get up every other morning to move it from one side of the street to the other. And it costs a small fortune to garage it."

"You're preaching to the choir, Tonya. It was cheaper for me to take a car service than have a car when I lived there. By the way, how's Nydia?"

Tonya smiled. "She's great. She loves the apartment and the neighborhood. I couldn't have asked for a better person to sublet my place, because she's quiet and fastidious. And I must say she's quite the cook when it comes to preparing Latin dishes. She taught me how to make sofrito and mojito, which is a garlic dipping sauce that's out of this world."

Hannah nodded. "I couldn't get enough of her rice and peas when she came down last summer."

"I can make them, too," Tonya said boastfully.

"You know you're going to have to put your money where your mouth is," Hannah teased. "Maybe one of these nights you can make us a traditional Latin dinner."

"Consider it done." Tonya wanted to tell Hannah that Nydia moving in November rather than January proved beneficial to them both. Nydia didn't have a landlady clocking her every move, and she had more privacy and a lot more room than she had had in the studio apartment.

"How is she making out with her boyfriend?" Hannah asked.

Tonya shook her head. "I wouldn't know, because she's never mentioned him again after she moved in. And if she's not seeing clients, or spending hours doing their books, then she's visiting her relatives, who happen to live within walking distance."

"I'm glad everything's working out for her." Hannah pushed to her feet. "I'm sitting here running my mouth when you need to settle in and unwind. If you want to hang out together, then send me a text. St. John and I are hosting a Super Bowl party this year, so I'd really appreciate it if you can give me suggestions for a menu. I want something different from the quintessential wings, guacamole, and chips."

"Why don't you have Eustace cater it?"

"I would if he didn't have several other parties he's catering the same day. However, he did say he would stop by later."

Tonya smiled. "Not to worry. I'll come up with something a bit more unconventional. How many are you expecting?"

"Twenty have committed to coming."

"I'll make enough for thirty."

Hannah held up a hand. "I didn't ask you to help so you'd have to—"

"Stop, Hannah," Tonya interrupted in a quiet voice. "I want to cook because it's free advertising for once I open the supper club. How will folks know what I can do if they don't get the opportunity to sample my dishes?"

Hannah's pale eyebrows lifted slightly. "You're right about that. You can do the cooking, but only if you allow me to pay you. I need you to give a shopping list, and I'll make certain you'll have whatever you need."

Tonya bit down on her lower lip. "If you mention paying me again, I'll cut you."

Throwing back her head, Hannah laughed until she nearly lost her breath. "Now you sound like me."

"Do you think you have a monopoly on threatening to cut folks?" She remembered Hannah threatening to cut her when she attempted to pick up the check for a restaurant dinner they had shared with Jasmine and Nydia, and then again when they threatened to sleep with St. John if she did not marry him.

"I really wouldn't have cut anyone."

"Neither would I, because I don't like violence." Tonya's mind was working overtime as to what she would put together for the Super Bowl gathering. "Give me a few days to come up with a menu you like, then we'll go shopping together."

"You've got a deal, partner."

Partner. The word lingered with Tonya long after

Hannah walked out. After drawing all the shades in the house, she picked up the weekender and removed a bag containing bottles of bath gel, shampoo, conditioner, and body moisturizer. After a shower, she planned to brew a cup of coffee with plenty of milk, then get into bed and read. Some people watched television before going to sleep, but Tonya found reading a lot more relaxing. Although she had downloaded many books onto her tablet, she still liked holding a physical book. There were some nights when she fell asleep and woke to find the book had fallen off the bed onto the floor.

Forty minutes later she climbed into bed, pulled the sheet and lightweight blanket over her shoulders, and went to sleep, knowing when the sun rose she would mark her first day as a transplanted Louisianan.

Tonya woke, slightly disoriented, and then she remembered where she was. Stretching her arms above her head, she smiled. Today marked the first day in her journey to fulfill her destiny. Although it would be months before she opened the restaurant, she felt as if she had been wrapped in an invisible cocoon of peace and happiness she had not experienced since she held her infant daughter in her arms for the first time.

Turning over, she reached for her cell phone on the bedside table. It was minutes before four. It was apparent her body's circadian rhythm was still in the Eastern time zone. And although she had not had to get up early since being downsized eight months earlier, old habits were hard to shake. Then she had to be at the bank at six to help prepare breakfast for the employees or their elite clients. She had worked long hours, but she was generously compensated for what would routinely become twelve-hour workdays.

A silent voice told her to stay in bed, but Tonya had never been one to laze away the morning. There were boxes to unpack. She had packed and shipped all of her clothes and personal items to DuPont House two days before she left New York to drive to Florida, leaving several outfits she would wear during the week she spent with her parents. She had also called Eustace to inform him that she was returning to New Orleans and she would stop in and help him prepare dishes for Chez Toussaints' lunch crowd.

Sitting up and swinging her legs over the side of the four-poster bed, Tonya flicked on the bedside lamp and walked out of the bedroom to the bathroom.

The sun was up and the Garden District was alive with activity when Tonya got into her car and drove to Tremé. It had taken her less than an hour to unpack the boxes and put everything away. She had brought several heavy jackets and two winter coats despite the fact that the temperatures rarely dipped below fifty degrees.

She managed to find the restaurant without using the Honda's GPS and pulled into the parking lot behind the building. It was six thirty, and there was one other vehicle in the lot along with the two white vans. She recognized the SUV immediately. It belonged to Gage. Her brow creased in worry. Had something happened to Eustace since their recent conversation?

Tonya did not want to think the worst when she got out and rang the back doorbell. The door opened and she came face-to-face with Gage Toussaint. It was obvious he was surprised to see her as he stared at her for several seconds.

She met his gray-green eyes, wondering what was going on behind the luminous orbs. "May I come in?"

"Sure . . . yes," he stammered and opened the door wider.

Tonya did not want to believe the man was even more attractive than she remembered. He had covered his hair with a black baseball cap. A sprinkling of gray in his stubble served to enhance his masculine beauty. A white tee, relaxed jeans, and running shoes were not what she considered required attire for a high school teacher.

"I called the other day and told Eustace I was coming in."

"Eustace didn't say anything to me."

She narrowed her eyes. "Does your brother tell you everything?"

A hint of a smile tilted the corners of Gage's mouth. "Apparently he doesn't. Put your stuff away and come into the kitchen."

Tonya resisted the urge to salute him as she slipped out of her lightweight jacket and left it on a hook in the storeroom. Reaching into her oversize tote, she took out a large bandana and covered her head, and then removed a rolled-up canvas with an assortment of chef's knives and walked into the kitchen. It was ablaze with lights, while a large stockpot simmered on the stove.

"Where's Eustace?" she asked Gage when he handed her an apron.

"He's working out. He'll be here around eight."

She blinked slowly. "Working out?"

"Yes. His New Year's resolution is to lose weight, lower his cholesterol and blood pressure before his high school's fortieth reunion, and I've offered to come in early Mondays, Wednesdays, and Fridays to cover for him."

Tonya smiled. "That's great."

Gage flashed a warm smile. "What's great is that he's already lost five pounds. His goal is to lose ten pounds a month. By the time his reunion rolls around in May, he wants to tip the scales at two hundred."

She quickly did the math in her head. "Your brother weighs over two-forty?"

Gage nodded. "Eustace was always a big boy. He weighed ten pounds at birth. He takes after Pop's side of the family, while I'm built more like the men in my mother's family."

"He should've played football."

"He was offered full athletic scholarships to play ball at several colleges, but he turned them down to help Pop run this place. At that time they were open six days a week serving lunch and dinner."

Tonya remembered Eustace telling her how he had to decrease the hours and days of operation, which made her think about how many days and hours she would devote to the supper club. "Did he ever regret not playing ball?"

"I've never heard him complain about it. Chez Toussaints is a family business that hopefully will be around for generations to come. Once Eustace hangs up his apron, my nieces will take over. They're trying to convince their husbands to come into the business, but right now they're not ready to change careers. Melinda's husband is a firefighter, while Nicole's is a sheriff in Baton Rouge."

"What about you, Gage?" Tonya asked. "Have you considered stepping in when Eustace retires?"

Gage went completely still. It was a question his brother had asked him so many times that he had lost count, and occasionally it was a topic of contention between the two of them. Eustace had insisted he decide whether he wanted to be a chef or a musician, but at this time in his life, Gage did not have to make a decision as to one or the other. As long as he was able to teach during the week, play at Jazzes on the weekends, and assist Eustace whenever he had to cater a party, then he did not see the need to change his current lifestyle.

"No!" He gave Tonya a direct stare when she opened her mouth, but then closed it quickly. He hadn't meant for his response to come out so harsh, but it was too late to retract it. "I'm sorry. I didn't mean to bark at you."

Tonya lowered her eyes. "Apology accepted, even though you seem to do that a lot."

His brow furrowed. "What are you talking about?"

"The last time we were together you were rather condescending when I told you I wanted to run my own restaurant, and your comeback was 'good luck with that, chef.'"

His eyebrow lifted. "I said that?"

"Yes, you did."

Crossing his arms over his chest, he angled his head. A few minutes ago, when the bell had rung, he had opened the door and was shocked to find Tonya standing there. In that instant everything he had remembered about her came rushing back like frames of film: her flawless skin, sexy mouth, and the scent of the hauntingly hypnotic perfume that lingered inside his car for days.

"I don't know what had gotten into me to have said something like that."

A smile parted Tonya's lips, the gesture bringing his gaze to linger on them. In that instant he wondered if she knew just how sexy she was. He had known a lot of women who did not hesitate to capitalize on their looks when in the company of men, but there was something about Tonya that indicated that wasn't a part of her feminine repertoire when it came to interacting with a man. It was as if she were oblivious to her looks and undeniable sensuality.

"Perhaps it was lack of sleep that brought out the bear in you." She extended her hand. "Let's start again. Hello. I'm Tonya Martin."

Gage ignored the proffered hand; instead he rested his hands on her shoulders and kissed her on both cheeks. "It's a pleasure to make your acquaintance, Tonya Martin. I'm Gage Toussaint." He had registered Tonya's intake of breath when he kissed her, hoping he had not overstepped the line. It was apparent he and Tonya would get to see quite a bit of each other now that she was working with his brother. "Now that we have the formalities out of the way, chef, can you please put up a pot of beef stock?"

The dimples in her cheeks winked at him when she smiled. "No problem, chef."

He watched Tonya wash her hands, dry them, and then slip on a pair of disposable gloves, pretending interest in his stockpot with crushed crab claws and crawfish shells. She moved around the kitchen with a minimum of wasted motion as she heated a heavy stockpot over medium heat and added soup bones and oxtails until they were browned all over before she added two coarsely chopped carrots, and then several gallons of water. Once the pot came to a light boil, she lowered the flame to barely a simmer.

They worked well together. Now he knew why Eustace had sung her praises when she halved the time it would have taken him to cater the book club party. Gage opened the oven to check the water level in a pan of roast beef, adding more until it was at least two inches deep.

"Are you teaching today?" she asked after a long, comfortable silence.

Gage glanced up at the wall clock. "My first class isn't until eleven. Right now I'm a permanent substitute for the orchestra teacher, who was the victim of a hit-and-run. I got the call late yesterday afternoon from the principal that Mr. Murdock was taken to the hospital and the prognosis is he won't be able to return to work for at least four to five months."

"That sounds serious."

"It is. He has a spinal injury, along with two broken legs. Thankfully someone copied down the license plate of the driver before he drove away, so it's just a matter of time before they catch the heartless bastard."

"How many classes are you teaching?"

"Two, but then there's after-school practice. This year the orchestra has qualified to compete for the state championship."

"Do you ever give private lessons?"

He shook his head. "No. Most of the kids can't afford private lessons. I'll usually stay after practice to work with a student who may need extra help."

"When do you sleep or even have time for a social life?" Tonya asked.

"Are you asking me if I'm involved with a woman?"

"No . . . of course not," she said quickly. "I just asked if you take time out to have some fun."

Gage sobered. If he was truly honest, then he would say he didn't have an active social life, and he had not had one in a while. "Teaching and playing at Jazzes and helping Eustace with catering take up a lot my waking hours. And I haven't been in a relationship for a while because I don't have the time to make it work."

"All work and no play makes for a dull boy."

Picking up the pot of fish stock, he poured it through a strainer into another large pot and discarded the solids. "I've never thought of myself as dull. And to prove it, I'd like you to hang out with me one night when I'm not playing at Jazzes."

Tonya gave a sidelong glance. "Are you asking me out on a date?"

He lifted a shoulder. "It really wouldn't be a date, because I don't want to be responsible for you cheating on your man."

Several seconds went by. "I don't have a man. But if you just want to hang out, then I'm okay with that."

Gage successfully concealed a smile. There was something about Tonya he liked—a lot—and he instinctively knew hanging out with her would not only be fun, but also stimulating, because they both were chefs, had lived abroad, and when it came to marriage—been there, done that. In the past he had dated so many women who were so immature that he had begun to think maybe there was something wrong with him. He extended his hand. "Give me your cell and I'll program my number."

"It's in my tote. I'll give you my number, and you call me whenever you're free."

"Are you staying with Hannah and St. John?"

"No. I'm living in one of the guesthouses at DuPont House until the renovations are completed."

Reaching into the back pocket of his jeans, Gage handed Tonya his cell phone, waiting until she tapped in the numbers. He studied the phone number, committing it to memory. "It's been a long time since I've seen a two-one-two area code."

"Do you miss New York?" she asked.

"Sometimes I do, but not enough to live there again. What about you? Do you think you'll adjust to living down here?"

"I'm good as long as I don't have to deal with snow-storms and below-freezing temperatures."

"Maybe I should go back home and take the day off, now that you two seem to have everything under control here."

Gage turned to find Eustace standing at the entrance to the kitchen. "That's not happening, brother, because in a couple of hours I'm going home to change for my *real* job."

Eustace strolled across the kitchen and gave Tonya a bear hug. "Welcome back."

Going on tiptoe, she kissed his cheek. "Thank you. It's good to be back, and I'm here to help out any way I can."

Gage smiled as he watched the interchange between his brother and the woman who unknowingly had en-snared him in a web of longing he hadn't felt in a very long time. He liked her because she was direct; she was nothing like some women he knew who were into playing head games. A few had set up scenarios in an attempt to make him jealous, but it always backfired. There was no way he was going to confront a man about the woman with whom he had been physically involved. But on the other hand, everything about Tonya appealed to him as a man, and the fact they shared a love of cooking was something he could not ignore. He wasn't looking for a relationship, and he suspected neither was she, so that meant they could begin as friends and then see where that would take them.

Chapter 7

Tonya stood at the prep table chopping, dicing, and mincing onion, celery, red and green bell peppers, garlic, thyme, and parsley for the various dishes on the day's menu board. The distinctive voice of Billie Holiday singing the poignant protest song "Strange Fruit" flowed from the radio speakers, and in a moment of shared emotion she met the eyes of Eustace and Gage. She may not have grown up in the South during segregation and Jim Crow, but she knew the strange fruit Billie sang about were victims of lynching.

Eustace must have registered the somber mood, because he picked up the remote device and changed the radio station to music that was more contemporary and upbeat. "That's better," he said under his breath as he returned to the stove.

Gage had removed several large bowls filled with

chicken from the refrigerator and sprinkled them with the house Cajun seasoning. He did the same with slices of catfish, while Eustace poured a couple of tablespoons of oil in a large Dutch oven and heated it before browning the chicken pieces for chicken-andouille gumbo.

"How often do you change your menu?" Tonya asked Eustace as she set the bowls of chopped ingredients on the countertop.

"Not too often. We try to have customer favorites every day, and that includes gumbos, red beans and rice, fried catfish, and Cajun jambalaya."

"What's the difference between Creole and Cajun jambalaya?"

"Gage can answer that for you."

"Cajun jambalaya is brown, never made with tomatoes, and always has smoked sausage or tasso," Gage explained. "Creole jambalaya is reddish, a color it gets from tomatoes, and always contains shrimp."

"Which do you like best?" she asked him.

"I like both."

"I'm going to have to sample both before I make a decision which I like best," Tonya said. She glanced at the menu board again. "I've heard of shrimp, oyster, and sausage po'boys, but I see you're serving roast beef po'boys."

Eustace patted his belly over his apron. "I love roast beef po'boys. There's something about thinly sliced beef and gravy on fresh French bread with lettuce, tomatoes, mayo, and pickles that's out of this world." He patted his belly again. "It's one of the reasons I got this corporation up front."

"Speaking of bread," Gage said, "where the hell is the bread man? He should've been here hours ago."

"I don't mind making the bread," she volunteered. "I'm

not bragging, but I *can* make incredible authentic French baguettes."

Gage shared a look with his brother. "Are you sure that's what you want to do?"

Tonya gave him a long, penetrating stare when he met her eyes. "I wouldn't offer if I didn't want to make them."

"Well, we do have baguette trays in the storeroom, so if you want to bake baguettes, I don't have a problem with it. What do you say, Eustace?"

A beat passed, and then Eustace said, "Yes. But I have to pay you for baking the bread, and close your mouth and don't say anything because I'll fire you if you—"

"You can't fire me," Tonya said, cutting him off. "I'm a volunteer, not an employee," she added, smiling. "And I won't accept money from you, because whatever I learn in this kitchen can't be measured in dollars and cents. Don't you realize you're offering me a free education when it comes to perfecting regional dishes?"

Eustace paused, as he appeared to be deep in thought. "You're probably right about that."

She flashed a smug grin. "I know I'm right. Starting tomorrow I'll make baguettes for your po'boys."

The words were barely off her tongue when the bell chimed. "I hope that's the bread man," Gage said under his breath. "I'll get it."

Tonya waited until he left the kitchen before she moved closer to Eustace. "I didn't mean to sound overbearing, but I told you before that I'm willing to help out anyway I can, and if that means baking bread then I'll do it. It may be six months or even nine months before I will be able to open my supper club, and when I do, I want to hit the ground running. People come to New Orleans for the food and music, and that's something I need to perfect if I want to stay open. I can't compete with other restaurants, because they're just too many, but when folks leave my place I want them to think about coming back again, and that's not going to happen if I don't offer dishes that represent this city."

Eustace chuckled softly. "I wouldn't fire you even if you were an employee. I know what you can do, and I'm certain there are a lot of things I can learn from you, because your wings were a big hit with the book club women. I tried making them again, but they didn't turn out like yours. My stepmother taught Gage to make the bread we use for the pudding, while I'm completely useless when it comes to working with dough. So, if you want to bake bread, then just do it. I'm going to give you a key and the code to the alarm, so you can come in whenever you want."

Tonya felt a warm glow through her. It was apparent Eustace trusted her not only with his family's secret recipes but also respected her suggestions. "Thank you."

"No thank *you*, Tonya. It's too bad we can't go into business together because then I'd let your run Chez Toussaints with my daughters, while I devote all of my energies to expanding my catering business."

"That can't happen, because I've committed to running the café and supper club for the inn."

Eustace winked at her. "You can't blame a dude for trying. Hannah knows I'll do any and everything I can to help her business succeed because she's family."

Tonya nodded. Hannah told her that once she married St. John McNair, she was also considered a Baptiste and a Toussaint. And because of her partnership with Hannah, Tonya was now privy to secret recipes handed down through generations of Toussaints.

Gage returned to the kitchen with two large paper bags filled with loaves of French bread. "The driver said he had a flat tire and didn't have a spare."

That's another reason for baking your own bread, Tonya mused. Chez Toussaints could not compare to the restaurants where she had worked that were staffed with personnel ranging from executive, sous, and pastry chefs, along with a broiler cook, baker, fry/sauté cook, servers, and bus person, but it could be run just as efficiently. Once she opened her restaurants, she would bake enough bread to supply her place and Chez Toussaints.

Tonya sliced tomatoes, washed and dried lettuce leaves for the po'boys, placing them in plastic containers before they were stored on shelves in the walk-in refrigerator. She shelled and deveined countless pounds of shrimp that would be battered and fried for the sandwich.

"Are you certain you'll sell out all of these today?" she asked Gage when he moved over to stand next to her.

He nodded. "We usually sell out of shrimp po'boys before noon. It's one of the most requested items on the menu. We call them firecracker shrimp because we add cayenne to the dry seasonings. That and a spicy garlic mayonnaise made it an instant hit the first time we put it on the menu."

"Do you make your own mayonnaise?" She had noticed a large glass jar in the fridge labeled mayo.

"Yes. But that's another family secret."

"Garlic mayonnaise by another name is aioli."

"That is it," he confirmed with a wide grin, "but we add chilies in addition to Tabasco sauce to give it an extra kick. There's nothing better than our shrimp po'boy with an ice cold bottle of beer."

"That sounds good."

He dipped his head and pressed his mouth to her ear. "It is."

Suddenly Tonya felt as if he was too close, that his body's heat had seeped into hers and made her feel warm. He smelled of soap and clean linen. She wanted to tell him that he had invaded her personal space, which made her more than aware that something about Gage, other than his looks, excited her. He was a reminder that she was a woman who was still capable of passion.

Unfortunately, her ex had made it difficult for her to form a relationship with a man; she did not want to become so involved that she would lose her independence, and for Tonya independence was the single most important factor in her life. Gage had suggested they hang out together, and she would, because she knew their relationship would never progress beyond friendship and a mutual respect for their shared profession.

"What is your favorite sauce?" she asked. She felt the need to say something to make herself ignore the fact that she found his nearness slightly overwhelming.

Gage blinked as if coming out of a trance. Standing inches from Tonya and inhaling her perfume conjured up the moments when she had sat next to him in his vehicle. Every time he opened the door and sat behind the wheel, her scent lingered until after a while it faded completely. He had tried recalling the timbre of her voice, the stunning flawlessness of her bare face, and the mature, lush curves of her body that threatened to send his libido into overdrive. He did not know what there was about the woman that intrigued him so much, but he intended to discover what it was, and that was why he had asked her to go out with him.

"I'm partial to béarnaise. It goes well with chicken pontalba."

"Is that a Creole dish?" she asked.

"Yes. It was name for the Baroness Micaela Pontalba, who earned fame for supervising the construction of the Pontalba buildings on the uptown and downtown sides of Jackson Square. One of these days I'll make it for you, and you have to let me know if you want to put it on the menu when you open your restaurant."

She flashed a dimpled smile. "I'd like that."

Gage glanced above her at the clock and took off his apron. "I have to head out now, so we'll talk later."

Tonya nodded. "Later." She pretended interest in chopping the red bell pepper, green onions, and sprigs of fresh tarragon for crab cakes rather than watch Gage walk out. She reminded herself she had relocated to New Orleans to go into business—not fall under the spell of a man whose very presence seemed to suck the air of out of the room.

Gage walked into the general office to sign in for the day. He nodded to the two women who were the eyes and ears for the principal who ran his school like a four-star general. The high school had undergone several changes over the years, and the result was higher test scores and lower dropout rates. The school board called an emergency meeting and conducted a search for an administrator with strong leadership qualities. They eventually hired the former headmaster of a military school who within two years had turned Lafitte High School into a model for success.

The principal's secretary handed Gage a large kraft envelope. "Mr. Toussaint, Dr. Carter wanted me to give this to you. He's assigning you to Mr. Murdock's class as a permanent teacher for the remainder of the school year. You'll now be paid out of the regular school budget *and* the grant. Any after-school activities will have to be reported on the hourly professional personnel time report. Those forms are also in the envelope. If you have any questions, then please see me. I also made up a timecard for you, so beginning tomorrow you'll be required to punch in at eight and out at three. We've temporarily deactivated Mr. Murdock's email and added your name to the school's email list, so you'll be able to log on to his computer using your own password."

She had spoken so quickly that Gage had to listen intently to catch every word. "Thank you." He was taken aback that the district had hired him as a permanent teacher. Louis Murdock was a department head, which meant he would not only cover the man's classes, but suspected he would have the responsibility for running the music department. And having to come in at eight would conflict with his covering for Eustace at the restaurant on Mondays, Wednesdays, and Fridays.

He left the office, nearly colliding with Dr. Carter. Although he had recently celebrated his sixty-third birthday, the West Point graduate and former career officer appeared years younger with his slender, ramrod-straight posture, lightly graying hair, and smooth nut-brown face.

"I see Miss Gibbons gave you the envelope. The school board and the superintendent have agreed to appoint you as a permanent teacher rather than a sub. With you in Murdock's position, you'll be responsible for organizing the spring concert. A group email was sent to the faculty and staff that your office has been changed from the band room to Murdock's office."

Gage's impassive expression did not reveal what he was thinking at that time, and he doubted the principal would want to know. He didn't mind stepping in and picking up the slack because of a colleague's medical emergency, but becoming a permanent faculty member was something he hadn't planned. If he had wanted to teach full-time, then he would have applied for a position as a full-time teacher. Eustace had asked him whether he wanted to be a chef or a musician and he had been unable to give him an answer, because at this time in his life he was willing to devote only a portion of his free time to teaching students who were seriously considering a career in music.

He had earned a graduate degree in education as a backup in case he ever tired of being a session player for various bands; however, in less than twenty-four hours, his well-ordered life had changed. Now he would spend the next five months teaching, running a department, playing at Jazzes on the weekend, *and* assisting his brother whenever he had to cater for any party for more than twenty-five.

Gage smiled, but the gesture did not reach his eyes. "Murdock is a hard act to follow."

Dr. Carter nodded. "That he is, but I have no doubt you'll be able to build on what he has accomplished with our students, because what you've done with the jazz band is phenomenal."

"That's because I'm working with a group of very talented young musicians."

"Don't be self-deprecating, Toussaint; the kids are close

to worshipping you." He glanced at his watch. "Classes are about to change, so I'm going to let you go."

Gage nodded, turned on his heel, and headed down the hall. He opened the door to the band room at the same time the bell rang. Within seconds the hall was filled with students pouring out of classrooms. He entered the room and draped his jacket over the back of the desk chair. Murdock had pasted on the desk a printout of the orchestra with the various sections and the names of the students and where they were seated. He studied the printout, then picked up the sheet music resting on the stand in front of a stool. A yellow Post-it was attached to a page of Dvorak's Symphony No. 9 in E minor op. 95 "From the New World."

Gage wrote his name on the white board, and then nodded to each student as they filed into the room. He saw surprise cross the faces of his jazz band students. It was apparent they were not prepared to see him directing the orchestra. Once all were seated and had taken out their instruments, he sat on the stool.

"For those who are not familiar with me, I'm Mr. Toussaint and I'm going to be your teacher for the rest of the school year. Unfortunately, Mr. Murdock has experienced a medical emergency. Those who are in the jazz band know me well and what I expect from them. I will have the same expectations from the orchestra." He paused briefly. "I know the fall concert was a rousing success, but it's usually the spring concert that is the musical highlight of the school year.

"This spring I would like to try something different, but that all depends on how hard you all are willing to work. I expect you to practice whatever we go over in class, and if called upon, you will play in front of your classmates." Glances were exchanged amid whispers. "It's not to put you on the spot, but for me and your peers to acknowledge your musical genius." Laughter, high-fives, and fist bumps followed his compliment. "I'm going to give you three minutes to warm up, and then I want Mr. Santos to come up and play for us."

A rush of color flooded the boy's face. "I didn't get a chance to practice it."

"Mr. Murdock doesn't make us play if we don't practice," said one of the viola players.

Gage resisted the urge to shake his head in exasperation. "Well, I'm not Mr. Murdock, and if you don't practice at home, then you'll practice in front of the class." Minutes later, he beckoned to the clarinetist. "Mr. Santos, please bring your music." The band room was so quiet he could hear breathing coming from those sitting closest to him. Gage did not want to embarrass the boy, but if he was a serious music student, then it was incumbent upon him to practice. He slipped off the stool and waited for the student to sit and arrange his music. "We're listening, Mr. Santos."

The first few notes came out in high-pitched squeaking until he settled down and played the piece flawlessly. There was deafening silence for several seconds before the room erupted in applause, Gage clapping along with the others. "Excellent." The boy returned to his seat, exchanging high-fives and handshakes with his classmates.

A French horn player raised his hand. "Mr. Toussaint, may I play my solo?"

"Me, too," came a chorus from the assembly.

The students asking to play solos meant they were confident enough to play in front of their peers. His eyes swept over their eager faces. "Okay. We're going to begin with the violins, then the violas, and follow with the cellos and bassist. Each section will play their part, and then it will be the woodwinds' turn, followed by brass and percussion. Once everyone has their turn, then time permitting we'll play the entire movement."

It had only taken one class for Gage to assess the students as quite accomplished when it came to reading and playing music. Two months before, they had performed in the winter concert, and now it was time they practice for the spring frolic, and the compositions Mr. Murdock had chosen did not match their ability to play different genres. Gage had spent years playing classical music, but it wasn't until he was introduced to ragtime, jazz, and the blues that he felt alive, as if the music was personally talking to him.

He glanced up at the wall clock as the students packed away their instruments. There was still another three minutes before the bell rang. "Can anyone tell me what the first instrument was?"

Several hands went up. "It was the drum," called out the percussionist.

Gage smiled. "Even before that." He was met with silence and blank stares. "What about the voice? Did not man have the ability to sing even before the first drum was constructed?"

"Word!" yelled Mr. Santos. "I saw an a capella group competition, and they made music with their voices that sounded like instruments."

Gage nodded. "You're right. We'll talk about this at the end of the next class."

He watched the students file out of the band room as ideas in his head tumbled over one another. This was his last year teaching under the two-year grant, and he wanted to leave more of an impact on the school than just starting a jazz band. Reaching for the leather portfolio case with his initials stamped on the front cover, he opened it and took out a pen and legal pad. Fifty minutes later he had jotted down several ideas he wanted to present to the instructors chairing the drama and choral clubs.

He found Murdock's office, opened the door, and slowly walked in. Framed posters of musicians from bygone eras to the present lined three of the four walls. Gage didn't know why, but he felt like an intruder. The music teacher had not spent more than twenty-four hours in the hospital and already he had been replaced. It was a sobering reminder that everyone was replaceable. He stared at the photographs of Louis with his wife and children during happier times when they visited Disney World and the Grand Canyon. Gage made a mental note to call the hospital to ascertain when Murdock would be able to receive visitors.

As he had booted up the desktop and programmed a password, he reminded himself that he had to call his brother and apprise him of the change in his work schedule. Eustace had confided to him that when he had checked with his physician before embarking on an exercise regimen, the doctor ordered a battery of tests, and some of the results were not good. Not only was he overweight, but his blood pressure was elevated and his cholesterol levels were much too high. It had become a wakeup call for Eustace to change his current lifestyle. He stopped eating fried foods and decreased his sodium intake. He had sworn Gage to secrecy because he did not want his wife to know what she had suspected for years— that if he didn't change his diet, then he was going to have either a heart attack or stroke.

Gage transcribed his notes into a memo, revising it several times before emailing it to those assigned to the music and art department. Slumping back in the chair, he stared at the computer monitor, and recalled Tonya's words: *All work and no play makes for a dull boy.* He did not know when she had said it how prophetic the statement would be. Gage was aware that he could have rejected the offer to become a member of the school's faculty, but he now realized it would have a negative impact on the students if they had to wait for the district to search for, interview, and hire a replacement.

Well, Tonya, he thought, *you're right, because for the next five months it will be all about work.* Not only would he work with both the orchestra and jazz band, but also plan and rehearse for the upcoming spring concert, which was coming to resemble opening day for a big Broadway play. It would involve musicians, singers, actors, and stage designers. Ruminating about the concert was not going to solve the dilemma of his going into the restaurant to prep before Eustace arrived at eight.

Reaching for his cell phone, he tapped the number to the restaurant. It rang three times before his niece answered. "Nicky, can you please put your dad on the phone?"

"Hold on, Gage, he's right here."

"What's up, bro?"

It took Gage less than a minute to explain to Eustace the change in his status at the school. "I have to clock in at eight, so I'm not going to be able to cover for you the days you work out."

"That shouldn't be a problem now that Tonya's here. I gave her a key and the code to the security system. I'm almost certain she wouldn't mind coming in early, but just in case I'm being presumptuous, you should let her know why you won't be here. Hold on, and I'll give you her number."

"Don't bother. I have her number."

There came a noticeable pause. "You have her number?" Eustace asked.

"Yes. She gave it to me this morning. I know you guys are busy now, so tell her I'll call her later on this afternoon."

"No problem. Congratulations, professor. Or should I say maestro."

Gage laughed. "Neither."

"I gotta hang up now and get back to the kitchen because my girls are giving me the stink eye."

Gage ended the call, smiling. Tonya had appeared on the scene like a fairy godmother. When she left New Orleans following his cousin's wedding, Hannah had mentioned Tonya planned to return at the end of January. But by some miracle she had come earlier than predicted. Circumstances could not have been better if he had planned it. Eustace could continue to work out as recommended by his doctor; Tonya had volunteered as a baker and sous chef for the restaurant; while he was stepping in for a fellow musician who had selected Gage to become an artist-in-residence. Although he and Louis Murdock had grown up in the same Tremé neighborhood, they rarely saw each other. By the time Gage entered grade school Louis had left New Orleans for Potsdam, New York, to enroll in the Crane School of Music. They were reunited years later when Louis returned to his hometown after three decades of teaching music education in various New York City and Washington, D.C., public schools.

A reply to his email appeared on the monitor. It was from the director of the marching band. Like Gage, he was paid from a discretionary budget to rebuild the band after the former director had been fired the year before. He indicated the days and times he was available to meet with Gage to discuss the plans for the concert. By the time he left the office to pick up lunch from the faculty lunchroom, he had received two more replies.

He had a jazz band class at two, followed by an hour of practice, and then he planned to call Tonya to update her on his teaching schedule and ask whether she would be willing to cover for him.

Chapter 8

Tonya worked well with identical twins Nicole Dupree and Melinda Shaw, who arrived together at eight-thirty and greeted her as warmly as if she were a long-lost cousin. She had met them for the first time the summer before at St. John's family reunion. The thirty-five-year-old women had inherited their father's complexion and height, and their mother's doll-like features.

Both had graduated college, earning degrees in social work like their hospital-based social worker mother, but after marriage and motherhood they were stay-at-home mothers until their children were school age, and then opted to work in the family-owned restaurant. They told her they left promptly at two in order to arrive home to meet their children's school buses. Nicole, the mother of two sets of twins, admitted she didn't miss counseling clients or updating case notes, because now she could spend more time with her children, while Melinda admitted she had always preferred working with her hands, because her first career choice had been to study art.

Melinda adjusted the hairnet covering her short natural hair under a baseball cap before she unlocked the front door. "Tonya, you can work the counter with me, while Nicky will take care of table service."

"Are you ever filled to capacity?" Tonya asked as she placed a tray of white rice in one of the aluminum pans filled with hot water. Several other trays were filled with red beans, shrimp etouffée, chicken-andouille gumbo, dirty rice, and jambalaya.

"Not too often. Most times our customers fax their takeout orders, and a few will begin calling around ten thirty for an eleven o'clock pickup. Then we have some folks who have a standing order, so once we hear their names we know what they want."

"What happens when you sell out of a particular item?" Tonya asked.

"We don't replenish it," Melinda said. "If there are leftovers, then Daddy will donate them to our church for their soup kitchen. He believes it's a sin to throw away food."

Tonya nodded in agreement. She had worked at several New York City restaurants that had joined City Harvest and donated food to organizations dedicated to feeding the hungry rather than throw it away.

As soon as the first customer walked through the door, the work continued nonstop until closing time. There was nothing left to donate, because everything had sold out. Melinda and Nicole tossed their aprons in the laundry bin, kissed their father, and rushed out to make it home before the buses dropped off their children. Tonya cleaned off tables and stacked chairs in a corner, and then swept the floor. By the time she returned to the kitchen, Eustace had filled the dishwasher with dishes, flatware, and pots.

"It's quitting time for you, young lady," Eustace announced loudly. "As soon as I clean the stovetop and mop the kitchen, I'm out of here."

"Do you want me to clean the stove?"

Eustace pointed in the direction of the back. "You're done for the day, so I'm ordering you to leave."

Tonya affected a snappy, "Yes, sir, boss!" Both were laughing when she took off her apron. "I'll see you tomorrow bright and early."

Eustace wiped his shaved head with a paper napkin. "Not too early. Remember, I'll be here around six."

"And I'll see you at six, because I have to put up the bread dough for the baguettes."

"Thank you for reminding me that I have to call the bread man and cancel tomorrow's delivery."

She left Chez Toussaints eight hours after she had walked in, feeling more alive than she had in months. Working in the kitchen alongside Eustace had revived her passion for learning to prepare dishes that were not in her repertoire. She managed to sample a spoonful of each dish and concluded red beans and rice with grilled chaurice—a Creole hot sausage—was one of her favorites. Tonya knew if she did not carefully monitor what she ate, she would regain the weight she had lost.

When she had gone for her annual health checkup, the results of her tests indicated she wasn't overweight, but over the years the pounds had begun to creep up, and there were times when she felt winded climbing subway stairs, especially in the winter when wearing a heavy coat.

But once she began shedding the pounds, she had a lot more energy.

Tonya left the restaurant and drove in the direction of the Lower French Quarter, where she planned to buy fresh produce. Hannah had stocked the guesthouse with meat, fish, and staples, but Tonya had made it a practice to eat several servings of fruit and vegetables every day. She managed to find parking and walked to the market with its graceful arcades that spanned six blocks.

Within seconds she felt as if she had been transported back in time to when residents went down to the river, where fishermen, farmers, and artisans called out to customers to purchase their products. She passed trinket stands and shopkeepers selling pralines, muffulettas, and fresh herbs. By the time she left, her tote and several shopping bags were bulging with her purchases.

She was five minutes into the return drive to the Garden District when her cell phone rang and Gage's name and number appeared on the dashboard screen. Tapping a button on the steering wheel, she activated the Bluetooth feature. "I'm sorry, but I can't go out with you tonight because I have to get up early and bake bread," she said teasingly.

A deep chuckle came through the speaker.

"I'm not calling to take you out tonight, because both of us have to get up early. But I do need to see you."

Tonya stopped for a red light at Jackson Square. Her pulse quickened. The first thought that came to mind was something had happened with Eustace. "Is Eustace okay?"

"He's fine."

She exhaled an inaudible breath of relief. "When do you want to see me?"

"Now. That is if you're not busy."

"Right now I'm not home. Can you give me about fifteen minutes to get back to the Garden District?"

"I'm already here. I'm parked on the street outside the house."

Her eyebrows lifted with this disclosure, wondering what could be so pressing or important that Gage had come to her home. "Okay. Once I'm close enough, I'll open the gates for you to park near the garages."

"I'll be here."

She tried coming up with different scenarios as to why Gage would have to talk to her in person rather than tell her on the phone, and each time she dismissed the possible situations. In the end she knew she would have to wait to hear it from him.

Lengthening shadows shrouded tree-lined streets as she maneuvered down the block leading to DuPont House. Reaching for the remote device under the visor, she punched a button, and the gates to the imposing mansion opened. She saw the taillights of the white Audi SUV come on and disappear when Gage drove through, she following his vehicle. Tonya tapped another device, and the doors to a three-car garage opened smoothly. The garage was empty, indicating LeAnn and Paige were both out. She knew even if she did occupy a first-floor suite, she doubted whether she would see much of the now retired schoolteachers. She drove into the garage and cut the engine. Gage was out of his car to meet her when she opened the hatch to remove her purchases.

He reached around her. "Let me get those for you."

"Thanks."

Tonya gave him a sidelong glance, silently admiring the turned-back cuffs on the crisp pale-blue shirt. A pair of tailored navy slacks and black leather slip-ons had replaced his jeans and running shoes. The lingering scent of his cologne wafted to her nose. Notes of jasmine, musk, and sandalwood were the perfect combination for his body's natural pheromones. And in that instant, she pondered why someone with his looks and talent was still single. She suspected maybe his ex-wife had soured him when it came to a forming a committed relationship, or perhaps he was so used to women coming on to him that he simply ignored them. She did notice women staring, whispering, and pointing to him when she had sat in Jazzes with her friends listening to live music, and she had been no exception. However, it wasn't as much about his attractiveness as it was his musical talent. He had played a horn solo, the muted notes so hauntingly beautiful that it left her spellbound.

Her focus wasn't on getting involved with a man but putting all of her energies into starting up and making her business viable, because when it came to love she always found herself on the negative side of the ledger. Once she committed, she went all in, and in the end she wound up the loser. It had been that way with Samuel, and the result was that she could not give Darius what he wanted or needed for them to have a satisfying relationship.

"What on earth did you buy?" Gage asked as they followed the flagstone path leading to the guesthouses.

Tonya smiled. "A little of this and a little of that. I could've spent the entire day at the French Market, but some of the vendors were closing for the day."

"The flea and farmers' markets open at nine and close at six depending on the season and the weather, while retail stores open every day from ten to six."

"I haven't seen that much of the city, but right now the French Market is one place I plan to visit over and over."

"When I take you around the city, I'm going to begin with the nightlife, and after you recover we can visit some of the other parishes."

Tonya walked up the steps to the guesthouse located farthest from the main house, unlocked the front door, and punched in the programmed code on the wall keypad to deactivate the security system. She had left the table lamp on in the entryway because she did not like walking into a dark house. She flipped a wall switch, and the table lamp and a crystal chandelier in the living room flooded the space with warm, golden light. She slipped out of her shoes and left them on a thick straw mat.

"Do you always take off your shoes when you come into the house?"

Tonya dropped her keys on the drop-leaf oaken table. "Yes. It's a habit I picked up when living in Asia. I'll take those," she said to Gage, reaching for the bags as he, too, slipped out of his shoes.

"I know you profess to be a strong, independent woman, but damn, can't you allow me be chivalrous just this one time," he teased, smiling.

Tonya patted his shoulder and felt solid muscle under the cotton fabric. "Yes, my liege. Come with me and I'll show you where to put them." She led the way across the living room to the kitchen.

"I've been to DuPont House a few times, but I've never been in any of the guesthouses," Gage admitted as he followed Tonya into the eat-in kitchen. "They're as large as some of the cottages where I grew up in Tremé." He placed the bags on the floor next to the refrigerator, and then walked over to the French doors spanning the back porch. There was still enough light for him to see the gardens.

"Do you still live there?"

Gage turned and stared at Tonya. He still found it hard to believe she was fifty when she could easily pass for a woman ten years younger. He had celebrated his forty-sixth birthday last November, and there were times when he felt much older, especially when it came to dealing with his ex-wife and son. It was only after constant threats to cut him off that Wesley finally finished high school, and now at twenty he found every excuse known to man not to attend classes at a local junior college. Fortunately for Tonya, she wasn't faced with the same dilemma because come May her daughter would graduate college.

He returned to the kitchen, rested a hip against the countertop, crossed his arms over his chest, and watched Tonya as she emptied bags filled with seasonal fruits and vegetables. "No. I live in the Upper French Quarter between Dauphine and Burgundy Streets."

"How far is that from Bourbon Street?"

"About two miles; far enough away where I'm not kept awake from the constant nighttime debauchery."

Tonya rolled her eyes upward. "Do you hear yourself? I was under the impression that musicians stay up all night and sleep during the day."

"For me it's only two nights a week. Monday through Thursday nights I'm usually home because I have to teach the next day. Speaking of teaching, that's why I wanted to talk to you."

She held up a hand. "Have you had dinner?"

"No. Why?"

She met his eyes. "You can tell me over dinner, but first I'm going to light a few candles, turn on some music, and change my clothes, and then I'll make something for us that won't take a lot of time." Tonya continued to set plastic bags of shrimp, avocado, fresh cilantro, scallion, red onion, fresh ginger, red bell pepper, salad greens, and several types of cheese on the countertop.

"Are you planning for us to have a romantic dinner?"

Her hands stilled. "Why would you say that?"

"Dinner with candles and music goes hand-in-hand with romance."

Tonya scrunched up her nose. "Sorry to burst your bubble, there will be no romance tonight. I usually light scented candles to mask cooking aromas, and listening to music always relaxes me." She patted his shoulder again. "If you're looking for romance, then you should join an online dating site. I know a few guys who met their future wives like that."

Gage was unable to form a reply as he replayed her suggestion. "Do you really think I need to go online to find romance?"

"I wouldn't know."

"Well, I don't. Would you go online to find someone?" he asked her.

Tonya shook her head. "No. I don't like the idea of someone hiding behind a much too perfect to be true profile, and then when I get to meet them in person I'm ready to run in the opposite direction."

He angled his head, meeting eyes that reminded him of pools of dark, rich coffee. "At least we can agree on that."

A hint of a smile played at the corners of Tonya's mouth. "I'm willing to bet we will agree on a lot of things. After all, we're both chefs."

"True." Gage nodded. "I can't believe you'd want to cook when you've spent most of the day on your feet."

Tonya went still. "I like cooking for others, but I love cooking for myself."

"Is there anything I can help you with?"

A beat passed. "Would you mind standing in as my sous chef?"

Gage bowed gracefully from the waist. "I'd be honored, Madame Chef. What's on the menu?"

"Asian shrimp cakes with avocado-wasabi sauce, a mixed citrus salad with red onions and escarole, and hazelnut gelato for dessert. I'm going to give you an apron so you don't stain your clothes." Tonya opened a narrow closet and took out two bibbed aprons, handing one to Gage.

"Did you make the gelato?" he asked, as he slipped the apron over his head.

"No. Hannah knows how much I like gelato, so she bought some for me. I'll be right back, so don't run away," she teased.

He watched her leave the kitchen, and seconds later the house was filled with the melodious voice of Sade singing "The Sweetest Taboo." Gage wanted to tell Tonya that he couldn't run away even if he wanted to. There was something about her that so intrigued him that he wanted to know what had happened in her life to make her who she was today. She had more than her share of confidence—a trait she needed in order to become successful in what was still a man's profession. And in addition to confidence, she projected an air of independence, like a badge of courage.

He washed the fruit and then emptied the bag of shrimp into a bowl of cold water while he waited for Tonya to return to the kitchen. Opening and closing drawers and cabinets, he selected knives, spoons, plates, a grater, bowls, and measuring spoons. Then he examined the inside of the refrigerator and discovered it was fully stocked. All of the ingredients needed to make the shrimp cakes were stacked on a plate when Tonya returned dressed in a pair of gray sweatpants and an oversize white tee. The baggy attire concealed her curves.

"What do you want me to begin with?" he asked her.

"I'd like you to please peel, devein, and finely chop the shrimp, and then toast two tablespoons of sesame seeds." She opened a cabinet and took out a bottle of sesame oil. "I found a Vietnamese vendor at the market who has an extensive inventory of Asian products. He stocks wasabi rhizomes, powder, and paste, and many other things I need for my Asian-inspired selections." Tonya handed him a cutting board after he cleaned and patted the shrimp dry with a paper towel.

Gage finely chopped the shrimp and placed them in a mixing bowl. "Are you planning to offer the same tapas every night?"

"No. Other than the more popular local dishes on the menu, I want to offer special tapas every night. Tuesdays will be Spanish and/or Caribbean-inspired dishes. Soul food Wednesdays, barbecue Thursdays, fish Fridays, and Asian Saturdays."

He gave her a quick glance. "What about Sunday and Monday?"

"I plan to close on those days."

Gage silently applauded her. Preparing breakfast for the inn's guests seven days a week and serving dinner guests at the supper club for five was certain to be exhausting, even with a fully staffed kitchen. "If you want to operate a supper club, then should I assume you'll provide some type of music?"

Tonya nodded. "I'll offer prerecorded music Tuesday through Thursday, and a small combo playing live music on Fridays and Saturdays."

"I like what you've come up with."

Tonya halved an avocado and scooped out the fruit with a tablespoon. "You do?"

Gage stared down at her staring up at him. "Of course I do. Why would you believe otherwise?"

The seconds ticked as she gave him a lingering stare. "I don't know. For some reason I thought you would have something disparaging to say."

"Like what, Tonya?"

"Like you don't believe a woman can run a successful restaurant."

Gage set down the knife. "I know we didn't get off on the right foot the first time we met, and I may have said a few things that made you believe I doubted you because of your gender, but it has nothing to do with you being a woman. It's just that there are so many eating establishments in New Orleans that if you're going to open one, then in order to remain viable, it has to be exceptional."

"I have no doubt it will be exceptional."

There was a quiet assurance in Tonya's voice that indicated she refused to accept failure—another feature Gage had come to admire in her. A flash of humor crossed his features. "I'm certain it will, and I'd like to volunteer my services to make certain you do succeed." He was certain he shocked her with the offer when her jaw dropped.

"How?" The single word came out in a whisper.

"After you finalize your menu, I want you to prepare the selections and I'll grade you on each. I promise to be open-minded *and* unbiased. And if I find something a little off with a particular recipe, then I'd like for you to be open to my suggestions as to how to make it better."

She blinked slowly. "You'd do that?"

Gage returned his attention to chopping the shrimp. "Why wouldn't I? Have you ever heard of the expression, 'one hand washes the other and both hands wash the face'?"

"No, I haven't."

"Well, it goes both ways. I'm willing to help you, but I also I have a favor to ask of you."

"What is it?"

Gage told her about the change in his teaching schedule and that he needed her to cover the restaurant three mornings each week to allow Eustace to continue his exercise regimen. "If you can't do it, then I'll have to try and find someone else to come in—"

"Stop it, Gage," Tonya admonished quietly, interrupting him. "Of course I'll do it. Your brother already gave me a set of keys and the code to the security system, so that lets you off the hook for volunteering to become an official taster."

He curbed the urge to kiss Tonya until both were breathless. "No, it doesn't," he countered. "If you think I'm going to turn down the opportunity to sample what you make, then you don't know how stubborn we Toussaints can be. Not only will I judge, but I also want to be there to observe when you make each dish."

Her dimples winked at him when she smiled. "Just when are you going to find the time to watch me cook, now that you're a full-time teacher?"

"I'm usually free on Sundays. Either you can cook here or at the restaurant."

Her smile grew wider. "Well, well, well. It looks as if I have an official judge. *Merci*."

"You're welcome." He averted his head so Tonya could not see his smug expression. When he had called Tonya to ask whether he could talk to her, it had not entered his mind to critique the dishes she planned to serve to her patrons. And his offer meant he would get to see her at least once a week. Gage pointed to the fresh ginger. "How much ginger do you want me to grate?"

"One teaspoon, and please make certain it is finely grated."

"Yes, chef."

A slight frown furrowed Tonya's forehead. "Can you please stop calling me that when we're alone together?"

"What?"

"Chef."

"What do you want me to call you?"

"Tonya."

He nodded. She had berated him when he had referred to her as a cook, and now she had taken issue with him because he called her chef. "Then Tonya it is."

There was a comfortable silence as Tonya worked side-by-side with Gage. She concentrated on mashing the avocado with a fork before adding lime juice, salt, and wasabi paste.

"Now it's my turn to ask a favor of you."

Gage angled his head. "Talk to me."

"Hannah asked me to help her plan a menu for her Super Bowl get-together, and I need your opinion as to a more fusion menu besides wings, guacamole, and chips. I thought spring rolls, sesame prawn toasts, deep-fried bite-size spare ribs, Moroccan-style meatballs, and miniature shrimp and crab cakes would be a welcome addition and surprise."

Wiping his hands on a towel, Gage splayed his fingers at her waist. "I know my cousin's wife will be more than pleased with your eclectic menu choices, and so will I."

"Why you?"

"After I help Eustace with his catering orders, I'm joining St. John and Hannah for the game." He dropped a kiss on her hair. "Just make certain you put aside some of your kick-ass wings for me."

Tonya laughed softly. "I'll make certain to put aside a little of everything for you."

Gage eased back, staring down at Tonya. "I'm willing to predict that after the Super Bowl party, you will become a much sought-after chef in this town even before you open your restaurant."

Her eyebrows lifted slightly. "Aren't you being premature with your prediction?"

"Not at all. And one of these days I'll take extreme pleasure in telling you I told you so."

"And hopefully I'll be gracious enough to accept it."

"Believe me, you will, Tonya."

Tonya felt a warm glow sweep over her body with his prediction. She did not doubt that she could prepare palatable dishes, because she had proven herself over and over; she could broil steak to a diner's precise specification, and cook a pot of rice so all of the grains were light and fluffy. Her spareribs were tender enough to fall off the bone, and she had perfected tuna tartare, eliciting raves from those favoring sushi and sashimi. However, the thing that nagged at her was the worry her restaurant would become just another eating establishment in a city where food and music were responsible for attracting tourists to the Big Easy.

Picking up a spoon, she scooped up a small portion of the wasabi-infused avocado. She extended the spoon to Gage. "Let me know if you like this." She held her breath, waiting for a reaction from him as he slowly chewed the smooth mixture.

"It's incredible," he said after a long moment.

Her smile was dazzling. "I have to chill it until the shrimp cakes are ready."

"The chilled avocado will counter the heat from the wasabi, and the sauce is the perfect complement for crab, shrimp, or salmon croquettes. I hope you'll include it for your fish Fridays."

Tonya affected a saucy grin. "What grade are you going to give me?"

Gage leaned over and brushed a light kiss over her parted lips. "A-plus."

She went completely still when she felt the pressure of Gage's mouth on hers. He hadn't actually kissed her, but she could not stop herself from fantasizing what it would be like for him to really kiss her. The heat in her face had nothing to do with the warmth from Gage's body but was a result of her own traitorous thoughts. They flooded her mind with unbidden memories of long-denied passion. Darius had accused her of sleeping with another man because his lovemaking left her frustrated, unfulfilled, and after a while she refused to let him touch her.

"My, my. I had no idea my judge would be so liberal."

Gage kissed her again, this time on her hair. "Your

judge is open-minded, and that means he will always tell you the truth. By the way, I like your taste in music. Dave Brubeck's 'Take Five' is a favorite of mine."

"Yours and my father's. I grew up listening to my father playing jazz. He inherited a priceless collection of vinyl seventy-eights from his father. Collectors have offered him an obscene amount of money for them, but he refuses to give them up. I did manage to convince him to convert them to disks, so I have a set for myself. Let me know if you want a set, and I'll make a copy for you."

"Thank you. You are truly an angel."

Tonya felt closer to Gage than any other man she had encountered since her ex-husband. Within minutes of Samuel Alexander asking if he could sit with her in the high school cafeteria, she felt the envy of the other girls at their table. Samuel was good-looking, intelligent, and co-captain of the swim team. However, after a few years of marriage, the love of her life turned into her worst nightmare. She shook her head as if to banish the bad memories and concentrated on sectioning orange, grapefruit, and mandarin orange for the mixed citrus salad.

Chapter 9

Gage sat across the dining room table from Tonya, staring at her over the rim of his wineglass. The shrimp cakes topped with avocado-wasabi sauce accompanied by the salad with thinly sliced red onion, escarole, endive, citrus, and tossed with red wine vinegar with cubes of Gruyère and fine slivers of prosciutto, created an explosion of different textures and flavors. The bitterness of the escarole was offset by the sweetly acidic taste of the citrus fruits, and the subtle saltiness from the cheese and prosciutto were completed by the red wine vinegar.

"I can't say which I enjoyed more: the shrimp cakes or the salad." *Or the chef who prepared them,* he thought.

Tonya raised her glass. "Thank you for your assistance."

He touched his glass to hers. "It was my pleasure. Would you be opposed to standing in as my sous chef?"

Tonya smiled and then took a sip of rosé. "Of course not. When and where?"

Lines fanned out around Gage's eyes when he smiled. He didn't know why, but he hadn't expected Tonya to be that agreeable. "My place. Sunday afternoon."

She set down her glass. "How many people are you expecting?"

"There will be just the two of us. Will that pose a problem for you?"

She stared at him wordlessly and Gage wondered if perhaps he was moving too quickly for her. It actually wasn't his style to come on strong or even attempt to overwhelm a woman when he found himself intrigued by her, but Tonya was so very different from other women. First, she was closer to his age, mature and definitely more urbane than the others.

Her mouth curved into a smile. "No, Gage. It doesn't pose a problem."

"I don't want to insult you by coming on too strong, but I—"

"Don't say it, Gage," she said, cutting him off. "We're not teenagers playing head games. You know how old I am, and at this time in my life, I find that I don't have a filter when it comes to speaking my mind. Whether it is a date or just hanging out, I'm looking forward to our getting together because we share a lot in common. We both speak French, we're chefs, we've lived abroad, and we like jazz. However, you have one up on me because I don't play an instrument."

"Have you thought of taking piano lessons?"

"When am I going to have time to take lessons?"

"What's the projected date for opening the restaurants?"

"Hannah's still awaiting approval for the installation of an elevator, so the completion date for renovations on the main house and the café is the end of summer. Converting this guesthouse into a restaurant should take at least a month, which means I'm predicting an October grand opening."

"That gives you enough time to take lessons."

Tonya shook her head. "Have you forgotten that I'll have to interview, hire, and train my kitchen staff? Then I'll have to make certain to bring on an experienced dining room manager who will supervise and train employees. I'm hoping one of my former coworkers will decide to come in with Hannah and me to monitor the financial end of the businesses."

"Shouldn't your dining room manager take care of food and beverage costs and buying supplies?"

Tonya shook her head again. "I don't want to give him or her that responsibility. I lost my job at an upscale restaurant when agents from the IRS showed up one morning and padlocked the place. We later discovered the restaurant manager had been literally and figuratively cooking the books and owed the feds millions in back taxes."

Gage had heard of restaurants closing not because of less than palatable dishes or bad service but because of mismanagement. Chez Toussaints could not begin to compare with many of the larger restaurants in New Orleans, yet its longevity and viability were based on secret family recipes and the edict that it would always be owned and operated by a family member.

"I see your point. And you're certain you'll be able to trust your friend?"

He was asking a question Tonya did not have to think about. "I'm very certain," she said confidently. She trusted

Nydia to take care of her apartment, and she would trust her to manage the restaurants' finances. The astute accountant, in good faith, had given her twelve bank checks totaling a full year's rent rather than one totaling more than twenty thousand dollars. She said she didn't want to raise a flag with the IRS when Tonya deposited it. Her only other wish, other than opening the restaurants, was for Nydia and Jasmine to become innkeepers with her and Hannah. She had grown rather close to Jasmine and Nydia after Hannah moved to New Orleans. They met once a week for dinner, either at a restaurant, ordered in at Jasmine's condo, or Tonya prepared dinner for them at her apartment.

Dating Samuel in high school had had its drawbacks. She spent all of her free time with him rather than cultivating friendships with girls her own age. Then at nineteen, she found herself pregnant and married when she should have been at clubs dancing until all hours of the morning or traveling with a group of young women in between college semesters. She exhaled an inaudible breath, chiding herself for ruminating on her past. Tonya had come to the realization a long time ago that if she hadn't gone through what she had with Samuel, then she would not be who she was today. And it had all been worth it because of Samara. Becoming a mother had given her the strength to take the steps to secure not only her future but also her daughter's.

"I'll give you a penny for your thoughts."

Tonya blinked as if coming out of a trance. "Right now my thoughts are worth a lot more than a penny," she countered with a brittle smile.

"How much then are you charging?" Gage asked. "Because I'm willing to pay any amount just to know a little bit more about you."

Tonya lowered her eyes and stared at the tablecloth. She wasn't ready to talk about the circumstances surrounding her failed marriage. To do so was a reminder of how she had been innocently gullible, malleable, and unquestioningly trusting of a man who did not deserve her love and trust.

"I cannot accept your money at this time."

"In other words, you're going to remain an enigma?"

Tonya looked up, staring into the large gray eyes with glints of green that seemed to go through her, and tried to ignore the palpable virility he exuded effortlessly. *He's just a man*, the silent voice reminded. Gage may have been just a man, but he possessed something that stirred every emotion that appealed to her as a woman.

"I'm hardly an enigma, Gage."

"If not an enigma, then you're definitely a woman of mystery."

She gritted her teeth in frustration. It was apparent he had no intention of letting it go. "I can't believe you want me to tell you my life's story when this is only the third time we've been together." Tonya knew she had hit a nerve with Gage when he sat straight. "I'm sorry," she apologized.

"No, you're not. Weren't you the one who said you don't have a filter, and what comes to mind comes out?"

"That may be true, but I could've been a bit more tactful." Much to her surprise, Gage smiled.

"I don't want you to be tactful, Tonya. I want you to be outspoken—that is if we're going to have anything that resembles an honest and open friendship."

A powerful relief filled her once she realized Gage wanted friendship and not a relationship. At this time in her life Tonya did not believe she could balance starting up a new business with becoming involved with a man— no matter how attractive she found him.

She extended her hand across the table. "I guess this means what you see is what you'll get."

Gage took her hand, his thumb caressing her knuckles. "I happen to like what I see." He dropped her hand and came around the table to pull back her chair. "Come dance with me."

Tonya wasn't given time to protest when Gage looped an arm around her waist and led her into the living room. She had turned off the chandelier, and the only illumination came from candles lining the fireplace mantelpiece. Her defenses fell away as he pulled her into a close embrace. She closed her eyes, smiling when he sang along with Brenda Russell's "Piano in the Dark."

"I love this song," she whispered against the column of his neck.

"Me too," Gage agreed, as he spun her around and around in an intricate dance step.

"It appears the men in your family are wonderful dancers."

His deep chuckle caressed her ear. "If you're talking about St. John, then there's no comparison. I saw the video of the wedding with him dancing the tango with Hannah."

She eased back, trying to make out Gage's expression in the diffused light. "You've already seen the video?"

"Yes, and I have to say you were incredibly sexy in that orange gown."

Tonya laughed softly. "I spent the entire time praying

not to have a wardrobe malfunction and upstage the bride."

It was Gage's turn to laugh. "That would've been the talk of the town for a long time, and I'm certain the videographer would've replayed it over and over before editing it out of the final copy."

She playfully pounded his shoulder. "You're so bad."

"Bad like good bad?"

Tonya paused for several seconds. "Yes. I know Hannah and St. John take lessons, but where did you learn to dance?"

"My mother made me take lessons for a couple of years because my father had two left feet. His idea of dancing was to move his feet from side to side. I hated going, because at seven I didn't want to hold a girl's hand. Mom would drop me off at the front of the studio, and as soon as she drove away I went out the back. When the dance teacher sent a note home that I'd missed a number of lessons, my mother grounded me for the entire summer. I told her I didn't want to go back, but I was willing to take piano lessons. The first time I placed my fingers on the keys I knew I'd found my calling."

Lacing their fingers together and tightening his hold on her waist, Gage dipped Tonya until she was only inches from the floor. "I'll never forgive you if you drop me," she gasped in fear.

Gage eased her upright. "That's not going to happen. I can bench-press twice my weight, so there's no way I won't be able to hold on to you."

"Bragging?" she teased.

"No. I swim laps and lift weights."

"Where?" Tonya asked.

"At a downtown gym. Now that I'm teaching full-time, that's going to change. Instead of working out during the day, I'll have to switch to nights."

"You're definitely burning the candle at both ends with teaching, catering, working out, and playing at the club on weekends. Careful you don't overdo it, *old man*," she said teasingly.

Gage dipped her again. "Did anyone ever tell you that you have a smart mouth?"

Tonya nodded. "Yes, my grandmother. She used to call me 'miss sassy.' I was never disrespectful, just outspoken."

She didn't tell Gage that it was her straightforwardness that irritated Samuel whenever she refused to go along with whatever decision he made without first asking her input. In the end he would sweet-talk her, and in order to keep the peace she would give in to him.

"What about your mother?"

Tonya chose her words carefully. "My mother was born in Florida and came of age during the civil rights movement. As a high school student, she was involved in a number of peaceful demonstrations. The one time she was arrested for unlawful assembly, my grandfather bailed her out, and then warned her it was the first and last time he would go to the bank to withdraw money to get her out of jail. The ordeal left her traumatized, because she'd witnessed one of her classmates clubbed to death."

"That's something no one, regardless of their age, should have to experience."

Tonya nodded. "It took years before she was able to talk about it without breaking down."

"How did she meet your father?"

"They met at Bethune-Cookman College. He was a

math major and my mom was a nursing student. After graduating, they moved to New York and lived with Dad's sister and her husband until they saved enough money to buy their own home. They liked living in Queens, so they bought a place in St. Albans. My mother had a job at a city hospital and eventually became a nursing supervisor, while Dad taught math at a community college."

"Do they still live there?" Gage asked.

"No. After Daddy retired, he decided to move back to Daytona Beach. He fixed up the house where he'd grown up, sold it, and then he and Mama moved to a retirement community. One of the reasons I decided to accept Hannah's offer to go into business with her is to live closer to my parents and my daughter."

"Did you ever think you would become a Southerner?"

"No. I really love the Big Apple and all it offers, but I'm finding myself slowly falling under the magical spell of NOLA."

Gage cradled her face in his hands. "Good." He kissed her forehead. "I'm going to help you clean up before I leave."

Tonya held onto his wrists. "There's not much to clean up. Everything can go into the dishwasher."

"Are you sure?"

"Yes." He dropped his hands, and in that instant she felt his loss even before his leaving. "Go and get some rest before you have to get up tomorrow to deal with a bunch of rowdy high school students."

"They're not as rowdy as they used to be, but I'll tell you about that when I see you again."

Tonya walked Gage to the door, watching as he sat on an oak bench in the entryway to slip into his shoes. Rising on tiptoe, she pressed a kiss to his jaw. "Thanks again for helping me with dinner."

"I should be the one thanking you for covering for me at the restaurant."

"Please let's not get into that again."

He dipped his head and kissed her cheek. "You're right. Good night, Tonya."

She nodded. "Good night, Gage. I'll activate the gates so you can get out." He was there, and then he was gone. Tonya reached for her cell phone. Hannah had given her the remote device for her car and also sent her the link to download the icon to her phone.

Tonya walked into the living room and flopped down on the loveseat. She half listened to Kool & the Gang playing the hauntingly beautiful "Summer Magic." A smile parted her lips when she realized Gage would have been an incredible therapist. He unknowingly had gotten her to open up enough to talk about her family. Fortunately for her, he hadn't asked whether she had siblings, which meant she would have had to talk about her brother—a topic that usually left her in a blue funk for days. It had taken her years before she was even able to mention his name without crying. Not only had Ian been her older brother, but also her protector. Boys in the neighborhood knew not to mess with Ian's sister, or they would have to deal with him.

It was years before Tonya discovered her brother was living a double life. He worked as an occupational therapist during the day and sold heroin and cocaine at night. However, the lure of the streets and fast money proved too much for Ian, and he began a downward spiral once he became hooked on the drugs he sold to other addicts.

The ringing of her cell phone shattered her dark mood;

she saw the name and number come up on the screen. "*Hola, Señorita Santiago.*"

"Your Spanish accent sounds French."

"At least I'm trying, Nydia."

"And you get an A for effort. I wanted to give you a few days to settle into your new spot before calling you. How are you?"

Tonya got up and walked into the kitchen. "I'm good. Hannah had the guesthouse cleaned and fully stocked by the time I got here."

"You know Miss Thang is up on everything. How is she?"

"Ecstatic."

"That's because she's married to one of the finest brothers in the Big Easy. I'm not looking for a father figure, but if I met someone like St. John I'd be all over daddy-love like flies on a meat skin."

Tonya laughed. "I had no idea you liked older men."

"Not really, but I'm tired of guys my age who refuse to grow up. If they're not trying to shack up with a woman because they need someplace to lay their dusty asses, then they're living like a mole in their mama's basement."

She grimaced at Nydia's acerbic declaration. When Nydia had announced she was "so done" with her long-time boyfriend, Tonya was skeptical the thirty-one-year-old would keep her promise. "I'm glad you're finally getting your love life together."

"Right now I don't have and don't want a love life," Nydia admitted, "and for the first time in a very long time I'm enjoying my own company. That never would've happened if you hadn't offered to let me sublet your apartment. I come home, close the door, and shut out the world. I don't have a nosy-ass landlady watching to see who I invite over. Some of my cousins keep asking when they can come and see the apartment, but I've been putting them off because I know they'll want to use it as a hangout. And that's not going to happen, because every time I turn around they'll be in my face. Enough talk about me. How's the weather down there?"

"It's not bad. It was in the low sixties this afternoon."

"That's a lot better than it is here; it's snowing. They're predicting at least a foot before it's all over. This is when I envy you and Hannah. You don't have to deal with the cold and snow."

"You wouldn't have to deal with the cold and snow if you decide to come on down and work with us."

"Give me a couple more snowstorms and I'll definitely start thinking about it. Luckily, I don't have to go out until the weekend, and hopefully by that time most of the snow should be cleared away."

"Have you heard from Jasmine?" Tonya asked.

"She called yesterday to tell me she has the flu. I asked her if she wanted me to bring her some homemade chicken soup, but she told me to stay away because she's been barking like a seal."

"Has she seen a doctor?"

"Yes. He told her to stay in, get some rest, and drink plenty of liquids. He did give her a prescription for cough medicine, but she claims the codeine makes her feel loopy."

"Call her back and let her know you're going to order from Grubhub and have them deliver soup and whatever else you think she needs to keep up her strength, because we know she eats like a bird."

"That's a good idea. Why didn't I think of that?"

"It's because you're not a mother who's had to take care of a sick child."

"You've got that right. I'm going to hang up now and call a restaurant close to her place, and hopefully they'll deliver in this weather."

Tonya wanted to tell Nydia that blizzard conditions slowed down the city, but did not shut it down completely. "Tell Jasmine to call me once she feels better."

"I will. *Adios, mija.*"

"Good-bye, Nydia"

She disconnected the call and began the task of cleaning up the kitchen. After stacking dishes in the dishwasher, she turned off the radio, and settled down to watch television. The large flat-screen sat on a shelf in the massive, ornately carved armoire. When Tonya first saw the two-bedroom guesthouses, she likened them to luxurious suites in some upscale hotels. They were furnished with exquisite reproductions that only an expert in antiques would be able to authenticate. The electricity had been updated to include cable and Internet access.

Hannah had shown her the architect's renderings for the café and supper club, and Tonya was caught completely off guard with the incredibly beautiful depictions of her new restaurants. He had divided the café with an area for dining and another into a parlor with chairs, loveseats, and sofas where guests could relax before or after breakfast.

The supper club was designed for intimacy, with loveseats instead of individual chairs at more than half the tables. There was a dance floor and a raised stage for a band. He decided to keep the wood-burning fireplaces and replace the chandeliers with hanging fixtures resembling late-nineteenth-century gaslights. The kitchen, stream-lined to provide optimum dining room space, was to be equipped with top-of-the-line commercial appliances. The architect's specs also included a central cooling unit for each building. The supper club was configured with a capacity to seat forty at any given time. Once the club was open to the public, she planned to offer open seating Tuesday through Thursday, and reservations for Friday and Saturday.

Hannah planned for nine of the eighteen bedroom suites in the mansion to be set aside for guests, which meant at any given time Tonya knew she would have to prepare enough food for no more than twenty-five if the inn was filled to capacity. Seven suites were doubles, and the two remaining suites were triples.

She watched the news on CNN, then picked up the re-mote device and began channel surfing and saw that *The Best Man Holiday* was scheduled to begin in ten minutes. It was one of her favorite movies. The highlight for her was the scene when Morris Chestnut, Taye Diggs, Ter-rance Howard, and Harold Perrineau danced to New Edi-tion's "Can You Stand the Rain." Their smooth dance moves never failed to make her smile. Once the movie ended, Tonya turned off the television and made her way to the bathroom to brush her teeth and shower. No more sitting up late watching movies and talk shows or reading because she had to get up early to go into Chez Toussaints to bake bread.

Patting the moisture from her body with a thick velour towel, she walked on bare feet into the bedroom. How different, she mused, her new, although temporary, home was from her East Harlem apartment. She didn't have to walk up four flights of stairs or share the fifth floor with three other apartments. Tonya rarely encountered her neighbors, and when she did they usually acknowledged one another with nods, smiles, and not much more. They, like most New Yorkers, were in a hurry to get where they were going.

Opening a drawer in the mahogany chest-on-chest, she took out a cotton nightgown and pulled it over her head, and then climbed into the four-poster canopy bed draped in white mosquito netting and dotted with tiny embroidered yellow butterflies. Whoever had decorated the room favored butterflies, which were stamped on the window seat cushion and the padded bench at the foot of the bed. She thought of the bedroom as romantic and whimsical.

Although she had settled comfortably into the house, she still needed to unpack two more boxes that were in a corner of the smaller bedroom, boxes filled with books and magazines she still had not read. Reaching over, Tonya turned off the bedside lamp, plunging the room into darkness. In her second day as a transplanted Louisianan, she was involved in preparing the dishes that made Chez Toussaint a popular eating establishment. Spending hours in the restaurant kitchen reminded her why she had made the decision to become a chef. Although the activity was not as frenetic as it had been for her when working in larger, fully staffed restaurant kitchens, she still had to bring her A-game. Despite being professionally trained, she had a lot to learn about authentic Cajun and Creole cuisine with its unique flavors and textures.

Her day had begun with and ended with Gage. There was no doubt he was shocked to see her when he opened the door to her ring. And her day had ended with him when they shared cooking duties, dinner, and a dance. It wasn't vanity that communicated to Tonya that he was interested, if not intrigued, with her. There was something in his personality that reminded her of Cameron Singleton when he had questioned her about Jasmine. And it was obvious that if either man saw someone or something they wanted, they wouldn't allow anyone or thing to deter them, even if it meant it wasn't good for them.

Tonya recalled her grandmother's warning: *What may be good to you may not be good for you.* Her grandmother was right when she flew up from Florida to New York for her granddaughter's wedding to Samuel Alexander. Grandmamma Martin took one look at Samuel and tried to dissuade her from marrying him, even though she was carrying his child. In hindsight, she wished she had taken her grandmother's advice. She'd grown up when she had the option of terminating the pregnancy, bringing it to term, and/or choosing whether to marry or become a single mother.

She closed her eyes, smiling and wondering if becoming friends with Gage Toussaint was good for her. Tonya knew she had to be very careful or she would find herself succumbing to his captivating presence. He made her think about things that had nothing to do with a shared passion for cooking. Sleep was slow in coming, but after tossing and turning, she finally fell asleep.

Chapter 10

Gage knew it would take time to get used to starting his day at the high school at eight in the morning, although he did not have a class until later in the afternoon. But as a faculty member, and now an acting department head, he was required to clock in and out. He had emailed everyone involved in the school's concerts about a meeting, and fortunately they indicated they were all free to meet for lunch. He had visited the faculty lunchroom and ordered a salad plate and water, then returned to his office before the others arrived. Minutes after noon the art, drama, and choral teachers strolled in, carrying trays. Only the director of the marching band was missing. He'd emailed Gage earlier indicating he had a family emergency and would not make the meeting.

Gage pulled out a chair for the drama teacher, who smiled at him over her shoulder. He waited for the two men to sit before taking his seat at the round table. "Thank you for coming. Even though I never would've imagined I'd be sitting here taking over for Louis, I hope with your help, the transition will be a smooth one."

Karla Holcomb pressed a tissue to her nose. "I still can't imagine someone running him over and then leaving him bleeding in the street."

Gage met the drama teacher's tear-filled light-blue eyes. "I spoke to his wife earlier this morning, and she said he's still in ICU, but she predicts he will be moved into a private room by the weekend. She'll let me know when he's ready to receive visitors."

Karla sniffled loudly. "That's encouraging."

Bobby Mays rested a hand on Karla's back in an attempt to comfort her. "My brother-in-law who's a cop told me they have the license plate number and a pretty good description of the vehicle they were able to pull off a couple of traffic cameras."

Gage nodded with the art teacher's disclosure. "It shouldn't take the police long before they identify the driver." Then he changed the subject. I called this meeting because I need your feedback on some ideas I have about the spring concert."

"Like what, Toussaint?" asked the choral instructor.

He gave Cleveland Brown a direct stare. The students in the mixed chorus said Mr. CB was cool with them because he liked rap and hip-hop. "I was playing around with the idea of putting on a production chronicling the journey of music from human chants, drumming, classical, blues and jazz, R and B and to today's hip-hop, rap, electronic techno, and electro-funk. Not only would it cover different musical genres, but also dances from countries around the world."

Cleveland was grinning from ear to ear. "I like it!"

"Me, too," Karla agreed. "But how will the musical theater students be involved?"

Gage exhaled a breath of relief. It was apparent they were warming to his idea. "Several of them will be narrators, while others will have to be taught various dances to accompany the music genres."

Karla nodded, smiling. "That's not a problem. Is there money in the budget to rent costumes?"

"I'll check with the school's business manager," Gage said. "Once we decide which time periods we want to highlight, then we'll have to come up with a figure for costumes and other incidentals." He wanted to remind the drama teacher that the school charged admission to offset the cost of putting on the production, but decided it wasn't the time to bring it up.

"What about set decorations, Toussaint?" Bobby questioned.

"I don't believe we have enough time before we go into rehearsal for the art students to build all the sets, so I thought maybe you could create computer generated images and project them onto a blue screen like—"

"Yes!" Bobby shouted, startling everyone at the table with his effusive outburst. "I know a few students who are into graphics. They can design images of whatever you want."

Gage laughed loudly. "We'll start with an African landscape and the a capella group singing Swahili. There will be no drums, just voices. Can you work with your chorus to accomplish this, Mr. Brown?"

Cleveland ran a hand over his neatly braided shoulder-length hair, his dark eyes filled with laughter in an equally dark face. "My students can give you whatever you want. Give me a list of the songs you want them to perform and they'll bring it."

"Bragging, CB?" Karla teased.

Cleveland winked at the attractive blond teacher with a fashionable chin-length bob. "Of course. You should know by now my kids are the best in the city."

A flush suffused Karla's fair complexion, and Gage wondered if something was going on between the two. Even though the principal frowned on his teachers forming personal relationships, there was little he could do to prevent it.

"Before you start crowing, CB, let me remind you that the orchestra and jazz band can also bring it when need be," Gage countered.

"Damn, Toussaint. Why are you trying to throw shade?" Bobby asked. "Because I happen to have the most talent of all of you."

Karla shook her head. "Why is it men always have to resort to a pissing contest to see who can pee the farthest?"

The three men exchanged sheepish looks. "On that note," Gage said, "we'll conclude this meeting and get together next week, same time and same place, to go over what I've come up with. If any of you have any ideas, please put them in my mailbox or email us in advance."

Bobby stroked the full sandy beard that matched his long ponytail. "I must give you credit, Toussaint. You've come up with something completely different from the Broadway productions we've been putting on in the past."

"I agree," said Cleveland. "Maybe one of these days we'll put on a performance of *Hamilton* for those who will never get to the Broadway show."

"*Hamilton, Cats, Phantom of the Opera,* and *The Lion King* are my personal favorites," Karla said.

In between bites of food the quartet talked about plays they'd seen and those they wish they had seen. Gage had one up on them because he had attended college in New York City, and whenever he wanted to see a play he would go to 47th Street and Broadway and line up at TKTS to buy discounted same-day tickets for Broadway shows. During his freshman year there had been one time when he had spent most of his monthly allowance after attending three shows that month and had to eat pasta, rice, and beans for two weeks until his father deposited money into his bank account. He had been tempted to call his mother and ask her to send him money, but thought better of it because he didn't want his parents to know he had been that irresponsible in choosing pleasure over necessity.

The bell rang, and the three teachers picked up their trays and hurried out of the office before the start of their next classes. Leaning back in his chair, Gage laced his fingers behind his head. The meeting had gone better than he had anticipated; he hadn't been certain whether he would be met with acceptance or resentment. The other teachers could have viewed him as an interloper— an artist-in-residence who would only be there until the end of the school year.

He wasn't concerned as much about their reaction to him as their direct supervisor, but he was glad they were willing to work together to put on a musical production that would define Jean Lafitte High School's music and art program for years to come.

Gage went online and searched for local businesses specializing in costumes from those worn by Shakespearean actors to Cossack dancers as a sheaf of paper filled the printer's tray. He gathered the pages and locked them in the desk drawer. Time had passed quickly. His jazz class was about to start. After practice he would retrieve the pages and go over them at home. He had overheard teachers complaining about taking tests and papers home because they did not have enough time during the school day to go over them, and now he was about to do the same, but without complaining.

Music was his passion, and he felt he would be lost without it. However, Gage was realistic enough to know his tenure with the school would end in May, and it would be with no regrets, because he still had Jazzes.

Tonya saw it was minutes before closing time; she had just rung up the last customer's order when she saw Hannah standing in front of her. "What brings you to this fine establishment?"

Hannah smiled. "I'm here to buy something for tonight's dinner. St. John went up to D.C. to lecture at his alma mater as a visiting professor for a week, so I decided not to cook tonight. By the way, how is it to work for Eustace?"

"He's a teddy bear. What can I get you?"

Hannah's green eyes scanned the menu board. "I'll have a container of crabmeat and corn bisque, a small order of red beans and rice, and a couple of crab cakes." She paused. "Why don't you double the order and come over and eat with me?"

"Are you sure?"

"Don't be ridiculous, Tonya. I also want to give you a copy of the video and an album of photos from the wedding."

Tonya picked up a ladle and filled a large cup with the soup. "How did they turn out?"

"They're beautiful. The photos in the garden are breathtaking."

She remembered Gage's comment about how she looked in her gown, wondering if the neckline had been too risqué. "I can't wait to see them."

Hannah pointed to the bread basket. "When did Eustace start ordering baguettes?"

"I didn't," said Eustace. He'd come from the back in time to overhear Hannah's question. He walked over to the door and locked it. "Thanks to Tonya, we'll now have freshly made baguettes. And I must admit I like them better for our po'boys. I had one this morning right out of the oven with cheese and coffee and thought I was sitting at an outdoor Parisian café enjoying the sights and sounds of the city."

Hannah smiled. "It sounds as if you need to visit the City of Lights to experience Paris firsthand."

"That's not going to happen because I still have to work here," he said as he joined Tonya behind the counter.

"Maybe you'll be able to take a vacation once I'm able to duplicate all your recipes," Tonya volunteered. Eustace stared at her as if she had taken leave of her senses.

He shook his head. "No, Tonya. I can't have you take on that responsibility."

She scooped up rice and filled a round plastic container and filled another with red beans and then covered them with see-through plastic lids. "I don't mind. Don't forget that your daughters are here to make sure I don't mess up."

Eustace adjusted his baseball cap. "I'm not worried about you messing up. It's just that you have to be up before the sun is up *and* prep everything before my girls get here."

"I've been getting to work at the crack of dawn for the past thirty years, so it wouldn't make a difference if you took a couple of weeks off to go on vacation."

"What about catering orders?"

Tonya realized Eustace was inventing excuses not to leave his business for any appreciable amount of time. "Gage can help me with those."

Eustace stared at Tonya, and then Hannah. "I'll think about it."

"Don't think too long, Daddy," Nicole said, smiling. "You know Mama's been complaining that you never take her anywhere, so why don't you take Hannah and Tonya's suggestion and go on vacation. This place will not fall apart because three women are running it."

Eustace pushed out his lips. "I said I'll think about it."

"Keep thinking, and Mama will ask another man to take her away," Nicole mumbled under her breath. "You know there's a doctor at the hospital that's been sparking at her for a while."

"What the hell!" Eustace shouted. "Is this some conspiracy?"

"What's up, Daddy?" Melinda asked as she approached the counter.

"These three," he said accusingly, pointing a finger at Hannah, Tonya, and Nicole, "are badgering me to take your mother on vacation."

Melinda threw a towel over her shoulder and rolled her head on her neck. "Make that four. We keep telling you that you're working too hard, but you won't listen until you're flat on your back. Look, Daddy, we have Tonya working with us, so you don't have an excuse not to take time off."

Eustace bobbed his head. "I'll talk to your mama and maybe we'll go somewhere after Mardi Gras. Satisfied, Mrs. St. John McNair?"

Hannah's smile was dazzling. "Quite."

"Tonya, give Hannah whatever she wants and don't take her money, because we never charge family. And that includes you."

Tonya's jaw dropped. "I'm not family."

He glared at her. "As long as you work in *my* kitchen you *are* family."

Nicole patted her father's back. "Give it a rest, Daddy. I don't think Tonya's the least bit intimidated."

Tonya wanted to tell Nicole she was right. She was long past being intimidated when working in a restaurant's kitchen. An executive or head chef could scream at her until they lost their breath, yet she refused to take it personally. She knew who she was and what she could do and had enough confidence to know that if she decided to quit, she could get another position—even if it meant starting at the bottom. Fortunately, now she didn't have to start at the bottom, not when she was about to become owner and executive chef of her own restaurants.

Nicole gave her father a direct stare. "Mama's taking off Monday and we're closed for Dr. King's birthday, so why don't you take her on a dinner cruise on the steamboat *Natchez* to show her how much you still love her."

Eustace's dimples deepened as he smiled. "I like that idea."

Melinda narrowed her eyes. "Just make certain Mama doesn't come back pregnant, or I'll never appear in public again."

"Lindy, I can't believe you said that," her twin chastised. Nicole shook her head. "Hannah and Tonya, please forgive my tactless sister."

Eustace's smile faded as he glared at Melinda. "FYI, young lady, your mama couldn't have any more children after carrying you two knuckleheads. She spent most of her time in bed, and the last month of her pregnancy in the hospital, because her doctor feared she would lose her babies. Three weeks before her due date the doctors had to perform a cesarean to save you and your sister. Two days later she underwent a complete hysterectomy. So if you have jokes, then just keep them to yourself."

Melinda's eyes filled as she covered her mouth with her hand. "I'm sorry, Daddy. I didn't know."

Eustace beckoned her and Nicole closer. "Come and give your gruff old dad a hug."

Tonya watched as Melinda and Nicole hugged their father, feeling like a voyeur. It was apparent the Toussaints also had family secrets, just as she did. Rather than tell anyone that her brother was one of Harlem's major drug suppliers, she felt it more plausible to say he'd died from an OD after injecting himself with a speedball of heroin and cocaine.

"Is there anything else you want?" she asked Hannah, who'd averted her gaze from the exchange of affection between her husband's relatives.

"I'd like a baguette."

Tonya slipped the bread into a paper sleeve. "Anything else?"

Hannah smiled. "I don't think so. I have to watch what I eat or I'll blow up like a balloon, and goodness knows that at my age the weight will settle in my belly and butt."

Tonya shook her head. "Please, Hannah. You're talking to the wrong person about belly and butt. Whenever I gain weight it's always in the three B's: belly, breasts, and behind."

"Stop complaining, Tonya. You have the perfect body."

Tonya wanted to tell Hannah that it took a lot of hard

work to shed the weight that hung on to her like a good friend. However, she made certain not to obsess about her weight by counting calories, points, or even weighing and measuring her food. The reality was she felt better and now had more energy.

"What time do you want me to come over?"

"Any time you want. We can look at the video before or after we eat. The choice is yours."

Tonya glanced at the wall clock. Melinda and Nicole always left at two, leaving her and Eustace to clean up. "I probably won't leave here until four, and then I'm going home to shower and change into something that doesn't smell like Creole seasoning. Look for me around six."

"Six it is." She waited for Nicole and Melinda to leave with Hannah, and then closed and locked the door behind them. Forty minutes later she slipped behind the wheel of her car and headed for the Garden District.

Tonya parked on the street in front the two-story brick Southern-style farmhouse where Hannah lived with her husband. Driving through the Lower French Quarter to Faubourg Marigny was like stepping back in time with streets lined with handsome Creole-style cottages. She found herself falling more in love with her adopted city with each passing day. She wasn't certain whether it was the slower pace, warmer winter weather, the cornucopia of sights and sounds, along with the food, friendly people—or all of the above. She no longer felt like a tourist driving slowly along streets and avenues to find a particular neighborhood with the assistance of her vehicle's navigational system.

The front door opened as she exited the Honda, and Hannah walked out onto the porch. The portico light fixture bathed her in a halo of gold.

This was her second visit to St. John's home. The first was last July when she, her daughter, Nydia, and Jasmine drove down to visit with Hannah. St. John had been the designated host for his family's reunion, and he invited Hannah's guests to sleep over at his house rather than go back to the DuPont House. The reunion began with an early morning breakfast, and the celebrating continued with ubiquitous New Orleans dishes, music, and dancing. Tonya had volunteered to assist Eustace when they grilled together in the outdoor kitchen. While some homeowners had dismantled their outdoor kitchens, St. John and Hannah had elected to keep the structures. And Tonya could think of nothing better than cooking outdoors year-round.

Hannah extended her arms and hugged Tonya. "Did you have a problem finding this place?"

Tonya returned the hug. "No. I remembered certain landmarks when you drove us here last year."

Wrapping an arm around Tonya's waist, Hannah led her inside the house. "I can't believe so much has happened since last year."

"The most momentous being you getting married."

"And don't forget you moving down here to open a restaurant," Hannah reminded Tonya. "And I'm praying that will happen before the end of the year. When I first moved back I found myself obsessing about converting the house into an inn before Mardi Gras, but now I realize that was totally unrealistic."

Tonya followed Hannah into the kitchen, where she had set a table for two. She suspected Hannah did not want to eat alone while her husband was out of town. It was apparent her friend had quickly grown accustomed to sharing her life with another person. Tonya had been single so long that she was accustomed to living by herself.

She communicated with Samara several times a month, because she didn't want her daughter to think she was monitoring her whereabouts or prying into her life. One time she didn't contact her for two weeks and Samara called her in a panic, believing something had happened to her. Tonya relieved her daughter's anxiety when she revealed a former co-worker had asked her to help him launch his new restaurant in a newly gentrified Brooklyn neighborhood while she was still employed by Wakefield Hamilton. She had gone directly from the bank's kitchen to his, and when she returned home close to midnight it was to collapse fully dressed across her bed. She woke at dawn, showered, and dressed to do it all over again until he found someone to replace her. His flagship restaurant had been so successful that two years later he opened a second one in Brooklyn Heights.

Hannah set a bowl filled with salad greens, chick peas, avocado, cherry tomatoes, thinly sliced Bermuda onion, Kalamata olives, capers, and marinated artichoke hearts on the table. "I know how much you like having salad with your dinner."

"To tell you the truth, I could have salad for breakfast, lunch, and dinner," Tonya confessed as she made her way to the bathroom off the kitchen to wash her hands.

She stared at her reflection in the mirror over the vanity. It was time for a haircut; she made a mental note to call Callie and make an appointment. Shorter hair complemented the shape of her face and her lifestyle, because she no longer had to search for hair bonnets large enough to fit over her then braided hair when cooking.

"Do you want wine, sweet tea, water, or lemonade?" Hannah asked when she returned to the kitchen.

"I'll have water."

"You really do eat healthy."

"Not that much. I had wine last night."

Hannah filled a pitcher with water from the dispenser on the refrigerator door. "What were you celebrating?"

"Actually, nothing. Gage came over to talk to me, and we ended up cooking and eating together."

Hannah went still. "You and Gage Toussaint?"

Tonya met her startled gaze. "Yes. Why?"

Setting the pitcher on the table, Hannah pulled her lower lip between her teeth. "I . . . I don't know. Somehow I can't imagine you and Gage together."

A shiver of annoyance snaked its way up Tonya's spine as she glared at Hannah. "There's nothing to imagine because there's nothing going on between Gage and me."

Hannah didn't seem the least bit affected by her sharp tone when she smiled. "Not yet."

Tonya frowned. "Why would you say something like that?"

"I don't know Gage that well, but from what I've observed, he's rather standoffish when it comes to women. I met him for the first time when St. John took me to Jazzes before you guys came down, and I've lost count of the number of women trying to get him to notice them."

"Maybe it's because he was involved with someone."

Hannah made a sucking sound with her tongue and teeth. "If Gage's involved with anyone, then it's with himself."

"Why would you say that?"

"You'll find out if you continue to see him," Hannah warned.

"I suppose I will, because I'm having dinner with him on Sunday."

Turning slowly, Hannah gave Tonya a long, penetrating stare. "You like him." It was a statement.

Tonya narrowed her eyes. "Get your mind out of the gutter, Hannah. Gage and I are chefs, and that translates into sharing a passion for cooking. I asked him for his feedback for the menu for your Super Bowl party, and he was quite helpful."

"Oh, shit!"

"What are you shitting about?" Tonya asked.

"I don't know why I forget he's also a chef, because it's stuck in my head that he's a professional musician."

"All that means is he's multitalented."

"That and drop-dead gorgeous," Hannah added, smiling.

"I never noticed," Tonya replied, deadpan.

"That's BS and you know it. Let's eat, then I'll show you pictures from the wedding."

"I can't wait to see them. By the way, where's Smokey?"

"He's probably sleeping on St. John's desk. We won't allow him in the kitchen, and don't you dare mention anything about him sleeping on the bed, because I'll lose it."

Tonya chuckled under her breath. Hannah confided to her that the only thing she and her husband disagreed about was having the cat sleep at the foot of their bed; she told her friend if that's all they had to argue about, then not only was she lucky but blessed to have had a second chance at love.

Chapter 11

Tonya sat on the porch waiting for Gage to arrive. He had sent her a text to let her know he would pick her up around two-thirty. Just hearing his voice brought back images of them cooking, eating, and dancing together, while at the same time it reminded her just how long it had been, aside from Hannah's wedding, since she had danced with a man. In fact, it had been almost a year since she had gone out on a date with Darius, because of his fluctuating work schedule.

She still couldn't believe how much her life had changed in less than a week. She woke to the sound of birds instead of honking horns, sanitation trucks picking up garbage along her street, and an occasional slamming door and the voices of her fifth-floor neighbors.

The instant she'd closed the door to her apartment after a trio of men carried out the last box with her personal items to be shipped to DuPont House, Tonya had experienced an emotion bordering on anxiety. Doubt had crept in, making her question her decision to give up all she had in New York to move to start up a restaurant in a city known for its own unique cuisine.

Her anxiety was short-lived when, a week before Christmas, she picked up her new SUV and hugged Nydia while wishing her the best.

She drove south, stopping overnight in Charlotte, North Carolina, and then continued on to Daytona Beach, where she spent Christmas and celebrated the New Year with her parents. Samara called on both holidays, and although pleased to hear her daughter's voice, Tonya had come to the realization that her adult daughter was exercising her independence for the first time. A sense of strength came to her during the drive from Daytona Beach to New Orleans as she remembered when she'd left the States to live abroad. She'd traveled without a companion and survived.

She was now a Louisianan, and not only would she survive living in a new state, but she was also confident she had made the right decision to go into business with Hannah.

A smile parted her lips as she recalled watching the video of Hannah and St. John's first dance together as husband and wife. They were as graceful and fluid as professionals as they floated across the ballroom floor, much to the awe and shock of their guests.

It was as if Tonya had viewed the wedding, the cocktail hour, dinner, and reception through the eyes of the videographer, because he had captured expressions and nuances of everyone in the garden and ballroom. Her former apprehension that her gown revealed too much cleavage was belied when she stared at her image as Hannah's maid of honor.

What she found blatantly obvious was Cameron Singleton's entrancement with Jasmine when they danced together. Although Cameron was not a man whom she found attractive, she wasn't ready to dismiss him as someone who could help Jasmine get over her ex-husband's duplicity.

Jasmine had called her earlier that morning. Her voice was still raspy, but she wanted to let Tonya know she was feeling better and that Nydia was coming over to cook for her. Tonya did not know why, but she felt more like a mother rather than an older sister to Nydia and Jasmine— although she *was* old enough to be Nydia's mother. When she had mentioned this to Hannah, Hannah explained it was because they both were mothers, and although their children were adults, their maternal instincts were always front and center.

Sitting there and waiting for Gage to come pick her up for their date, Tonya realized she liked him, although she felt they had not gotten off on the right foot during their first encounter, for which he had apologized. She had met so many men in her male-dominated field who would become combative rather than admit they were wrong.

Tonya stood up as she saw Gage's SUV maneuver up the winding path and come to a stop in front of the house. He got out and met her as she descended the steps. It was impossible to see his eyes behind the lenses of a pair of sunglasses. However, his smile indicated he was glad to see her. Her gaze lingered on the slight cleft in his strong chin.

"Hey, beautiful," Gage crooned as he kissed her cheek.

At that moment Tonya felt beautiful as she leaned into

him, savoring his warmth and strength. She had gotten an appointment with the stylist who'd cut her hair for Hannah's wedding, tipping her generously for her handiwork.

"How are you?" she asked breathlessly.

Gage eased back, his smile still in place. "Better, now that I see you again. You look incredible."

She inclined her head. "Thank you."

Tonya had been in a quandary when she couldn't decide what to wear: slacks, dress, or skirt. Garments were piled high on her bed before she decided to go with a long-sleeved black sheath dress with an asymmetrical neckline; the dress ended at the knees and hugged every curve on her body. She'd tried on several pairs of shoes and in the end slipped her bare feet into a pair of three-inch-heel black leather pumps. She had also applied a light cover of makeup to accentuate her eyes and mouth.

"Do you have to get anything before we leave?"

She raised her left arm, from which dangled a wristlet. "Everything I need is in here."

"Do you always travel this light when you go out with a man?"

"It all depends on whether I'm forced to bring pepper spray or a Taser."

His expression changed, suddenly becoming grim. "I hope you're teasing."

Tonya rested a hand on his shoulder. "I am."

His eyebrows lifted behind the glasses. "You had me worried for a minute," he said as he assisted her up onto the passenger seat.

She waited until Gage was seated and belted in, then said, "Thankfully, I've never been in a situation where I had to fight off a man because he didn't want to believe that no meant no."

Shifting into drive, Gage gave her a quick glance. "Good for you, because I've heard stories from women who weren't as lucky."

Tonya stared through the windshield. "Can you answer one question for me?" she asked after a comfortable silence.

"What is it?"

"Why do some men feel the need to force a woman to sleep with them when there're some who are willing to give it up even without their asking?"

"I don't know. It's probably more about power and control. A woman who's that aggressive has usurped the man's power because he's no longer in control."

"A relationship shouldn't be about one having control over the other, but mutual respect."

Gage shot her a quick glance. "Is that what happened between you and your ex?"

Tonya closed her eyes as she recalled what Gage had said to her when he'd come to her house: *I don't want you to be tactful, Tonya. I want you to be outspoken—that is, if we're going to have anything that resembles an honest and open friendship.* And she did want an open relationship with Gage in which she could speak her mind and not have him judge her negatively, as Samuel had done whenever she attempted to talk to him about what she wanted for their future.

"Yes."

"Do you want to talk about it?"

"Not now, because bringing it up will just put me in a bad mood."

Draping his arm over the back of her seat, Gage caressed the nape of her neck. "That reminds me of the song from *The Wiz*: 'Don't Nobody Bring Me No Bad News.'"

"Amen," Tonya intoned.

"Are you hungry?"

"Not really. I had breakfast around ten."

"Was it an American or continental breakfast?"

"Moitié, moitié."

Throwing back his head, Gage laughed loudly. "It can't be half and half, Tonya. Either you went all in with grits, bacon, eggs, and biscuits or you had cereal, croissants, and fruit."

Turning her head, she hid a smile. "I had a cup of cantaloupe along with a spinach, mushroom, and feta eggwhite omelet."

"Do you always use egg whites?"

"No. Hannah stocked the fridge for me before I arrived, so I decided to use them rather than whole eggs. What's on the menu for dinner?"

"When you mentioned Asian Saturdays, I thought you could help me prepare a few Chinese dishes. I went online and pulled up recipes."

Shifting on the seat, she stared at his distinctive profile. "What do you have in mind?"

"Dumplings, barbecue spareribs, orange beef, and fried vegetable noodles."

Tonya was slightly taken aback. She had believed they were going to have a traditional Southern Sunday dinner, not Chinese. "What you want is more American than traditional Chinese."

"Aren't you going to offer Asian dishes most Americans are familiar with?" Gage questioned.

"Yes."

"Then, that's what I want you to help me make. To be honest, I haven't had good Chinese food since I left New York."

Tonya smiled. "No place can compare to New York when it comes to bagels, pizza, and Chinese food."

"Now you're preaching to the choir," Gage said in agreement. "There's nothing better than a slice of thin-crust Margherita pizza topped with fresh basil."

An audible groan slipped past Tonya's lips. "Stop or you'll have me craving pizza." It had been a while since she had had a slice of pizza, because one slice always led to two and sometimes three.

"Have you ever made pizza?"

"Yes," she admitted. "I always make my own moz-zarella, and use only San Marzano tomatoes for the sauce."

"Damn, girl. You're really good."

"That's because I took lessons from a master chef in Italy who lectured his students about taking shortcuts. He'd rip you a new one if you used ready-made sauce, even if it was highly recommended, for pizza. One time when I was in between jobs I helped a caterer friend pre-pare for a wine and cheese gathering, and we decided to turn it up a notch when we made individual pizzas topped with tuna and fresh salmon tartare, figs, and prosciutto. They were such big hits that another couple hired us and requested even more unorthodox toppings."

"What did you make for them?"

"Crème fraiche and red onion confit, salmon caviar and lemon crème fraiche, spicy shrimp, and a few with deviled crab with a tomato rémoulade."

Gage shook his head. "The caviar must have cost them a pretty penny."

"It did. I had caviar once, and I must admit I wasn't too fond of it."

"I suppose it's an acquired taste," he said.

"You're right about that. Do you have all the ingredients we need for our dinner?"

He nodded. "Yes. I managed to find everything at the French Market."

"Did you decide on Chinese to test me?"

A smile ruffled his mouth. "Not really."

"Either it's yes or no, Gage." Tonya waited for his answer as he signaled and turned off onto Esplanade Avenue, and then maneuvered down another tree-lined street and parked in front of a building with green-shuttered second-story windows and a fire escape leading from the second to the third story, both with decorative ironwork balconies.

Gage shut off the engine, unsnapped his seat belt, and then turned to face her. He removed his sunglasses, leaving them on the console between the seats. "No. I want you to test *me*. Don't move," he said. "I'll help you down."

Tonya undid her seat belt and waited for him to come around and assist her. Gage had called her an enigma, but she could say the same about him. Although she felt comfortable being with him, there was something about his mercurial moods that kept her slightly off balance. She found him candid almost to a fault, and then within seconds he would turn on the charm, making it nearly impossible for her to be angry with him.

He opened the door, extended his arms, and swung her effortlessly to stand on the sidewalk. She glanced at the building. "Which apartment is yours?"

Grasping her hand, he gently squeezed her fingers. "There's only one apartment," he said cryptically.

*   *   *

Gage knew he shocked Tonya when she went completely still. After his divorce he had rented a small furnished house in Tremé with the possibility that he would purchase it. His plans changed once he overheard a patron at Jazzes mention he wanted to sell his condo because he was moving his family to Austin, Texas. Gage approached him and asked if he could see the property.

A single glance at the rare Parisian-style garret located in the Lower French Quarter and he knew he wanted it even before entering the secure entrance leading to a lush, tropical courtyard. Once inside the three-bedroom, two-bath condo he found himself awed by the open floor plan, exposed beams, high ceilings, skylights, and Jacuzzi, while the upper floors offered views of the river, the city's skyline, and many church steeples. He was able to negotiate a price to which the seller agreed, and two months later he moved in with only a bed and a folding card table and chairs.

He was totally clueless when it came to decorating and asked his mother whether she would decorate his new home. The first thing she asked him when walking through the empty rooms was whether he was thinking of getting married again; his response was a resounding "never again." Desirée told him he was too young to be so bitter, and then gave him a look that dared him to refute her.

He unlocked the gate leading into the courtyard that spanned the width of the building and reached for Tonya's hand. "This is what sold me on the condo even before I saw inside."

The courtyard resembled an emerald city, with two towering trees, one an oak tree covered in Spanish moss and the other a red mulberry; ivy, and dozens of different ferns and flowering plants in massive clay pots. They provided shade and set the scene for beginning or ending the day in the verdant mini-jungle.

Tonya noticed strings of tiny globe lights and three lanterns suspended from the beams supporting the second-story balcony. Her gaze lingered on a gas grill and fire pit in a corner. "I see what you're talking about. You have your own private Garden of Eden."

Gage squeezed her fingers. "I come down here every morning to have coffee and read the newspaper. I now have birds to keep me company because a couple of weeks ago I installed a couple of feeders under the mulberry tree."

She pointed to several hanging baskets overflowing with colorful orchids. "Do you also take care of the flowers?"

"Thank goodness, no, or everything would be dead within a month. Come inside with me."

He led the way down the flagstone walkway to a door at the opposite end of the courtyard. Gage unlocked the door, and then tapped several buttons on a wall keypad to deactivate the security system. Despite the security cameras positioned around the building, and the gate leading into the courtyard, and bars protecting a wide window and the glass on the double doors on the street level, he felt a lot more secure after he had the property wired against potential intruders.

Gage stood aside, waiting for Tonya to enter, and then turned and closed the door. "Welcome to my humble abode."

Tonya blinked once as her gaze swept over the living and dining rooms. "There's nothing humble about this place."

"You like it?"

She turned to meet his eyes. "I more than like it. It's beautiful."

He caught her elbow as she bent over to take off her shoes. "You don't have to take off your shoes."

Tonya had already slipped out of her pumps, leaving them on a mat. She unzipped the wristlet and took out a pair of non-skid ankle socks. She walked on bare feet to a leather armchair and slipped them on, but not before he saw the bloodred color on her toes. He forced himself not to stare at her slim, shapely legs.

Leaving the wristlet on the chair, Tonya stood up. "Now I'm ready."

"What else do you have in that little bag of tricks?" Gage teased.

"Just my cell phone and lip gloss."

"No keys?"

Tonya shook her head. "I have an app on the phone that will activate the gate to the house."

Gage slipped out of his shoes and left them on the mat next to Tonya's. The only time he walked into the house without his shoes was after working at the restaurant. He always took them off and stored them in the room off the kitchen that doubled as the laundry and mudroom.

"Would you like to see the house first before we begin cooking?"

She smiled, dimples deepening in her cheeks. "Yes, please."

He reached for her hand. "We'll start upstairs and work our way down."

Tonya enjoyed the warmth of Gage's hand on hers as she walked up the winding staircase with wrought-iron railings that were so much a part of the city's architecture. She marveled at the high ceilings, beautiful wood floors, and exposed beams throughout the house. The third-story bedroom nestled under the eaves of exposed beams was reminiscent of the garret bedroom she had occupied when she lived in France. He'd partitioned off an area for a music studio with an electronic keyboard, desktop computer, and built-in bookcases packed tightly with CDs. Tonya peered through a set of French doors opening onto the rooftop which held a trio of bistro tables and chairs.

Gage pressed his mouth to her hair. "I don't entertain much, but I did host a rooftop party for some friends who'd come in from out of town last spring."

Tonya nodded. Seeing the rooftop seating reminded her of the time she'd spent in Florence, Italy, where she and those in her cooking class had visited a restaurant and requested rooftop service. The experience was ethereal as she watched the sun set over the historic Renaissance city.

"Do you ever sit out here at night?" she asked Gage.

He nodded. "Not enough."

Tonya registered the wistfulness in his voice, wondering if Gage's life was so hectic that he did not have time to enjoy his home. She knew he was now a full-time teacher, played at Jazzes on Friday and Saturday nights, and occasionally helped Eustace with his catering orders, which left him with few precious hours to relax other than drinking a cup of coffee in the courtyard.

"If you don't have time to help your brother with his catering orders, then I'm willing to step in for you."

Gage turned her to face him, and rested both hands on her shoulders. "No, Tonya. You're doing enough."

"Why don't you let me be the judge of that? If I don't stay busy, then I'm going to lose my edge before it comes time for me to open my place."

He leaned closer. "You'll never lose your edge, because you're a natural. When I asked you to make a pot of beef stock from scratch, you knew exactly what to do without hesitation. So, please don't try and sell yourself short. Hannah told me you're an incredible, innovative chef."

She closed her eyes for several seconds. "You asked Hannah about me?"

Gage's hands moved up to cradle her face between his palms. "No. When Hannah told me she was going to convert her home into an inn, she said it wasn't going to be just a B and B. She said she also wanted to turn one of the guesthouses on the property into a restaurant and that she had already selected the chef she wanted to run it. She hadn't mentioned your name, but said the chef had prepared meals for the bank's employees and private clients, and as the assistant had more international experience than the executive chef. That's why I was surprised when I found out you were that assistant chef."

"Were you surprised her choice was a woman?"

His lids came down, hiding his innermost feelings from her. "Yes. And I was even more pleasantly surprised to find you so naturally beautiful."

Tonya knew Gage was going to kiss her, and in that instant she wanted him to. He'd said she was beautiful, and whenever she was with him she felt beautiful, feminine, and desirable. Resting her hands on his chest, she leaned into his strength and warmth as his mouth covered hers in a tender, gentle joining; throwing caution to the wind, she surrendered completely to his expert seduction. She did not want to analyze whether he said what he had to gain her confidence so that she would sleep with him, but at that moment Tonya did not want to think about anything, just to enjoy the deep feeling of peace that entered her being—a peace that had eluded her for longer than she could recall.

Her arms curved under his shoulders, and she went on tiptoe to get even closer. She felt the heat of his body eddy down hers from her chest to the area between her thighs. She moaned as shivers of desire throbbed through her, and Tonya knew if she allowed Gage to continue to kiss her, she would beg him to make love to her. Then without warning he ended the kiss, both of them breathing heavily. She bit down on her lip as she waited for the pulsing in her nether region to subside.

Easing back, Tonya met his eyes. They were so dark, all traces of gray and green missing. It was obvious he was as aroused as she. Her gaze moved over his cropped hair, the tiny gold hoops in his lobes, and down to the rapidly beating pulse in his throat. Hannah's words came rushing back—*If Gage's involved with anyone, then it's with himself*—and she wondered if he'd kissed her because he felt himself attracted to her, or was it because it assuaged his curiosity?

"I think it's time we continue the tour before we do something we're not ready to do."

Gage exhaled, the nostrils of his straight nose flaring slightly as his hands fell away from her face. "You're right," he said after a pregnant pause.

They went downstairs to the master bedroom suite. California-king bed with a mahogany headboard carved with flowers and pineapples took center stage in the room decorated in colors of pale-gray, dark-gray, and white.

The intricately carved design was repeated on a massive armoire and a chest at the foot of the bed.

Tonya was drawn to the French doors leading to the balcony. How magical, she mused, it would be to wake up to the spectacular sight of the sun rising over the Mississippi River. The en-suite master bath was as dramatic as the bedroom, with a double vanity, large, freestanding shower stall, and a Jacuzzi. Gage led her into another bedroom with tall windows and a door that also opened out onto the balcony. Next to the bedroom was another bath, which overlooked the balcony at the rear of the house.

Minutes later they were on the first floor. Two fireplaces, skylights, and ceiling fans were strategically placed throughout the open floor plan for the living/dining room and modern gourmet kitchen. The kitchen wasn't as large as the one in DuPont House, yet it provided enough space for two people to work comfortably without bumping into each other.

Leather seating, area rugs scattered over glossy wood floors, mahogany tables with lamps, and a matching entertainment console with a large flat-screen TV and electronic components graced the living room. An oversize leather sofa was positioned to divide the living from the dining area with a table with seating for six.

"Did you have to do a major upgrade before you moved in?" she asked Gage.

Crossing his arms over his chest, he shook his head. "No. I installed central air and heating and redesigned the kitchen because I wanted stainless steel appliances and white cabinets."

"Everything about your home, including the design and the furnishings, is magnificent."

"I'll be certain to let my mother know you like what she's done."

"Your mother is an interior decorator?"

Gage curved an arm around her waist. "Not professionally. She was a window dresser who never had any formal training. When she was in high school she worked part-time in her parents' antique shop, and every holiday she would decorate the windows. After a while other shopkeepers hired her to do their windows. Even after she married my father she would go back to Lafayette to change shop windows. She's never said it openly, but I believe she regretted not going to college to become a professional decorator." His fingers tightened on her waist. "Unlike you, I only had coffee for breakfast, so if you don't mind I'd like us to start dinner."

Tonya smiled up at him. "Lead on."

Chapter 12

Tonya and Gage reversed roles when she became his sous chef. Both had covered their clothes with bibbed aprons, while the ingredients for the various dishes lined the quartz countertop. She hummed along with the music flowing from wireless speakers set up around the first floor as she concocted a marinade for the spareribs, made a chili-soy dipping sauce for the pork dumplings, sliced the ribs in small pieces, and cut beef and carrots into thin strips for the crispy shredded beef.

"I like your choice in music." Gage had put on a recording from *Evita*.

"Thank you. I'm rather partial to Broadway show tunes."

"Which one is your favorite?"

"I have too many to select from, because most of the plays had finished their run by the time I moved to New York to go to school," he admitted.

Tonya gave him furtive glances out of the side of her eye as Gage measured rice wine, sesame oil, sugar, and egg white into a bowl with the minced pork, bamboo shoots, and soy sauce, mixed the ingredients, and then added corn flour. He had halved the recipes, which would result in smaller portions.

"Now you're ready to fill the wrappers." She demonstrated how much mixture to place in the center of each wonton wrapper. "Brush lightly around the edges of the wrapper with water, and then bring the wrapper together in the center by pinching and gathering it at the top." She placed the wonton on a clean damp towel lining a bamboo steamer, and then handed him the teaspoon. "You try the next one."

Gage duplicated what Tonya had done, smiling when he accomplished it quickly. "I think I've got it."

She smiled. "Excellent. The spareribs need to marinate for a couple hours, so we'll start with the dumplings as appetizers."

He gave her a sidelong glance. "Will you share a cocktail with me to go along with them?"

"What do you have in mind?"

"What else but a Mai Tai."

Tonya laughed softly. "You're really going all the way with the Chinese theme," she teased. "Will I get an orchid and umbrella with my drink?"

He winked at her. "Sorry, babe, the best I can offer is pineapple garnish." He made quick work of filling the wrappers and placing them in the steamer.

The sound of falling rain against skylights lulled Gage into a state of total relaxation as he lay on the sofa, his arm resting on Tonya's waist and his chest pressed against her back. Once the sky darkened with storm clouds, he flicked on wall sconces and table lamps. The afternoon and early evening was nothing short of perfection. The dishes, with a little tweaking from Tonya, were comparable to what he had eaten in New York. Although he had selected recipes that were modified for the Western palate, he knew for certain if she did decide to offer several traditional Asian dishes, they would also become quite popular.

Over dinner she admitted experiencing bouts of guilt and occasionally sadness when she left her daughter with her parents whenever she had traveled abroad to expand her culinary training. Gage reassured Tonya that her daughter had not suffered too much from the separation if she was planning to graduate college in the coming months.

He wanted to tell her about his son, who appeared to have adjusted to his parents' divorce, because he had continued to provide monetary support and maintained a close relationship with Wesley until he turned fifteen. That was when his son's life took a turn for the worse when he began cutting classes and abusing drugs.

Gage closed his eyes, but he could still see the image of his son lying in a hospital bed with fluids running into his veins to flush out the poisons polluting his body after he OD'd for what would become the first of many more episodes. Exasperated, Gage told his ex-wife if she didn't agree to put their son in rehab, he would petition a court to grant him sole custody and cut off her child support. And it was obvious the money he sent Winifred meant more to her than the welfare of their son. Rehab had become a revolving door for Wesley, and the last time he'd had contact with him was the weekend St. John hosted their family reunion. He got a call from Wesley from a

Baton Rouge police station, saying that he had been arrested for drunkenness and public lewdness. And inasmuch as he wanted to give up on him, he drove up to the state's capital, posted bail, and dropped him off at his mother's house without going inside.

"Is it still raining?"

Tonya's voice shattered his musings. "Yes. I thought you were falling asleep on me," he whispered near her ear.

"Not yet."

"I know you didn't plan to sleep over, but I do have an extra bedroom if you don't want to go home."

Shifting, Tonya turned to face him. "Your invitation is rather tempting, but I'll pass this time."

"Are you saying there may be another time?"

Tonya placed her fingertips over his mouth. "No, I'm not. But if I come over again, I'll know enough not to accept a cocktail from you. You were rather heavy-handed with the rum."

Gage's fingers curled around her wrist and then pressed a kiss to her palm. "What's the matter, babe? You can't hang?"

She smiled. "I can hang as well as you can."

He winked at her. "I assume that's something we'll have to find out once I take you with me when we visit several local watering holes."

"Not if you plan to do shots like some silly frat boy."

His fingers tightened on her wrist. "I didn't do shots when I was sixteen, and at forty-six I don't plan to begin now."

A beat passed as a slight frown appeared between Tonya's eyes. "I figured we were around the same age."

"We are."

"I'm four years older than you."

Gage pressed his mouth to the nape of her neck. "That

hardly makes you a cougar. What's the adage about age is just a number."

Tonya laughed softly. "You're right about that."

He sniffed under her ear. "What perfume are you wearing, because you always smell delicious?"

"Chance."

"Who makes it?"

"Chanel." Tonya pulled back, her eyes moving slowly over his face. "Why are you asking?"

"I'd like to buy a bottle for my mother because she loves perfume."

Gage had told her a half truth. His mother did have a weakness for perfume, but she had worn the same scent for as long as he could remember. And when he asked her why she didn't try a new fragrance, she said it was the first gift his father had given her for their first Valentine's Day together; not only had she fallen in love with the perfume but also the man who had given it to her.

"How old was your mother when she married your father?"

"Nineteen. She met him her last year in high school when she and several of her girlfriends came down for Mardi Gras. Pop was passing by when he saw a group of men who'd had too much to drink trying to pick them up. He pretended to know them and offered to become their protector. Mom gave him her number, and they alternated calling each other Sunday nights. Meanwhile, Pop hadn't told her he was a widower with a young son."

Tonya was so engrossed in the story that she had forgotten to breathe until she felt constriction in her chest. "What happened when she found out?"

"She said she wanted to meet his boy. It was love at first sight between her and Eustace. He asked Desirée if she was going to be his mother, because she was the first woman Pop had introduced to him. My maternal grandparents tried to talk her out of marrying a man with a ready-made family, but it was too late. They were married on her nineteenth birthday, and I came along a year later. Mom moved back to Lafayette a couple years after Pop passed away to help her folks run the antique shop. Six months ago, she moved them into an assisted living facility because she didn't trust them to be alone while she went to work after my grandmother forgot to turn off the stove. I drive up to see them once a month."

Tonya smiled. "What a wonderful love story."

Smiling, Gage ruffled her hair. "So, you're a romantic."

"I really wouldn't call myself a romantic, but who doesn't want to hear about a happily ever after? Should I assume if your father hadn't died that he and your mother would still be together?"

"You're probably right. Anyone who met my parents could see they were madly in love with each other."

Stretching her arms above her head, Tonya struggled to sit up. "I'm sorry to be a party pooper, but I need to head home."

Gage pushed into a sitting position and swung his legs over the sofa. "Don't you want to wait until the rain stops?" He'd said the first thing that came to mind because he didn't want Tonya to leave. Four hours had gone by much too quickly, and he discovered he was more relaxed with Tonya than any other woman he had known. Initially he thought it was because she was a chef, but that was only a small part of what made her who she was. Gage liked that she was intelligent, straightforward, and not afraid to speak her mind. He appreciated her accepting her natural femininity without attempting to change

her appearance, and doubted whether she realized she
was sexier than a woman half her age.

"Give me a few minutes, and I'll take you home."

Tonya huddled close to Gage's side as he held an umbrella over both their heads. The rain had intensified,
coming down in torrents. One of her pet peeves was wet
feet. "I should've had you park closer."

Gage's free arm circled her waist. "I don't mind getting a little wet."

Tonya tapped the app on her phone to unlock the door,
and then turned to face Gage. Going on tiptoe, she brushed
a light kiss on his mouth. "Thank you for a wonderful
afternoon."

Attractive lines fanned out around his eyes when he
smiled. "I should be the one thanking you. We have to
cook together again. In the meantime, would you be willing to come to Jazzes to hear me play?"

"I'd love to."

"What if I pick you up Saturday at eight?"

She nodded. "I'll be ready." If Gage was to ask her
outright if she liked him, then she would give him a resounding yes. He was the first man with whom she could
speak without censoring herself. Being with Gage allowed her to feel completely liberated, and that was
something she hadn't been able to be with any other man.

Gage pulled her closer. "I'm waiting."

She met his eyes. "For what?"

"Did I pass or fail?"

Realization dawned for Tonya. He was asking her to
grade his cooking. "I give you a B for dinner and a C for
the cocktails."

Gage stared at her as if she had taken leave of her senses. "You're kidding!"

"No, I'm not. If I gave you an A, then there's no room for improvement. And the C is for trying to get me tanked. I took a sip of yours when you weren't looking, and it wasn't as strong as the one you made for me."

"That's because I put less rum in mine. After all, I was the designated driver."

Her mouth formed a perfect O. "If that's the case, then I'll give you an A for the Mai Tai."

He smiled, revealing straight white teeth. "That's better. What are we making next?"

Tonya thought of the dishes Nydia taught her to prepare. "Caribbean."

"You know the Caribbean covers a lot of territory."

"We'll concentrate on Puerto Rico and Cuba."

"Nice." Lowering his head, Gage kissed her forehead. "Talk to you soon."

Turning on his heel, he retraced his steps to his vehicle, Tonya watching his retreating back until he disappeared from view. She closed and locked the door, then slipped out of her wet pumps. Under another set of circumstances, if she had known him longer and if Gage had invited her to spend the night at his house, she would've readily agreed. His mention of her sleeping in one of the other bedrooms was a blatant indication that he either did not want or did not need to sleep with her, and for that Tonya was grateful. Although she found herself physically attracted to him, she wasn't ready to engage in a sexual relationship. She enjoyed making love with a man, yet as she matured, it was no longer what she considered the bedrock in any relationship.

Tonya walked into her bedroom and undressed, thinking about how far she had come from the nineteen-year-old girl who panicked once she discovered, despite using protection, that she was pregnant. It was as if her entire world had been turned upside down. The notion of terminating her pregnancy had not been an option, because she loved Samuel too much to destroy something they had created through the most intimate act that made them one with each other.

It was only after she miscarried that her grandmother urged her not to stay with Samuel. At the time she did not understand why the older woman had taken an instant dislike to the man she had married, but years later it was obvious her grandmamma saw something in Samuel she couldn't or refused to see. Even when she had decided to leave her husband, Tonya never regretted staying with him, because the best thing to have come from their marriage was her daughter. Samara was Samuel's "baby girl," until he remarried.

Tonya changed out of the dress and into a pair of gray sweats with a matching tee and thick white socks. It was too early to retire for bed, so she decided to put up several loads of wash. She had just finished sorting the whites from the colored when the doorbell rang. The gates had been closed when Gage drove her back, so she figured it had to be Hannah.

Peering through the security eye, she was mildly surprised to see the faces of LeAnn and Paige grinning at her. Tonya opened the door, smiling. Both were huddled under an oversize golf umbrella. They were dressed in cropped slacks and long-sleeved tees.

LeAnn handed her a bottle of champagne. "We missed your arrival, so when we saw Gage Toussaint drop you off, we decided this is as good a time as any to show you that we haven't forgotten our home training. The champagne is a welcoming gift."

Tonya took the bottle, and then opened the door wider. "Please come in."

Paige slipped out of her tennis shoes, her sister following suit. "We don't want to track water over your floor."

When first introduced to Hannah's cousins, Tonya never would've thought them related, even though their fathers were brothers. LeAnn and Paige were physically the opposite of tall, blond, green-eyed Hannah, while the sisters were petite, dark-haired, and dark-eyed. They were also much less reserved than their younger cousin. However, on occasion Hannah did drop the F-bomb, if only to prove a point.

"It's only water," Tonya countered. "Can I get you anything to eat or drink?"

The retired schoolteachers shook their heads. "Gracious, no," LeAnn said as she folded her body down to a chair with a matching footstool. "We just had dinner with one of our friends, and I'm full as a tick on a dog's back."

Tonya set the bottle on a side table, noting the label. They had given her a bottle of premium wine usually offered at upscale restaurants. "Thank you for the wine. I'll uncork it after the ribbon cutting for the supper club."

Paige sat on the loveseat and fluffed up her short salt-and-pepper hair with her fingertips. "It looks as if Hannah turning this property into a business is about to become a reality. She called to say the workmen are coming Tuesday to begin stripping wallpaper in the second-story bedrooms."

"That means we're going to have to pack up what we need by tomorrow night and move everything to St. John's house," LeAnn added.

Sitting on the sofa, Tonya crossed her feet at the ankles. "Why don't you move into the other guesthouse?" The sisters looked at each other. "Am I missing something?" she asked.

LeAnn blew out her cheeks. "It would be too crowded. I love my sister to death, but we're like the odd couple. I'm a neat freak and Paige, let's just say, is less than tidy."

Tonya was intrigued by this disclosure. "What happens when you travel together? Do you share a room or cabin?"

"Yes," Paige said quickly, "because there's always room service. And St. John has someone come in to clean his house."

Tonya wanted to tell the DuPonts that she hadn't grown up with someone picking and cleaning up after her and didn't mind doing housework. When Hannah had told her she had a cleaning service ready the guesthouse for her, she declined her offer to have them come in either weekly or biweekly to clean the guesthouse. Although her present residence was larger than her two-bedroom East Harlem apartment, cleaning it wasn't what she would consider overwhelming.

LeAnn shot her sister an angry stare. "Mama used to have a hissy fit whenever she walked into Paige's room, but after a while she gave up."

Paige waved a hand. "Enough talk about me. Do you miss New York?" she asked Tonya.

"Not yet. I spoke to a friend the other day, and she was complaining about the snow, and that's one thing I know I'll never miss. I'm okay with cold weather if I'm dressed for it."

"I love going to New York," LeAnn admitted. "Whenever I'm there I find myself hanging out at Times Square until all hours of the morning. I think it's the lights I find so addictive. It's as if they're calling me."

Tonya nodded. "That's why it's known as the city that never sleeps."

"Hannah told me you're working at Chez Toussaints," LeAnn said.

"I am. Right now I'm trying to learn everything I can about the local cuisine."

"I know Eustace probably wouldn't want to hear this, but he definitely should have a Zagat rating, because his dishes surpass some of the ones served in some of the so-called best restaurants in this city," Paige said passionately. "But a Zagat rating would probably make it hard for the locals, because tourists would crowd them out."

"You're right about that," Tonya said in agreement. "He's only open from eleven to two, and there's no way he'll be able to seat more than thirty at any given time inside the restaurant, and that means the lines will be out the door and down the block. Even if Eustace hired another chef, it would be impossible to keep up with the demand."

"And now that Gage is acting head of Lafitte High's music department, he definitely won't have time to help out his brother," LeAnn added.

Tonya looked at her in surprise. She wondered if Gage had told St. John about his new responsibilities at the school, and he in turn told Hannah, who'd passed the news on to her cousins. "You know about that?"

LeAnn smiled. "Honey, please. Everyone knew about that the day it was announced. I still keep in touch with a few teachers at the high school, and they couldn't wait to tell me that a few shameless hussies were practically throwing their panties at him. And knowing what I know about Gage, there's no way he's going to mess with any of them. He hasn't changed a whit since I had him in my twelfth-grade English class. He was always good-looking and I'd always shake my head whenever some fast-ass young girl wearing a skirt that barely covered the cheeks of her behind would bend over in front of him."

Suddenly intrigued, Tonya leaned forward. "How did he react?"

"He didn't," LeAnn said, "but that didn't stop them from trying. I had a parent-teacher conference with his mama and she told me he'd decided he wanted to go to New York for college. She was worried because he was only sixteen, but then I reassured her that I'd taught students who were eighteen and some nineteen who were not as mature as Gage. He was very intelligent, talented, and competitive because he took extra classes to accelerate and graduate a year ahead of his peers."

Paige crossed her arms under her breasts. "What had me shaking my head was why he married Winnie Fouche when everyone knew she couldn't keep her skirt down or her knees together."

"Maybe she was offering something he wasn't able to refuse," LeAnn countered, as a frown creased her forehead. "At least he came to his senses and divorced her before she saddled him with another baby. She probably thought giving him a son would make him stay, but I heard he had given up soon after the boy was born."

Tonya was barely able to control her gasp of astonishment. When she'd told Gage about Samara, he never mentioned that he had fathered a child. "Where is his son?" The question was out before she could censor herself.

Paige met Tonya's eyes. "The last I heard he was living in Baton Rouge with his mama. When they were living down here, the boy was bad as hell," she spat out. "He must have taken after his mama, because I've had many a

Toussaint in my classroom over the past forty years, and I never had a problem with any of them."

"Did you also teach high school?" Tonya asked Paige.

"No. I taught elementary. I've watched a lot of kids grow up, and thankfully those that stayed made something of themselves."

Tonya wasn't usually prone to gossip, because she had witnessed firsthand the fallout from *"you said, I said"* scenarios that escalated into verbal and occasionally physical confrontations, and she chided herself for asking Paige about Gage's son. If he had wanted her to know that he was a father, then he would've revealed it. The one thing she'd learned as she matured was to choose one's friends carefully and respect their privacy—something she preached to her daughter once Samara entered adolescence.

"When do you project opening your restaurant?" LeAnn asked Tonya, breaking into her musings.

"If all goes well, then it should be sometime in October."

"Are you excited?" Paige asked.

Tonya shook her head. "Not yet. Once I'm told to move out of here and back to the main house, then I'll know it's about to happen."

LeAnn tightened the elastic band on her short ponytail. "Are they going to work on the café for the inn's guests and the supper club at the same time?"

"No. As soon as the renovations to the house are completed, then they're going to convert the guesthouse closest to the inn into the café. The architect's plans include constructing a glass-enclosed, climate-controlled walkway connecting it to the inn. That way the guests won't have to go outside to reach the café."

"When Hannah first told me she was thinking of turning the DuPont House from a personal residence to a business, I thought she had gone and lost her mind," Paige said, "because I knew it would not be an easy undertaking. Thankfully, the house is structurally sound, or it would take more than a year to do everything she wants to do."

"I do like the idea of her putting in an elevator," LeAnn added. "That will make it easier for guests to get to the second floor."

"Are you going to become involved in running the inn?" Tonya asked the sisters.

Paige met her sister's eyes. "We initially told Hannah we wanted no part of running the inn, but if she needs our assistance with something, of course we'll step up."

"That's when we're not traveling," LeAnn reminded Paige.

Tonya sat, listening to the two women talk about the places they'd visited since retiring and felt a bit nostalgic when she recalled how much she'd enjoyed going to a new country and immersing herself in the culture and cuisine. When they asked if she had traveled abroad, Tonya regaled them with tales of how difficult it had been for her to grasp some of the languages until she began cooking. It was as if food didn't need any translation because it was an international language for bringing people together. It was close to nine when LeAnn and Paige left to begin packing for their move from the Garden District to Marigny.

She decided not to put up several loads of wash until the next day. After all, Chez Toussaints was closed because of the holiday, and she had all day to do laundry, clean, iron, and unpack the remaining boxes in the other bedroom.

Chapter 13

Gage rapped lightly on the door to his teaching colleague Louis Murdock's hospital room, successfully concealing his shocked reaction to the number of fading bruises and Steri-strips covering the man's tawny-brown face. It was more than a week since the hit-and-run, and Louis's wife revealed he was now able to receive visitors. She also reassured Gage that her husband was expected to have a full recovery, but only after several months of inpatient and outpatient rehabilitation.

"Room service," Gage announced cheerfully.

"I hope you brought some gumbo, because I don't know how much longer I'll be able to tolerate this hospital grub."

Gage sat on a chair next to the bed. "The food may not be what you want, but I must say your accommodations are rather nice."

Louis nodded. "It's not too bad. I have views of the river, flat-screen TV, and all the legal painkillers I want whenever I want to get high."

Any mention of narcotics to Gage was akin to someone shoving a sharp object under his fingernail. He wasn't a neophyte when it came to drugs; on occasion he'd smoked marijuana before it became legal in many states, but that was in his youth. It was only after he'd married and become a father that he stopped.

"Are you in a lot of pain?"

A pair of light-brown eyes met his. "It comes and goes. I usually take something to help me sleep through the night, but I hold off during the day." Louis closed his eyes. "I still can't believe that sonofabitch knew he'd hit me but still didn't stop."

Gage studied the face of the man whom he thought of as his mentor since becoming an artist-in-residence. During his tenure he met with him biweekly, although it wasn't required, to keep Louis abreast of the direction in which he wanted to take the jazz band. He thought of the man as a musical genius who was able to engage students to appreciate music that went beyond rap and hip-hop. Louis played high school basketball and was offered athletic scholarships from several colleges, but his love of music won out when he decided to go the Crane School of Music. Now approaching sixty, he had not changed much from the tall, gangly boy with a tawny complexion and sparkling light-brown eyes.

"It may take a while, but the police will eventually catch him."

Louis opened his eyes. "My wife told me they're checking every body shop within twenty square miles, because it's certain the vehicle has front-end damage.

You said you wanted me to look over the proposal for the spring concert."

Gage handed him a folder. Louis reached for a pair of half-glasses on the bed next to his right hand. "These are the preliminary strategies from those on the concert committee." He had spent countless hours researching the evolution of music and dance before presenting it to the committee for their input. In the end he was left with a healthy respect for the amount of time and energy it took to put on a production.

Five minutes later, Louis peered over his reading glasses at Gage, a slow smile parting his still bruised lips. "I like it. Karla's going to be in seventh heaven because her drama and musical theater students will have a major role in this production." He took off the glasses. "I knew I was right to recommend you to be an artist-in-residence, because your handiwork is all over this production."

"That's because I have an incredible mentor."

"Cut the bull, Gage. You got into Julliard while they rejected me."

"And do you think getting into the Crane School of Music is like a walk in the park?" he countered. "You've taught music all of your life, while I'm still dabbling in it."

Louis ran a hand over his thinning, cropped gray hair. "You don't have to dabble in it if you stay on as head of Lafitte's music department."

Gage shook his head. "No! I'll stay on until the end of the school year, and then I'm done. Done as department head and done as an artist-in-residence. I came back to the States twenty-three years ago to help my brother run the family business, and now it's time I step up and do it again."

"You're going to give up music?"

"Not altogether. I'll still play a few sets at Jazzes. And besides, you're too young to retire."

"Don't forget I'm sixty."

"You're still too young to retire," Gage repeated. What he wanted to tell Louis was that if he hadn't had any other options, he would accept the responsibility of becoming a full-time teacher. He'd only earned a degree in music education as a backup, but now it was obvious his backup had backfired. "I'm sorry, Louis, but my first priority is to my family, so I suggest you forget about retiring and come back to do what you do best. And remember, I'll always be available if you ever need my input on a project."

Louis nodded. "That's good to hear. I suppose I'm just indulging in a little self-pity because I spend most my day in this damn bed."

"When are you scheduled to leave the hospital?"

"My doctor said as soon as they get a bed at the rehab facility, I'm out of here. My coccyx is healing, so it's just my legs that don't work."

Gage patted Louis's hand. "You'll be up and running again in no time. And once you're settled at the rehab center, call me and I'll bring you some gumbo."

Louis smiled. "I'm going to hold you to that." He patted the folder. "Can I keep this?"

"Yes. I made that copy for you. I'll be in touch."

"Thanks for coming."

Rising, Gage nodded. Although the principal had permitted him complete autonomy in the music department, Gage still wanted to keep Louis apprised of what was happening in *his* department. He left the hospital and headed home. He had several hours before he was to pick

Tonya up and take her to Jazzes. He'd committed to playing one set because he wanted to spend as much time with her as possible.

Gage had deliberately kept busy so he didn't have to think about Tonya. He had interacted with a lot of women abroad and in the States, but she was the first one whom he believed was his alter ego. Whenever they were together, he could be himself because of her easygoing personality. What initially surprised him was her candor, but now it was something he expected and looked forward to.

Even Eustace couldn't stop talking about how she was now able to duplicate the family's recipes for gumbo and jambalaya, and that he sold many more sandwiches now that the bread was baked on the premises. And Tonya would remain after closing hours to put up dough for ciabatta, pita, and focaccia, along with the baguettes, and by closing time they were able to sell every loaf. While he had trained under a Michelin-starred chef, Tonya's extensive training far exceeded his, and once she opened her restaurant, he knew she would become a much sought-after chef in a city with a number of high-profile celebrity chefs.

He did not want to think of her romantically, but every time they were together Gage found it more and more difficult not to fantasize about making love to Tonya. Everything about her was lush, feminine, and sensual. Perhaps it was time he stop living in the past; marriage had made it hard for him to trust a woman, and divorce was even more bitter because he had lost custody of his son. If he had raised the boy, he was almost certain Wesley would have chosen a different lifestyle than the one that could only lead to him losing his life.

His cell phone rang and his mother's number appeared

on the dashboard screen. Tapping the Bluetooth feature on the steering wheel, he said, "Hello, Mom."

"Hi, Gage. I'm calling to find out whether you plan to come up next week to watch the Super Bowl with us?"

"I can't. I'm helping Eustace with a couple of catering orders, and then we're going over to St. John's to watch the game. Why?"

"Some of my friends are going up to Baton Rouge to hang out at Frank Lemoyne's place to watch the game."

Gage paused. This wasn't the first time his mother had mentioned Frank's name, and he wondered if something was going on between Desirée and her former classmate. "Make certain to have a designated driver," he warned softly.

"I'm going to be the designated driver, because the older I get the less I can tolerate alcohol."

"You sound like Eustace. He claims that if he has a couple of cocktails, then he's done for the night."

"I still remember meeting Eustace when he was only ten, and now he's planning to attend his high school's fortieth reunion."

"Time goes by so fast that sometimes it's hard for me to remember what I did the month before."

Desirée's husky laugh filled the interior of the vehicle. "You're much too young to talk about having senior moments."

"I'm busier now than I've ever been." Gage told his mother about the change in his teaching status. "I still play at Jazzes on Friday and Saturday nights, and help Eustace whenever he has to cater a large party."

"You boys are just like your father. You work too much. And it isn't as if you need the money, because André provided for all of us."

Gage nodded, even though his mother couldn't see him. The terms of André Toussaint's will designated his wife and younger son as the beneficiaries of two of his life insurance policies, and his older son the ownership of Chez Toussaints. "The restaurant has been in the family for nearly a century, and there's no reason why it can't be passed down to Lindy, Nikki, and their kids for future generations. I'm certain you feel the same way about grandma and grandpa's antique shop."

There came a pause before Desirée said, "You're right. I've been trying to get Jennifer to come and work with me, but she's having problems with Tommy cheating on her. She knew he was tomcatting before she married him, so I don't know what made her think he would stop after he became her husband."

"I hear you," Gage whispered. His mother's niece had married a man she couldn't depend on, while he had married Winifred, unaware of her reputation of sleeping around, but he had wanted to do the right thing when she told him she was pregnant with his child. "Talking to her is not going to solve her problem. She won't do anything about it until she's had enough and divorces him."

"It's not going to be easy for her, Gage. Remember she has three children all under the age of eighteen. I told her she could come and live with me, but she's afraid when her husband has too much to drink that he'll start in on me."

"That's never going to happen, Mom, because I'll drive up to Lafayette and stomp a mud hole in his ass. I know you don't want to get between them, but Jennifer is blood, and if you want, I'll talk to Tommy, because it's not only about Jennifer but also her kids."

"I don't know, Gage. Tommy may yes you to death, then after you leave he'll turn on her and the kids."

"We'll see. I'll come up to visit with you and grandma and grandpa in two weeks, and while I'm there I'll stop in to see Jennifer. Hopefully I'll get a chance to take Tommy aside and have a man-to-man talk with him. He may be a bully badass with his wife and kids, but I'm hoping he'll be civil with me."

"And what if he isn't?" Desirée asked.

"Then Eustace and I will invite him to a blanket party."

"What's that?"

"We'll throw a blanket over his head, and you can guess what happens next."

Desirée laughed until she was breathless. "I never imagined my boys would turn out to be thugs."

Gage smiled. There was never a time when his mother didn't refer to him and his brother as "my boys" or "my sons." "Everyone has a dark side, and remember we were raised to protect our women."

"I always remind folks that's how I met your father. Tell St. John I said hello, and send my best to Hannah. Did Eustace tell you that he and Janine came up to see me on Dr. King's birthday?"

"No, he didn't," Gage admitted. Eustace had mentioned taking his wife on the cruise, but not that he had traveled to Lafayette to see Desirée.

"He said they were going on a dinner cruise later that night because it had been a while since they'd spent some quality time together. I must admit he looks good now that he's losing weight."

"He's really stuck to his New Year's resolution."

"I know you're busy teaching, helping Eustace, and playing at the club, but are you taking time out to have a little fun?"

Gage's eyebrows lifted as he slowed and came to a stop at a red light. "What do you mean by fun?"

"Stop pretending to be obtuse, Gage! You know I'm talking about you seeing a woman."

He smiled. "I am seeing a woman. In fact, I'm on my way home to get dressed before I pick her up."

There came another moment of silence. "Who is she?"

"She's a chef who will oversee the restaurants at the DuPont Inn once it's up and running."

"When am I going to meet her?"

Gage chuckled. "It's not what you think, Mom. Tonya and I are friends who happen to be chefs, divorced, and have children in their early twenties."

"I didn't ask if you're getting married. I just want to meet the woman who can get my son to take some time out his hectic schedule to have some fun."

"I must admit I enjoy being with her." The admission rolled off his tongue so easily that Gage hadn't had to think about it.

"Good for you."

He maneuvered down the street leading to his condo and found a parking spot in front of it. "I'm home now, Mom, so I'm going to hang up so I can shower and change."

"I'll talk to you soon. Love you, son."

"I love you, too, Mom."

Gage disconnected the Bluetooth, and then sat staring out the windshield. He had admitted to his mother what he had been reluctant to admit to himself. Not only did he enjoy spending time with Tonya, but he was beginning to like her and want for their friendship to become much more. He wanted to become her lover.

He realized both of them had had previous unhappy

marriages that ended in divorce, yet both were mature enough to be able engage in a no-strings-attached relationship, to enjoy whatever they were willing to offer each other. Gage turned off the engine. Sitting in the vehicle thinking about Tonya and the possibility of their having an ongoing relationship was premature on his part, and he did not want to come on too strong or get ahead of himself, because she may not be that into him.

He finally got out and unlocked the door leading to the courtyard. Hopefully, before the night ended he would know exactly where he stood with Tonya, because it would be their first official date.

Tonya had quickly come to the conclusion that most of her clothes, other than her chef's tunic and checkered pants, were black. When, she mused, had she become the quintessential New Yorker sporting the ubiquitous black year-round? The daytime temperatures had dropped to the mid-forties, so she decided a black wool gabardine pantsuit, silk shell, and a pair of matching kitten heels would be appropriate for the evening.

She paid special attention to putting on makeup, something she had not been used to since moving to New Orleans. It was a blatant reminder that she had had little or no social life over the past few years, which translated into not having that many dates since her divorce. Joining co-workers for get-togethers did not count as dates, and the few times she and Darius had gone out in the year since she saw him exclusively were unremarkable.

Tonya peered at her reflection in the mirror over the bathroom vanity as she washed her hands. The deep raspberry color on her lips matched the faint shade under her eyebrow and the blush on her cheeks. Pleased with the results of her handiwork, she returned to the bedroom to fill the small cross-body bag with her cell phone, tiny compact, lipstick, mints, and tissues. She smiled when recalling what she had mentioned to Gage about carrying pepper spray. Whenever she knew she was coming home late, even if it was with a car service, she made certain to take the canister out of her bag before getting out of the car.

The doorbell rang, and she glanced at the clock on the bedside table. It was exactly eight o'clock. She had left the main gate open for him.

She left the bedroom and walked across the living room to the door. Peering through the security eye, she saw Gage. Smiling, she opened the door, her breath catching in her chest when he stood there dressed completely in black: mock V-neck sweater, slacks, and shoes. Her gaze lingered on his smooth, shaven jaw before moving up to the professionally barbered salt-and-pepper strands.

"It looks as if great minds think alike," he said, smiling. "We're both wearing black," he added when her eyebrows lifted, questioning.

"You're right. I didn't realize until I went through my closet that I had so many black clothes."

His lids lowered over his eyes. "I didn't think you could improve on perfection, but you have."

Heat flooded Tonya's face with the compliment. "Thank you."

"Are you ready?"

She slipped the strap of her purse over her shoulder and chest. "Yes."

Gage closed the self-locking door, making certain it

was firmly shut, then reached for Tonya's hand. "I reserved a table for us at Jazzes. I'm sitting in for the keyboard player for one number, so we'll have time to sit together and enjoy the music."

"Do you play there every weekend?" she asked as they followed the path to the front of the main house.

"Just say I play there most weekends. Fridays are amateur nights, but it's always the house band on Saturday. Most of the guys in the band grew up together, so whenever I need a break, there's always someone willing to step in."

"Do you always play the trumpet?" she asked as he opened the passenger-side door and helped her up. She stared down at him staring up at her, trying to see his expression in the diffused light coming from stanchions along the path leading up to the main house.

Gage closed the door and came around to sit beside her. "Yes. It's my favorite instrument. Even when I began taking piano lessons I aspired to be like Louis Armstrong, so when I went to middle school and took band, I selected the trumpet." He pushed the start-engine button, and the distinctive voice of Maxwell filled the SUV. "I can change the music if you want."

"No, please leave it. I really like his music."

"What other male vocalists do you like?"

"I'm partial to Anthony Hamilton."

Gage nodded, smiling. "He's a throwback to old school R and B. When it comes to R and B, I happen to like Jaheim. I never get tired of hearing his 'Remarkable.'"

"I don't recall if I've ever heard that song."

"I'll play it for you whenever you come over again."

Shifting into gear, Gage circled the driveway and drove along the winding path. Within seconds of the rear wheels driving over the metal plate, the gates closed automatically. He reached for Tonya's left hand, holding it in his loose grasp as he steered with his free hand.

"I can't say it enough, but I love cooking with you."

"It's the same with me."

He gave her fingers a gentle squeeze. "I find that I can't keep my hands off you, and I must confess I can't remember if a woman has ever affected me like this."

"What about your ex-wife?"

Gage sucked in his breath, held it for several seconds before slowly exhaling. He had mentioned to Tonya that he wanted to have an honest relationship with her, and that meant she had a right to know about his past. "I had a very unconventional relationship with my ex. She used to come into a club where I used to play, and one night in a moment of madness I went home with her and we had unprotected sex. We continued to sleep together, but always using protection, but I guess the first time proved to be the wrong time, because she came to me a couple of months later to tell me she was pregnant. Three weeks later we tied the knot and moved into an apartment not far from Bourbon Street."

He revealed how within weeks of their living together Winnie complained bitterly because she wanted to live in a big house with someone to come in and clean for her. Chez Toussaints was open full-time, and he left for work at dawn and returned home twelve hours later to find his wife in bed watching television while the sink was filled with unwashed dishes and dirty clothes were stacked in piles around the house.

"And because she claimed she didn't feel well, I decided not to press her about coming home to a dirty house. After Wesley was born, it didn't get any better.

There were times when she left the boy with her parents and disappeared for hours. And when she returned home she pretended nothing had happened. One day I found a stack of money she'd hidden in a drawer, and when I confronted her about it, she said she had gotten a part-time job to save enough money so we could buy the house she wanted. I later found out she was sleeping with a man over in another parish. When I confronted her she promised to stop, and she did, but only for a while."

"How long were you married?" Tonya asked, her voice barely a whisper.

"Six years. I only stayed because of my son."

Gage knew he couldn't tell Tonya that the final straw was when Winnie revealed Wesley wasn't his son, that she didn't know who had fathered the child because she had been sleeping with several men at the same time. They mutually agreed not to tell Wesley that Gage wasn't his biological father, and even after the divorce he continued to provide monetary support for the child. However, she broke her promise when Wesley turned fifteen and she told him Gage wasn't his father, that she was pregnant when she first slept with him, and she didn't know who his father was. The disclosure resulted in a downward spiral for the adolescent.

"Wesley was fifteen when his mother moved to Baton Rouge, and that's when his life changed dramatically. He and his mother were drinking and drugging together. I tried to get custody of him, but my ex fought me, because she knew she would lose the child support. The judge denied my request when she agreed they would both go into treatment. Even after a number of stays in a residential treatment program, Wesley can't stay clean. Last year I gave him an ultimatum to come work at the restaurant, and if he manages to stay clean, I'll buy him a car and help him get an apartment."

"How old is he now?"

"Twenty. He managed to finish high school and get into a local junior college, but he's missed so many classes they keep flunking him. Then the police contacted me instead of his mother because he'd been arrested for driving under the influence. The judge revoked his license for six months, and I took back the car I'd given him. If he's able to stay out of trouble I'll give him back the car, but that can't happen until April."

Tonya digested what Gage had just revealed and knew what he was going through. Her brother had started out selling drugs, and in the end they were responsible for taking his life. "I've worn out my knees praying my daughter will stay away from drugs or anything that will derail her education. But that's not to say she won't meet a knucklehead who could sabotage everything she's worked so hard to achieve."

Gage gave her a quick glance. "Is that what happened to you?" he asked perceptively.

She nodded. "I met my ex in high school, and we were practically inseparable. I'd just completed my second year of college when I found out I was pregnant. We married right away, and three months later I lost the baby. I'd planned to go back to college, but Samuel insisted I wait because he wanted a family. I had two more miscarriages before I finally had Samara. By that time I was almost thirty, and I knew I would never have any more children."

"When did you go back to school?"

"Samara was school age, and by that time I knew I

wanted to become a chef. My ex put up every roadblock he could to keep me from succeeding, and it got so bad, I left him, filed for divorce, and sent my daughter to live with my parents while I attended classes in Rhode Island. I missed Samara, but in the end I knew the sacrifice was worth it."

Gage squeezed her fingers again. "Of course it was worth it, babe. You have a daughter you can be proud of, and I'm certain she's proud of you, because you're an incredible chef."

Tonya averted her head at the same time she blinked back unshed tears, because she wanted to cry for Gage's son. Once her brother started using, he alienated himself from his parents. Every once in a while Ian would call her, and they would talk for hours. He would admit going cold turkey, remain clean for months, once even for several years; but then he would relapse, because drugs took him to another place where nothing mattered. Tonya had just celebrated her thirty-eighth birthday when she got the call to come down to the coroner's office to identify a body. The only identification the police found on him was her name and telephone number. The hardest thing she had ever had to do was tell her parents that their son had died from a drug overdose. Her father arranged for Ian to be cremated. It was years later before they were able to talk about Ian and why he'd chosen the life he did, but they were still not able to come up with an answer, except that dealing drugs was exciting and his career as a therapist dull and monotonous in comparison.

Talking about their past cast a pall over the occupants of the vehicle as all conversation stopped, and there was only the sound of Maxwell's melodious voice singing "Fortunate." Pressing her head against the headrest, Tonya closed her eyes and listened to the music until Gage pulled into the parking lot adjacent to the jazz club. She waited for him to get out and come around to assist her after he retrieved the jacket from the rear seat. Even though she was wearing two-inch heels, he still towered over her, and she made a mental note that the next time they went out together for an evening affair she would wear stilettos.

A small crowd had gathered at the front door, waiting to gain admittance to the popular music venue. "We're going around the back to the employees' entrance," Gage whispered in her ear.

Tonya smiled. There had been a time when she had been willing to wait on line for hours to get into a concert or sporting event, but those days were in her past. Holding on to Gage's hand, she followed him around the building, where a man who'd been taking a smoke break opened the door for them. Gage led her past a kitchen and into the club, where tables were quickly filling up with those who had come to eat, drink, and listen to live music.

Chapter 14

Gage removed the "Reserved" sign from a table that was positioned with an unobstructed view of the stage and seated Tonya. He slipped off his jacket and draped it over the back of the chair opposite hers. "I'll be right back, as soon as I let the band know I'm here."

Tilting her chin, she smiled up at him. She had met Gage for the first time three weeks ago, yet it felt as if she had known him much longer. Hannah had confided to her that at their age they were mature enough to know what they did or did not want. Within minutes of reuniting with St. John and learning that he was no longer married, Hannah knew she wanted more than friendship. Now it was Tonya's turn to decide what she wanted. She could not deny the physical attraction that was evident, but was she willing to take their friendship to the next level?

Keep an open mind, the silent voice reminded her.

Whenever faced with a quandary, the inner voice would remind her not to overthink or overanalyze a situation. After all, she and Gage were adults with adult children, and potential grandparents.

Gage returned with a food and beverage menu. He shifted a chair and sat next to her, resting an arm over her shoulders. "Let me know what you want to eat, and I'll have one of the waitstaff get it for you."

She gave him a sidelong glance. "What are you having?"

He pressed his mouth to the diamond stud in her lobe. "I'll eat later. I'm only playing one set, so after that I'm all yours."

"What if I wait for you to eat?"

"You don't have to, Tonya."

"I want to. What do you want me to order for you?"

"I'll have what you're having."

Tonya gave the menu a cursory glance, and then recalled the tapas she had sampled. "The last time I was here I had tasso shrimp, crawfish with morel mushrooms, and deviled crab."

Gage smiled. "Have you ever tried the oysters en brochette?"

"No."

"I recommend you add the oysters and the spicy garlic shrimp. I'll tell the waiter to bring our order in half an hour. Meanwhile, what do you want to drink?"

"I'd like a glass of prosecco."

Tonya watched as Gage approached a waiter to give the young man their order. Everything about his body language communicated relaxed confidence. It was apparent he was comfortable *and* content with his current lifestyle, while she still hadn't settled into hers. She enjoyed cooking and baking for Chez Toussaints and dating a man who, unknowingly, was the missing piece to make her life complete. Before relocating to New Orleans she thought she had it together, but interacting with Gage was a constant reminder that she had been in denial—that she did want a man in her life.

Gage returned to the table and brushed a light kiss over her mouth; she held onto his arm until he deepened the kiss. It ended, and he stared at her, complete surprise freezing his features. "Thank you," Tonya said breathlessly against his parted lips. Easing back slightly, she rubbed her nose over his smooth cheek and inhaled the cologne mingling with his body's natural masculine scent.

He smiled. "I don't know what you're thanking me for, but I like it."

Tonya stared up at him from under lowered lids. She rubbed the pad of her thumb over his mouth. "I'll tell you later. And lipstick doesn't become you," she teased.

Gage blinked once. "Ms. Martin, are you flirting with me?"

She winked at him. "As a matter of fact I am. Does that bother you?"

"Hell, no! To tell you the truth, you don't flirt enough. There was a time when I thought maybe you didn't like me very much."

"That's where you're wrong, Mr. Toussaint, because I happen to like you a lot."

His expressive eyebrows lifted a fraction. "What are *we* going to do about it?"

"Roll with it."

Gage made the peace sign with his fingers. "We're going to have a lot fun together."

"You promise?"

He nodded. "Promise." He pressed a kiss to her fore-head. "I've got to meet the guys in the dressing room, so I'll see you later."

She watched his retreating back until he disappeared from view. A waitress wearing a white shirt, black slacks, shoes, and a red bowtie approached her table, balancing a tray on her shoulder. She set a coaster stamped with the club's logo on the table, along with napkins, two place settings, small plates, and a glass of prosecco.

"If there's anything else you need, please let me know."

Tonya nodded. "I will. Thank you."

She took a sip of the chilled, slightly fruity wine. She stared over the rim at the framed black-and-white photographs of jazz and blues greats lining the walls of the one-story wooden structure. When Hannah had invited her, Jasmine, Nydia, and Samara to accompany her to Jazzes, she had anticipated listening to live music. But when she discovered it was a supper club serving tapas, Tonya knew if she opened her own eating establishment it would mirror the iconic Tremé music venue. Unknowingly, Tonya had hit the proverbial jackpot when interacting with the Toussaints. As Eustace's apprentice she would learn from the best when it came to preparing local dishes, and Gage could assist her when it came to choosing and hiring local musical talent.

Gage had told her the owners of the club set aside Fridays as amateur night for those looking to break into the business; a few had been lucky enough to be picked up by an agent or record producer, some of whom occasionally came to the club searching for new talent. Now the house lights dimmed, followed by applause as members of the band walked on stage. Tonya couldn't pull her eyes away from Gage as he sat at the black shiny concert piano and rested long fingers on the keys. A strategically positioned spotlight turned him into a figure of gold.

The instant he played the opening notes to Vince Guaraldi's "Cast Your Fate to the Wind," cheers went up from the assembly. She closed her eyes and lost herself in the jazz composition, which had always been a favorite. Even children were able to recognize the piece of music as the theme from the *Peanuts* comic strip.

The quintet, consisting of a bassist, percussionist, sax, horn, and pianist, improvised solos for several minutes before returning to the rhythmic melody that had everyone nodding their heads and tapping their feet. Ten minutes stretched into fifteen, and finally into twenty as only the sound of the piano and congas echoed in the room, until they faded away to a hushed silence.

Tonya was up on her feet with the other patrons, applauding and cheering for an encore.

The saxophonist introduced each member of the band as they came to the center of the stage and bowed to thunderous clapping. There were whistles and screams when Gage took his bow. The band leader tapped his handheld mic. "We're going to take a short break, and then we'll be back, hopefully to play some of your favorites." The house lights went up, and then dimmed slightly as prerecorded music filled the restaurant.

A waiter with a tray hoisted on his shoulder approached the table at the same time Gage walked over. "I have your order, Mr. Toussaint."

Waiting until the plates were set on the table, Gage reached into the pocket of his slacks and pressed a bill to the young man's hand. "Thank you, Jules."

The waiter smiled, displayed a mouth with upper and lower braces. "Thank *you*, Mr. Toussaint."

"Could you please being me a Sazerac?"

The waiter bowed slightly. "Of course."

"You were wonderful," Tonya said softly when Gage sat next to her.

He gave her a sidelong glance. "I'm only as good as my bandmates."

"I'd never take you for someone who would be so self-deprecating."

"I'm not. What you have to understand is that I'm a part of a band. Sade Abu may have been the lead singer, but it was the band that was Sade."

"Have you ever thought about branching out on your own?"

A hint of a smile lifted the corners of Gage's mouth. "No. And where would I find the time? Right now I enjoy the camaraderie that comes from playing with other musicians. We may occasionally argue about how we want to play a particular composition, yet in the end we come to a consensus. What's nice about playing jazz . . ." His words trailed off when a woman from the waitstaff whispered in his ear. Pushing back his chair, Gage stood up. "I'm sorry, babe. I have to talk to someone."

Tonya nodded. When Gage had invited her to the club, she didn't expect to have his undivided attention. Picking up a fork, she speared a golden brown oyster with a butter sauce and crisp, thick-sliced bacon from the dish. Creole seasoning, lemon, and Worcestershire sauce were the perfect complement for the fresh oysters and smoky bacon. Tonya made a mental note to thank Gage for suggesting she order it. The dish was one she knew she had to add to her culinary repertoire. All of the tapas on the table were fish appetizers, and Tonya knew, living in New Orleans, she could very easily become a pescatarian.

Gage came back to the table, and this time he wasn't alone. Unbeknownst to him, Karla, Cleveland, and Bobby had come to Jazzes to hear him play. He met Tonya's questioning gaze as a waiter pushed a table close to theirs, while another brought over three more chairs.

"Darling, I'd like you to meet some of my colleagues. I hope you don't mind if they join us?"

Tonya's dimples creased her cheeks when she smiled. "Of course I don't. The more the merrier."

He waited until everyone was seated, then made the introductions. "The lovely lady seated next to you is Karla Holcomb, Lafitte's drama teacher extraordinaire." A becoming blush turned Karla's face a bright pink. "Next to her is our very talented choral director, Cleveland Brown. And last but definitely not least is Bobby Mays, who heads our art department and is also a brilliant graphic designer. Good folks, I'd like all of you to meet someone who's very special to me. Tonya Martin."

Tonya inclined her head. "It's nice meeting all of you."

Bobby angled his head and stared directly at Tonya, his gold-brown eyes sparkling like shiny pennies. "We're sorry about intruding on your date, but we wanted to surprise Toussaint. We've all witnessed the results of his teaching, but this is the first time we've actually heard him play."

"I may sound a little biased," Tonya said, "but I happen to think he's pretty amazing."

"He's beyond amazing," Karla countered, smiling. "Did

he tell you about what he's come up with for our school's spring concert?"

Tonya shook her head. "No, he hasn't."

"Shame on you, Gage," Karla chided softly. "Do you usually keep secrets from your woman?"

Gage was slightly annoyed at Karla taking him to task about something he had planned to discuss with Tonya, if only to get her feedback on which songs he should include for the final program. "No, I don't."

"Whenever Gage and I are together, we usually don't discuss our work," Tonya said matter-of-factly.

If he could, Gage would've kissed Tonya for her quick response. And she had told the truth. They had not seen each other that often, and when they did it was to cook together. Tonight was the first time they had gone out on what he deemed a real date. It had been his intention to share dinner, listen to music, and then take a tour of some of the other rock, blues, and jazz music venues. Le Bon Temps Roulé, located uptown on Magazine Street, was his favorite spot to listen to live local bands.

"I hear you," Cleveland intoned, "because that's why my last girlfriend left me. She said she got tired of me talking about work every time I opened my mouth."

"That'll learn you," Bobby teased.

"Tonight's not about work, but eating and listening to good music. You were given tickets when you paid the cover charge, so the first drink is on the house," Gage informed his co-workers. "After that I'll cover your tab."

Running both hands over his braided hair, Cleveland leaned back in his chair. "Toussaint, you may come to regret that offer, because give us a few hours, and Bobby and I can drink this joint dry."

Karla glared at Cleveland and then Bobby. "I didn't volunteer to become the designated driver tonight to have you act up like a couple frat boys and barf in my car."

Gage smiled. "Not to worry, Karla. If I'm paying, then I'll know when to stop them."

Bobby reached into the breast pocket of his jacket and placed a credit card on the table. "If Toussaint's paying for the drinks, then I'll cover the food."

Not be outdone, Cleveland also placed a credit card on the table. "I'll split the food with you, Bobby, because I intend to order everything on the menu."

Karla pressed her shoulder to Tonya's. "See what I have to put up with," she whispered. "They may be grown, but they're still big boys."

Tonya nodded in agreement. "It was the same when I used to go out with the guys who worked at several restaurants with me."

"You're a chef." Karla's remark was a statement.

"Yes."

"Good for you. Where are you working?"

"Right now I'm working at a small place in Tremé to learn how to prepare some of the local dishes." Tonya did not want to advertise that she was working at Gage's family-owned restaurant.

"You're not from down here, are you?"

Tonya smiled. "No. I'm a born and bred New Yorker. And I can tell from the way you speak that you're also not from down here."

"No. I'm a dyed-in-the-wool Green Bay Packers cheese-head from Wisconsin."

"I thought I detected a Midwest inflection. And I wouldn't brag about being a cheesehead because you're in 'Whodatnation.' I've lost count of the number of times

I've heard folks say 'who dat say dey gonna beat dem Saints.'"

Karla pushed out her lips. "And I'm not scared. I always wear my Packers' para whenever they play here."

Tonya nodded. "Good for you, because I intend to do the same whenever the Giants come to town." She and Karla executed fist-bumps to seal their decision.

The drink orders arrived, and everyone touched glasses to toast old and new friendships. Tonya took an instant liking to Karla, a free-spirited actress turned drama and musical theater teacher, as they shared glasses of prosecco, while the men drank hurricanes and Sazerac. Small plates of appetizers covered nearly every inch of surface on the table.

In between bites of food when the band was taking a break, Karla revealed that after graduating college she had married a fellow aspiring thespian. Their marriage lasted more than ten years and then came to an abrupt end when she came home unexpectedly from rehearsing with a Chicago-based theater company to find her husband in bed with their neighbor's wife.

"They were so busy getting it on that they never knew I was standing there. Even though I was in shock, I managed to get a camera from a drawer in the home office and took pictures of his naked hairy ass. Once the whore realized they weren't alone, I snapped a picture of her face frozen in shock and fear. Her husband worked for a private military company, and she told me she was deathly afraid of him."

Tonya made a sucking sound with her tongue and teeth. "Apparently she wasn't that afraid if she was willing to screw her neighbor."

"You've got that right," Karla said, smiling. "I turned

a deaf ear to the cheating bastard when he pleaded with me not to leave him. I called my father to pick me up because the car I drove was in that snake's name. I wanted nothing from him except my maiden name, but my father, who just happens to be an attorney, was so angry that he had cheated on his baby girl that he threatened Langdon that he was going to present the photos as evidence during the divorce proceeding if he didn't agree to a quickie divorce and a generous settlement. My ex came from a very wealthy family, and by the time he took control of his trust he was worth more than twenty million dollars. Once he agreed to give me a million for every year of our marriage, I signed a statement verifying that I'd destroyed the photos, and I changed the reason for the divorce from adultery to irreconcilable differences."

Tonya bit down on her lower lip to keep from laughing. Karla's ex cheating on her wasn't as funny as her turning the tables on him. It appeared that many of the women she'd talked to lately had had unfaithful husbands: Jasmine, Hannah, and now Karla. Samuel may have been controlling, but she doubted whether he had ever cheated on her.

"What happened to the trick?"

"I don't know. Langdon sold the house and moved back to L.A. even before the divorce was finalized. I'd read somewhere that he'd gotten a recurring role in a television drama filmed in Vancouver. I managed to stay involved in the theater, and after a while I realized I was a little long in the tooth to play the ingénue and decided I needed a change of scene. My agent wanted me to try out for Broadway, but I was already in my mid-thirties, and I didn't want to compete with much younger actresses trying to break into the business."

"When did you move to New Orleans?"

"Three years ago. I came down to visit a cousin, liked what I saw, and decided to stay. I was an English major in college with a minor in theater, so I applied for a position to teach English at one of the local high schools. Once I was hired, I bought a condo in the Warehouse District and convinced my cousin to sell her house and move into the first floor unit."

"Everything fell into place for you."

Karla nodded. "Just like a well thought-out plan. By the way, when did you move down?" Karla asked Tonya.

"January fourth."

Karla tucked several strands behind her ear. "So you're really a newcomer. Do you have any friends here?"

Tonya nodded. "I'm lucky to say I have quite a few." She could count Hannah, St. John, LeAnn and Paige DuPont, Eustace, his daughters, and Gage as friends.

"Good for you. I invite a few of the teachers over to my place for informal get-togethers several times a year. My brothers come down with their families during the summer, and they always complain about the heat. I don't have any kids, but don't tell that to Lola. She's a Pomeranian and a ball of fur. She is *so* spoiled and monopolizes all of my attention when I'm home."

"And I bet you wonder who spoiled her."

Karla lowered her eyes. "Guilty as charged. After all, she is my baby."

"I had a dog when I was younger, but as an adult I spent too many hours away from home to take care of a pet."

"What about now?" Karla asked.

Tonya shook her head. "It still wouldn't work because I leave my place before six in the morning, and I don't get home until around four. And there's no fenced-in yard where it could run around." She didn't tell Karla that a dog, whether large or small, might get into the garden, destroy the flower beds, or ingest a weed that might prove fatal.

"It's different for me because my cousin takes Lola for walks along with her poodle. Thank goodness I had her fixed or I'd end up with a bunch of puppies, because Oreo still hasn't been neutered." Karla dabbed the corners of her mouth with her napkin. "We've talked about everything but you and Gage."

Tonya stared straight ahead, purposely ignoring Gage's eyes. Throughout dinner she had noticed him staring at her and Karla as they whispered softly so not to be overheard by the others at the table. "What about him?" she asked.

"Did you just meet him, or were you previously involved with each other?"

"I saw him for the first time last summer. But once I relocated we began seeing each other." Tonya hadn't lied. She did see Gage for the first time when she had come to Jazzes with her friends in July, but she did not know he was Eustace's brother until he revealed it to her following Hannah's wedding. "Why are you asking?"

"There's a lot of talk going around about him at the high school because no one has ever seen him with a woman."

Tonya's eyebrows lifted as she gave Karla an incredulous stare. "Are they saying he's gay?"

"No!" she countered. "It's just that he's very quiet and a tad mysterious, and because of this he's become the topic of quite a few conversations among the female staff and faculty."

Tonya wanted to tell Karla there were some men who preferred keeping their private lives private, while others were more open about their relationships. Initially Gage hadn't told her he had a son, but once he felt comfortable with her, he had opened up to her. And she knew he was disappointed that his troubled boy was abusing drugs, which may have contributed to his not letting anyone get close.

"I've found Gage to be a very private person," she said in defense of the man with whom she found herself enthralled.

Karla sighed. "He's definitely a trifecta: private, talented, and kind on the eyes." Tonya and Karla laughed loudly, causing the others at their table to stare at them.

"Do you want to let us dudes in on your little joke?" Bobby asked.

"No!" the two women said in unison.

Gage smiled and shook his head. "Well, while you ladies were deep in conversation, we dudes decided we're going club hopping. Are you in or are you out?"

Tonya exchanged a look with Karla. "I'm in."

"So am I," Karla agreed.

Gage signaled a waiter, settled the check, while Bobby and Cleveland tossed large bills on the table for the gratuity. "Karla, you can leave your car here in the lot, while I drive everyone over to the Quarter. Afterwards, I'll bring y'all back."

"That's fine with me."

Tonya winked at Gage when he reached for her hand and led her out of the club and into the cool nighttime air. "I like your friends," she said in a quiet voice.

He dropped a kiss on her hair. "I had to tell Cleve to back up because he wanted to know if you're available."

"What did you tell him?"

"I told him hell no!"

Tonya felt something inside her she thought she would never feel again—a relationship. Being with Gage made her aware that she had unconsciously closed herself off from becoming romantically involved with a man. Even the few she had slept with after her divorce accused her of being cold, standoffish; she was neither, but she held back, unable to give all of herself because she feared she would lose what she'd fought so hard to acquire: independence.

Chapter 15

It was after three when Gage drove through the gates to DuPont House. They had spent more than five hours going from club to club, lingering to listen to jazz, R & B, blues, and Zydeco. Strolling through the French Quarter reminded Tonya of Times Square, with crowds of locals and tourists all jostling for space in the streets and on sidewalks. She knew it would take a while for her to get used to people carrying plastic go-cups and open containers—something that was illegal in New York City.

"I'm going to impose on you and ask you to make me a cup of coffee before I head home."

Tonya had noticed Gage yawning when he drove the others back to Jazzes' parking lot for Karla to pick up her vehicle to drive Cleveland and Bobby home before going back to her condo. "Why don't you stay over and sleep in the other bedroom? You look as if you can't keep your eyes open."

Gage yawned again. "Your offer sounds very tempting."

"It's not an offer but an order. I'm not going to be responsible for you wrapping your car around a pole. You can sleep in as long as you want, and when you get up, I'll serve you breakfast in bed."

He flashed a lopsided grin. "Are you going to join me in bed?"

Tonya patted his shoulder. "Nah. Maybe next time."

"Will there be a next time?" he asked, then covered his mouth to smother another yawn.

"Turn off the car and come inside with me before you fall on your face." Tonya didn't want to remind Gage that he shouldn't have joined Bobby and Cleveland when they decided to participate in sampling new concoctions during a raucous bartender challenge. Although the samples were poured into shot glasses, the cumulative effect was evident after three rounds. "And don't move. I'll come around and help you out."

"I'm okay."

"You're not okay, Gage. You may not be legally drunk, but you certainly are under the influence. Now, please don't argue with me because you're going to lose."

He punched the stop-engine button. "Dammit. You have to be so bossy?"

"Yes, I do." Tonya had punctuated each word.

Gage emitted an audible groan as he threw an arm over his face. He knew he should have dropped out of the challenge after the second shot, but his machismo overruled his so-called common sense. And he remembered his mother telling him that common sense wasn't that common.

Tonya gave him what he needed to brush his teeth, shave, and shower and showed him where he would sleep. The mattress was extra firm, the way he liked it, but he would have preferred that she share the bed with him. Making love with her was out of the question. He didn't have protection, and he doubted whether he could achieve an erection while it felt as if someone was playing congas in his head.

"Never again," he whispered in the darkened room. Gage recalled telling Tonya that if he hadn't downed shots at sixteen, then it wasn't going to happen at forty-six. He didn't know at the time that weeks later he would do exactly that.

Karla, Cleveland, and Bobby showing up at Jazzes had been a pleasant surprise, but even more surprising was Bobby's revelation that he was dating Karla, though Gage had suspected something was going on between her and the choral director. Bobby told him they had decided not to go public with their relationship because it would just generate too much gossip at the school. Bobby and single father Cleveland had become good friends when Bobby coached Cleveland's son's little league baseball team.

Gage had noticed when he came to the high school as an artist-in-residence that many of the teachers and staff had formed in-groups based on the subjects they taught. He was now acting head of the music department, and in socializing with those on the concert committee, they had formed their own in-group.

Lowering his arm, he stared at the shuttered windows, wondering if Tonya had gone to bed. She had refused to join him when he sat at the dining area table sipping from a cup steaming black coffee, with the excuse that she didn't need it because she was feeling just fine. Her veiled reprimand had become a signal that she hadn't approved of his overindulging. Talk about the pot calling the kettle black. Now, in retrospect, Gage experienced a modicum of shame that he had talked about his son driving drunk, while he himself was also guilty of imbibing more than he normally would.

"I don't want to lose her. I can't lose her," he said aloud. Not when he had just found a woman who made him believe that he could share whatever he had with her. Gage had lived long enough to realize that when something or someone good came his way, if he didn't grasp it, he couldn't bitch and moan after it was gone.

When he met Tonya for the first time last year, he had known immediately that he liked everything about her. It wasn't only her natural beauty but her confidence, candor, and that she was able to make him laugh—something he hadn't done often enough. He enjoyed preparing meals with her, dancing, and kissing her. He hadn't planned to kiss her, and what shocked him more than his impulsiveness was her kissing him back. And if he hadn't stopped himself, he knew he would have asked whether he could make love to her.

There hadn't been a time since he brought her to his home that he hadn't imagined her living with him. He had fantasized about them going to bed together, making love, falling asleep, and then waking up to make love again before they prepared to go to work. And more than anything he wanted to come home and find her waiting for him. It was something he had wanted when he married Winifred, because as a boy he saw the love between his parents. His father kissed his mother every morning before leaving to go to the restaurant, and kissed her again when he returned home.

André Toussaint wasn't ashamed to announce to the world that he loved his wife and that he had the best sons a man could ever have. Perhaps it had been Gage's naïveté or he had been in denial when he stayed in a marriage that had been doomed from the start. Even when he heard the whispers that his wife was sleeping with other men, Gage refused to believe it. And even when he convinced himself to stay with her because of their son, he knew it was detrimental to his own emotional stability. Then Winifred told him that Wesley was not his son.

He walked out that night and stayed with Eustace; he did not want to admit to his mother that she had been right when she warned him not to marry Winifred, even if she was pregnant with his baby. Desirée had wanted him to wait until after the baby was born and then get a paternity test. And it never dawned on him that he hadn't fathered Wesley when Winifred always referred to the baby as hers and never as his son. In the end she was right, because he wasn't the father.

Wesley may not be his biological son, yet Gage did not plan to give up on the boy. He would give him as many chances as he needed to straighten out his life. He owed him that because legally he still *was* his son.

Turning over, he buried his face in the pillows under his head and closed his eyes. Minutes later he succumbed to deep, dreamless sleep.

* * *

Tonya's head popped when she saw Gage walk into the dining area. "Good afternoon, Sleeping Beauty. You're looking well." He had shaved, showered, and dressed.

He ran a hand over his damp hair. "Thanks to you, I feel like a new man. I can't believe you washed my socks and briefs."

She saved what she had typed on the laptop and shut it down. "I figured you wouldn't want to put on dirty socks and drawers after your shower. I had to put in a load of dark clothes, so it was no trouble."

Gage leaned over and kissed her. "Thanks for taking care of me."

She scrunched up her pert nose. "No problem. Maybe one of these days you'll return the favor."

"I doubt that, because you know your limits."

Tonya stared into his eyes when he sat next to her, marveling how strangely beautiful they were. Now they appeared more green than gray. "I'm not going to lecture you about drinking, because you're a grown man and you're more than aware that your actions have consequences. But if we go out again and you want to get into a drinking contest, then I want you to give me the fob to your car, because there's no way I'm going to let you get behind the wheel."

"That's the first time I've ever done something like that."

"Don't apologize, Gage, because there were a few occasions when I had too much to drink and I had to stay over at a hotel because I couldn't make it home."

The lashes that touched his cheeks came up. "When?"

"At prom. Even though I wasn't old enough to drink, someone managed to sneak bottles into the suite. It was the first time that I had alcohol, and after a couple of glasses I was pissy-eyed drunk. My date called my parents to tell them I'd eaten something that didn't agree with me, so we were going to stay at the hotel until the next day."

"What did your parents say when you showed up the next day?"

"Apparently I didn't look well, so I assumed they believed me. It wasn't until years later that my mother told me she knew I'd been drinking because all she could smell was mouthwash."

Gage dropped an arm over Tonya's shoulders. "Why is it parents always know?"

She smiled. "I suppose they know what tricks they played at that age. I usually spend Christmas and New Year's with my daughter, but she said she had prior commitments for the holidays. This is the first time since she was born that we didn't celebrate those holidays together, and intuition tells me that she's involved with a man."

"Does that bother you, Tonya? That your little girl is now a woman."

"No. She's twenty-one, and when she graduates in May she will become totally emancipated. I told her I'll help her out financially to get an apartment and a car, but it's up to her to find gainful employment. She'll graduate with honors with a degree in economics."

Gage whistled softly. "That's heavy. Does she have any jobs lined up?"

"She said a professor at Georgia State wants to hire her as his assistant, but she has to have at least ten graduate credits."

"Is she willing to take his advice?"

Tonya nodded. "She's already applied to their graduate program, and based on her current grades they should accept her." She rested her head on Gage's shoulder. "Are you ready to eat?"

Cupping the back of her head, he pressed a kiss to her ear. "I'm ready for breakfast in bed."

She laughed softly. "Sorry, darling, but it's too late for breakfast. The best I can do is offer brunch."

"Brunch in bed?" he whispered in her ear.

"What if we have brunch in bed at your place and breakfast in bed here?"

He flashed a wide grin. "I like the sound of that. The next time we go out you can stay over at my place. Just make certain to bring an overnight bag, because I'm not adept when it comes to washing lingerie."

"What if I make it easy for you and don't wear panties?"

Gage covered his mouth, smothering a groan. "Don't, Tonya, because I'm very visual."

Tonya laughed when seeing his strained expression. "I'm sorry about that."

He dropped his hand. "No, you're not. Now if I have to resort to masturbating I'm going to curse the hell out of you when I ejaculate in the shower or sock and not you."

Tonya's mouth dropped open, completely stunned by his bluntness. "No, you didn't just say that," she whispered.

"Yes, I did. Please don't tell me I shocked Miss I Have No Filter."

She closed her eyes for several seconds, and when she opened them she noticed Gage was smirking. It was apparent he was enjoying her uneasiness. "Only for the moment," she said, unwilling to let him know he had bested her. "After all, I am a grown-ass woman."

"You forgot to say sexy. You're a grown-ass sexy woman who's gotten under my skin like an itch I can't scratch."

Tonya wanted to tell Gage that although she was physically attracted to him, she feared if they did sleep together, he would want more than she would be willing to give him.

Removing his arm from around her shoulders, Tonya pushed back her chair. "I don't know about you, but I need to eat."

Gage held her arm, not permitting her to stand. "What's the matter, Tonya? Does it bother you that I want to sleep with you?"

She stared at his hand until he dropped it. "No. We're not kids trying to figure out should we or shouldn't we. And if you want to know the truth, then it's yes, I'm looking forward to sharing your bed. But for me sharing your bed doesn't necessarily translate into sharing your life. And as long as we sleep together you will never have to concern yourself with me sleeping with another man, because I'm not emotionally able to carry on two relationships simultaneously."

Gage's expression was a mask of stone. "You said all of that to say what?"

"That I'm looking for being friends with benefits."

"Is that really what you want?"

She nodded. "Yes."

He gave her a long, penetrating stare. "Okay. Friends with benefits."

"Do you want to shake on it?"

"No, babe. I'd rather kiss on it."

He angled his head and brushed a light kiss over her mouth. The joining was so tender Tonya thought she had imagined it. Something deep inside her said Gage didn't deserve to be on the receiving end of the rancor she still carried because of her ex. She knew she hadn't been kind or receptive to Darius when he wanted to see her, and because of that he had accused her of sleeping with other men. If he had blamed her for being indifferent to him she wouldn't have been so angry. But if she was truly honest with herself, then she had to accept the responsibility for their relationship systematically going downhill.

Shifting slightly, she cradled his face and deepened the kiss. "I'm afraid," she whispered against his lips.

Gage's hands covered hers. "Afraid of what?"

"Although I feel more relaxed with you than I have with any other man in my life, I still believe we're moving much too quickly. And I know I say things that may shock you because . . ."

"That's because you feel comfortable enough to say it," he said when her words trailed off. He smiled. "What we have isn't that one-sided, Tonya. Most people, other than my family, don't know that I have a son who has a substance abuse problem, and there's no doubt if he lived here instead of Baton Rouge there would be a lot of gossip about me. Some of these sanctimonious parents would probably say there's no way I could be a role model for their children when my own kid is strung out on drugs."

"But you can't live your son's life."

"I know that and you know that, but people tend to be very judgmental. Now back to you speaking your mind. I wouldn't have it any other way, because my pet peeve is a woman into playing head games. I'd rather know what you're thinking than not. So can we now drop this subject?"

Tonya felt as if a weight she had been carrying for far too long had suddenly been lifted. "Yes."

Gage kissed her again. "Let's get in the kitchen and fix something to eat before it's time for dinner."

Tonya glanced around the sunroom. Seating groupings were arranged to provide an unobstructed view of the large flat-screen. The TV was tuned to pregame festivities, but muted, so as not to drown out softly playing jazz coming from wireless speakers.

The room was spacious enough to accommodate the twenty friends and family members Hannah and St. John had invited to join them to watch the Super Bowl. Earlier in the week Tonya had emailed Hannah a shopping list of what she needed to prepare for the McNairs' get-together, and given her training and experience she knew she had outdone herself. It was only after she finalized the menu that she felt confident in offering something different for her friend's guests. She had chosen to create a charcuterie and cheese platter on wooden boards spanning the length of a six-foot table that had been hewn from a single tree trunk.

She came to Marigny earlier that morning to slice prosciutto, salami, and Spanish ham, and a variety of cheeses and veggies. Cherry tomatoes and heirloom tomatoes sliced in big chunks were covered with olive oil and sea salt, and marinated artichoke and pickles were presented in martini glasses. She had added sweetness to the platter with fresh figs, sliced pears, and red, black, and green grapes, and crunch with some nuts. Jars of pepper jelly and honey and sliced baguettes and bread and crackers rounded out the well-balanced cheese plate that was pleasing not only to the eye but also the palate.

"What do you think?" Tonya asked Hannah when she joined her in the sunroom.

"It's an incredible gastronomical work of art."

"What's a work of art?" asked St. John as he entered the sunroom. He'd exchanged his walking shorts and t-shirt for pair of khakis. "Sweet heaven," he said softly when he stared at the table. "It's almost too pretty to eat."

Tonya smiled at the tall, slender college professor who, though nearing sixty, was still able to turn a woman's head regardless of her age. His cropped silver hair and goatee were the perfect complement to his tawny-brown complexion. Hannah looped her arm with her husband's. "I've been telling Tonya that she's going to become a much sought-after caterer once folks eat what she's prepared tonight."

Crossing her arms under her breasts, Tonya shook her head. "I'm not accepting any orders until I open my restaurant. Right now I'm committed to working at Chez Toussaints until that time comes."

St. John smiled, and attractive lines fanned out around his light-brown eyes. "You sound like a Toussaint."

A slight frown appeared between Tonya's eyes. "What does a Toussaint sound like?"

"We Toussaints have a rule that we won't work at another restaurant unless it's owned by a family member."

Tonya wanted to tell St. John that she wasn't a Toussaint, although Eustace had come to regard her as family. He also told her St. John's paternal grandmother had been a Toussaint.

"I'm not going to bake the Thai and General Tso's chicken until your guests arrive because they should be served immediately," she announced, deftly directing the topic of conversation away from the Toussaints.

She had decided to make three Asian chicken dishes: baked General Tso, Thai sweet chili, and spicy Korean wings. Thanks to Eustace she now felt confident enough to prepare grilled honey Cajun shrimp. Her extensive menu also included bourbon whiskey meatballs and a spicy green salsa. She rounded out the menu with tabbouleh, a basil pesto hummus, and a vegetable platter for vegetarians.

Reaching into the pocket of his shirt, St. John removed a folded check. "Hannah told me you won't give her a bill for catering the food, but I'm not my wife, so I want you to have this."

Tonya held up both hands. "I can't, St. John."

"Yes, you can." He took her hand, placed the check on her palm, and closed her fingers over it, glaring and daring her to refuse it. Nodding, she slipped it into the pocket of her black pinstriped pants. "That's better." The doorbell rang, and he reached for Hannah's hand and kissed the back of it. "That must be our first guest."

Hannah nodded, smiling. "Let's get this party started."

They left to answer the door, and a minute later LeAnn walked into the sunroom. "Oh, my goodness," she whispered under her breath. "I've never seen a charcuterie and cheese spread like this one."

Tonya laughed at her stunned expression. "I decided to go with a different theme from the usual buffalo wings, guacamole, and chips."

"Honey, you really outdid yourself with this banquet. Like Emeril says, you really kicked it up a notch. It's funny that I never thought of you as a chef until now. Maybe it's because you're wearing your outfit."

Tonya glanced down at the white three-quarter-sleeve chef's coat and black pinstriped chef's pants. Tonight she had covered her hair with a pinstriped black skullcap instead of her usual bandana, and black leather clogs added several inches to her five-five height. She wanted to tell LeAnn that she hadn't worn her chef attire since last May when she was downsized from Wakefield Hamilton.

She heard a familiar baritone, and then she saw Gage with Hannah. Her eyes met his, as a slow smile parted her lips when he set down a plastic crate near a portable bar. Not seeing him for a week made her senses spin so that suddenly she felt like a breathless girl meeting her idol for the first time. It took all of her self-control not to launch herself at him and kiss him with all the desire coursing through her body. There were times when she wanted Gage so much that she had to bite her tongue not to blurt out to him to make love to her. Then her mind played tricks on her in which she would dredge up old fears that made her a prisoner of her own emotional fear: the trepidation that she'd fall in love and it would result in her letting her heart overrule her head. Tonya found it ironic that she could tell Jasmine and Nydia how to deal with the men in their lives, and now she needed someone to tell her how to deal with hers.

"Tonya, are you okay?"

She blinked as if coming out of a trance and she turned to look at Hannah. "I think so. Why?"

"Because you look like a deer caught in the headlights."

"I'm going to need your opinion about something."

Hannah rested a hand on Tonya's back. "Is that something named Gage Toussaint?"

Tonya went completely still, wondering whether Hannah was that perceptive or she was that transparent. "You know?"

Hannah smiled. "I only know because of the way he's staring at you. And I must confess that my cousins mentioned they saw him bring you back to the house."

"That's the day he took me to his house for Sunday dinner."

"So, you're seeing each other?"

"Yes. But that's not what I want to talk to you about."

"I think I know what's bothering you, because I went through the same thing when I got involved with St. John. Come over tomorrow after you leave the restaurant and we'll talk."

Gage picked up a bottle of water, opened it, and took a long swallow before making his way over to Tonya. A single glance at the table with the meat, cheese, and fruit epitomized her training and extraordinary creativity. It was the perfect blueprint for a still life.

Wrapping an arm around her waist, he kissed her forehead. "You are amazing. Everything looks incredible and much too pretty to eat."

She smiled up at him through her lashes. "I did not get up at dawn to put all this together for folks not to eat. What time did you and Eustace begin cooking?"

"Not until nine. My brother cussed the entire time he had to fry more than fifty pounds of wings for two parties. We dropped off the last order an hour ago. Eustace went home to shower and change, so he's probably right behind me." Gage glanced over her head. "Are you finished with everything?"

"No. I still have to grill the shrimp, fry the Thai sweet chili chicken, and bake the General Tso's chicken."

He leaned in closer, and the clean masculine scent of his cologne wafted to her nostrils. "I'll wait until everyone gets here, then I'll grill the shrimp for you."

"Thank you." Tonya exhaled an audible sigh. "I'm going to wait for the halftime festivities, then I'm going home to take a bath and relax."

"Do you want company later?"

She gave him a tired smile. "As tempting as that may sound, I'm going to say no."

Gage chided himself for being selfish. It was apparent Tonya had been on her feet since dawn cooking and preparing for Hannah and St. John's guests, while he'd shared cooking for two parties with his brother. "I'm sorry—"

"There's no need to apologize," she said, interrupting him. "We can always see each other over the weekend."

"I've made plans not to work next weekend. And because I did promise to take you around the city, maybe you can clear your calendar and pencil me in."

She laughed softly. "I'll jot you down for Saturday morning through Sunday night."

Gage resisted the urge to pump his fist. He didn't want to believe he would have Tonya all to himself for more than forty-eight hours. "Thank you, babe."

Eustace joined them, putting an arm around Gage's neck in a mock chokehold. "I need you to help me, brother."

"With what?"

"We have to figure out how we can steal Tonya away from Hannah, so we can increase our catering business."

Reaching up, Gage forcibly removed Eustace's arm. "You're wrong *and* that's cold, brother."

Eustace gave Tonya a bear hug. "You can't blame me for trying."

"No harm, no foul, boss," she mumbled against his broad chest.

He released her. "I can't believe you put all of this together by yourself."

"Hannah and St. John did help slicing the veggies."

Eustace angled his head. "Don't be so modest, Tonya. Your presentations are works of art."

"That's where we agree," Gage said to Eustace. He took Tonya's hand, threading their fingers together. "Come, babe, and show me what else you need to do so you can get off your feet."

Chapter 16

Tonya pulled alongside the curb in front of Hannah's house and parked. She had kept her promise to leave the party at the beginning of the halftime entertainment, and she drove back to the Garden District. She had accepted compliments from the McNairs' guests, while graciously rejecting their offers to cater parties for them. With the exception of Eustace and Gage, LeAnn, and Paige, the other attendees were St. John's colleagues and his and Hannah's former high school classmates.

She had filled the bathtub with her favorite scented bath salt and lost track of time soaking in the water until it cooled too much for her to remain. Fortified with a glass of wine, she crawled into bed and went to sleep.

* * *

Tonya woke early Monday morning refreshed and ready to begin her day mixing dough for bread. Eustace was unusually quiet, and when she asked if he was okay, he grunted that he had wrecked his diet and now had to work out twice as hard to shed the extra pounds he gained from overindulging at the party. She had decided not to remind him that he could have chosen from the vegetarian platters instead of wings, meatballs, and sweetened chicken dishes. Nicole and Melinda, sensing their father's dark mood, kept their distance, and the day ended with little or no conversation. She stayed an extra hour after closing to put up several batches of dough to get a jump on the next day's baked goods before returning home to shower and change.

Hannah was waiting on the McNairs' porch when she shut off the engine and alighted from the Pilot. She climbed the steps and hugged her friend. "You don't look any worse for wear after last night," she said, smiling.

Hannah rolled her eyes upward. "I may look okay, but I'm still recovering from eating too much."

"Now you sound like Eustace."

"That's because the man's on a mission to lose weight before his high school reunion." She looped arms with Tonya. "Come inside and rest yourself. St. John won't be home until six. Thankfully, there're still a few leftovers so I don't have to cook tonight."

"Do you cook every night?"

Hannah shook her head as pale, layered strands grazing her chin swayed with the motion. "No. St. John and I take turns, depending on what we want to eat. Most times LeAnn and Paige don't join us. I still believe they're not comfortable living here, even though I told them this is as much their home as mine."

Tonya walked with Hannah into the sunroom and sat on facing cushioned chaises. "Maybe if you and St. John weren't newlyweds, they wouldn't feel like interlopers."

"Their bedrooms are at the opposite end of the hallway from ours, so we rarely run into one another. Just the other day they hinted about taking another cruise, this time to the French and Italian Riviera."

"It's nice when you have the time to globetrot."

"My cousins never married or had children, which meant they always lived their lives by their leave. They were the sole heirs to my uncle's estate, so they don't have to subsist on a fixed income."

"Good for them."

Turning fifty had been a reawakening for Tonya; she sat down to prioritize her future. The first item was learning to live healthier, which meant losing weight and eating clean. She had also directed her financial planner to unload her shares in several Wall Street–traded companies and purchase tax-free municipal bonds. The seven years she worked for Wakefield Hamilton allowed her financial stability with a salary commensurate with her education and experience, and she had anticipated working for the investment bank until she retired.

"Where are my manners? Can I get you anything to eat or drink?" Hannah asked, breaking into her musings.

"No, thank you." Tonya sucked in a lungful of air, and then slowly exhaled. "I need your advice about how I should proceed with Gage."

"You're not sleeping with him." It was a statement.

"No, but it's not as if I don't want to."

"Has he hinted that he wants more than friendship?"

Tonya nodded. "Then what's stopping you? You're both consenting adults."

"My attraction to your husband's cousin is similar to what I experienced when I first met my ex."

"Weren't you in high school when you got involved with your ex-husband?"

"Yes, but—"

"No buts, Tonya. Fast-forward thirty years and you are not the same wide-eyed young girl you were then."

"I know that, Hannah! It's not about age, but my initial reaction to him." Tonya saw pinpoints of red dotting her friend's fair complexion. "I'm sorry I snapped at you." She covered her face with her hands. "I may as well tell you the whole story about my marriage."

She watched Hannah's expression change from curiosity to shock when she told her about having to defer her dreams in order to save her marriage. "After my divorce I swore I'd never get so involved with a man that I'd have to give up or sacrifice my own happiness for him."

"Do you think you have a monopoly on loving and losing?" Hannah questioned. "I was still in high school when I fell in love with Robert. And he wasn't that different from your Samuel, because he tried to talk me out of going to law school, and if he hadn't been away so much, I probably would've given in to him. There are some men who resent independent women because they want them to need them. Are you in love with Gage?"

"Not yet."

A smile flitted over Hannah's lips. "Does 'not yet' translate into you are falling in love with him? And has he asked you to give up anything?"

"Yes to your first question and no to the second."

"Then what's your problem, Tonya?"

"When I fall in love, I don't go halfway but all in, because I don't know how to separate what's good *to* me from what's good *for* me. I've have a couple of relationships since my divorce, and each time I put up a wall to keep the men at a distance because I'm not emotionally equipped to love and lose. I lost my younger brother to a drug overdose, and it still haunts me to this day."

"I'm sorry, Tonya. Again, we're not that different because I, too, lost a brother. He was nine years old when he died from meningococcal meningitis. Has Gage said anything negative about you having your restaurant?"

"No."

Hannah shook her head. "You keep telling me that Gage hasn't tried to change you, so I don't know why we're having this conversation. I'm an attorney, not a therapist, but you have to learn to accept that people we love we will also lose. I loved and lost Robert even before he passed away. Once he confessed to sleeping with other women, I was devastated, and I actually thought about killing him but I knew he wasn't worth me spending the rest of my life in prison. I moved out of our bedroom and never slept with him again. In my naïveté I'd believed I had a faithful husband, yet in twenty-nine years of marriage he'd slept with so many women that he couldn't remember their names. And even before becoming a widow I'd lost both my parents."

Tonya closed her eyes. "I must really sound selfish and gauche."

Reaching over, she held Tonya's hand. "No, you don't. You're only human. You have a fear of loving and losing, while I feared sleeping with a man because I was married to a philanderer. If Gage is anything like St. John, then you should have a wonderful relationship with him. I don't know whether he's told you, but his first marriage wasn't something to write home about."

"You know about that?"

Hannah smiled. "Yes. Don't forget that even though I was a DuPont, I'm also a Baptiste and a Toussaint because I'm married to St. John, which means I'm privy to family secrets. Should I assume Gage told you about his ex?"

"Yes, he did."

"Then he's also familiar with loving and losing. Correct me if I'm wrong, but I believe some of your anxiety is coming from how quickly you're falling for him."

Tonya forced a tight smile. Again she wondered if she was that transparent. "You're right."

"Now we're getting somewhere," Hannah crooned as if she had discovered a map leading to buried treasure. "I hadn't realized I'd fallen in love with St. John when we were in school because we were dating other people. But when I returned for the reunion last year and found out he was single, I invited him to DuPont House with the excuse that we had to catch up on what had been going on in our lives."

"Did he come?"

"Not at first. He took me out to dinner, and after that it was all she wrote. I wasn't back two weeks when I realized I wanted to sleep with him, and by the time you guys came down we'd been screwing like rabbits." Hannah counted on her fingers. "And five months later we were married. I never could've imagined being this happy, and it was all because I was willing to risk falling in love again. My grandmamma used to say, 'opportunity is like a baldheaded man; you have to catch it when it's coming towards you or your hand will slip off and it's gone forever.' In other words, Tonya, you're being given the opportunity to start over in a new place with a business you've always wanted, and with a new man who respects you for you. Gage has a reputation of being into himself, and if he's willing to open up and share himself, then you'd be a fool not to accept him. Remember, we all have an expiration date, and none of us know when that is, but I'll be damned if I'm not going to enjoy what time I have left on this earth."

Tonya digested everything Hannah said and knew she was right. She had spent the past sixteen, almost seventeen, years living in the past because the man she had married and vowed to love in the good times and bad times had turned into a Dr. Jekyll and Mr. Hyde.

She nodded. "I'm glad we had this talk. And as my grandmamma used to say, 'tomorrow isn't promised,' so I'm going to make the best of what life is offering me. None of us knew that day when we went to Wakefield Hamilton that it would be our last day. And their offering us a severance package could not soften the shock of suddenly finding ourselves unemployed."

"Remember I needed a pep talk when I went back to clean out my apartment and told you guys that I wasn't marrying St. John."

Tonya grimaced. "Please don't remind me of what we said to you, because I don't know where that came from."

"You said what needed to be said, other than knocking my hard head up against a wall. I'd been so hung up on Robert cheating on me that I didn't want to hear what St. John had to say about why he'd cheated on his wife. Once he told me, I couldn't stop crying, because he'd stayed in a marriage where his wife wouldn't let him touch her because her uncle had sexually abused her when she was a child."

"Oh, no!" Tonya gasped.

Hannah nodded. "So we're not alone when it comes to screwed-up marriages."

"How right you are, because if Jasmine's ex had done to me what he did to her, I know I would be serving time right now. I would've cut that SOB so low he would have to walk on his knees to get around."

Pressing a hand to her chest, Hannah laughed until tears rolled down her face. "Same here, but I would've waited for him to go to sleep and give him a Lorena Bobbitt and then tossed his junk down the garbage disposal."

It was Tonya's turn to laugh hysterically, although what Jasmine's husband did to her was no laughing matter. "How dare he get another woman pregnant and then cheat his wife out of becoming a mother when he underwent a vasectomy."

"That's why I gave her the advice she needed to get what she deserved when going through her divorce," Hannah said. "I couldn't believe it when she told me everything he'd done to her. At first I wasn't going to help her, but when she said she suspected her attorney was being paid by her ex to screw her out of everything she'd worked for, I knew I had to help her."

"Was he working for the other side?"

"Damn straight he was. I called and told him I was going to report him to the bar for violating his ethics if he didn't refund her retainer. It took exactly twenty-four hours for him to messenger a bank check to her. I referred her to another attorney, and she got what she wanted."

"The last time I spoke to Jasmine she was just getting over the flu."

Hannah laced her fingers together as she stared at the bright pink polish on her toes in a pair of sandals. "I'm not one to spread gossip, but the last time I spoke to my investment banker, he asked me about Jasmine."

Tonya grunted softly under her breath. It was apparent Cameron had taken her advice to ask Hannah about Jasmine. "That's what I told him. He'd asked about her at your wedding, and I told him if he wanted to know anything about Jasmine or Nydia, then he should ask you."

Hannah grimaced. "I like Cameron, but not for Jasmine."

"What's wrong with him?" Tonya asked.

"He's not what I'd call a dog—it's just that he's a serial dater. Cameron will take a woman out for a few months, drop her, and then it's on to the next one."

"I really don't know Jasmine as well as Nydia, so I can't give you my opinion one way or the other. What I did glean from sitting next to him at the reception is that he doesn't need her money, and he's willing to go after whatever he wants."

"That's because Cameron comes from a moneyed family. And I can testify that he is resolute when he decides he wants a woman. Even though I'm ten years his senior, he's asked me out a few times."

Tonya's dimples creased her cheeks when she smiled. "I never took you for a cougar."

Hannah waved her hand. "Even if I was younger I'd never trade St. John in for all the money in the world."

"You really love him, don't you?"

Closing her eyes and shaking her head, Hannah said, "More than you could ever imagine." She opened her eyes, and they were shimmering with unshed tears. "St. John is good to me and for me. There had been a time when I agonized over wanting to open the inn in time for Mardi Gras, and he would tell me, everything in its own time. He was the one who suggested converting the guest-houses into eating establishments."

"What was your original plan for them?"

"I didn't have one," Hannah admitted. "I couldn't convert them for guests because that would increase the number of rooms from nine to thirteen and make the inn a hotel. And I wasn't willing to repeat the process of filing new applications and licenses and wait months for them to be approved. The approvals for the restaurants are pending, and with the installation of the elevator I can project a fall completion. St. John and I have talked about opening on the same day as our wedding anniversary."

"You'd really have a reason to celebrate twice."

Hannah nodded. "That, and St. John can't come up with the excuse that he forgot our anniversary."

Tonya pushed to her feet, Hannah rising with her. "I've taken up enough of your time with my bitchin' and moaning. I suppose I knew why I was being ambivalent, but I needed to hear it from someone else." She extended her arms and wasn't disappointed when Hannah hugged her. "Thank you. You've become the sister I wish I'd had."

"That goes double for me, Tonya." Hannah eased back. "The next time you talk to Jasmine, try and feel her out about going in with us. I don't want to call her and have her think I'm trying to pressure her. Now that the workmen are beginning to renovate the second-story suites, I know as soon as the summer ends we'll have to begin interviewing and hiring staff. And I can't think of someone more qualified to do that than Jasmine."

Tonya had to agree with Hannah. She and many other employees couldn't believe that Jasmine hadn't been promoted to director of personnel when her supervisor had been fired for leaking personal information on one of the vice presidents. It was a slap in the face when the board hired someone from the outside to run that department.

"Thanks again for lending me your ear."

"Any time. I'll walk you out."

Hannah stood on the porch, waiting for her to get into the SUV. Tonya executed a U-turn and waved out the open driver's-side window as she reversed direction and drove home. She marveled at how easy it was for her to think of the guesthouse as home when for most of her life, New York City had been home. It was where she was born, raised, and with the exception of spending some time in Rhode Island and abroad, the majority of her life she had lived in three of the five boroughs.

Now home was New Orleans, the Crescent City, NOLA, or Nawlins. Unconsciously she had settled into the predictable rhythm of getting up at dawn to bake bread, roast and grill meat and fish, and cut, chop, and sauté ingredients for gumbos, bisques, and other soups, while refining her expertise when it came to sauces, dry rubs, and seasonings.

Strolling through the Quarter reminded Tonya of Greenwich Village with its historic buildings, distinctive architecture, funky bars, antique shops, art galleries, and sidewalk cafés crowded with tourists and native bohemians. She had become accustomed to the differing dialects, which, like the food and music, she found hypnotic.

She was four blocks from the house when Gage's

number appeared on the navigation screen. Smiling, she tapped a button on the steering wheel. "What's up, darling?" The endearment had slipped out unconsciously.

"That's what I should be asking you, babe."

"What are you talking about?"

"Eustace."

Tonya's heart rate quickened. "Has something happened to him?" When she left him at the restaurant, he appeared to be all right.

"No. I just spoke to him, and he claims you were out of sorts today. He figured you may have been exhausted from yesterday."

She wanted to tell Gage it was his brother who was out of sorts, that, other than complaining to her about his early Monday morning weigh-in, he was practically monosyllabic. "I suppose I'm still a little tired," she said instead.

"You can't spend more than twelve hours catering a party and then get up early the next morning to begin cooking again."

"I didn't have a choice, Gage."

"Yes, you did. I could've asked one of the assistants at Jazzes if they wanted to earn some extra money, and I'm certain they wouldn't have turned it down."

She smiled. "Maybe next year."

"Next year you'll be open for business."

"Never on a Sunday." Signaling, she turned off onto the street leading to DuPont House.

"I remember you mentioning that you plan to close Sundays and Mondays."

Tonya slowed as she approached the centuries-old mansion and suddenly hit the brake when she saw the gates open. When she'd left, the contractors were still working in the main house. They always left promptly at five, and it was now minutes before six.

"Gage."

"What is it?"

"Someone left the gate open."

"What are you talking about?"

"The gate to the house is wide open and—"

"Are the workmen still there?"

"I don't think so. They usually park their trucks where I can see them from the road."

"Don't go in! Stay where you are, and I'll be there as soon as I can."

"Where are you, Gage?"

"Home. Hang up. I'm on my way."

Tonya disconnected the call and turned off the engine. The foreman of the construction company had been given a remote device to open and close the gate, yet it was apparent he had forgotten to activate it. The Garden District, having set up its own neighborhood watch, was relatively safe, but since Paige and LeAnn had moved to Marigny, Tonya had become very vigilant when leaving or returning to the property.

Gage knew he was speeding and prayed he wouldn't be stopped by the police before arriving at DuPont House. As soon as he hung up, he called St. John to tell him to alert Hannah that the workmen had left her property unprotected. St. John said he would handle it and that by the time Gage got to the house someone from a private security company would meet him.

He managed to make it to the Garden District without being pulled over; he spotted Tonya's Honda parked in front of the house. There was another dark vehicle idling in back of hers, and as soon as he turned off the engine and got out, the driver in the other car also emerged. Gage smiled when he recognized the man who'd been a guest at his cousin's Super Bowl party.

Mark Fitzsimmons, still sporting a military haircut, had attended the same high school as Hannah and St. John. He came from a military family, having serving thirty years in the Marine Corps as a drill instructor, and now operated his own security company.

Gage exchanged a handshake with Mark. The former marine was still in incredible shape for a man approaching sixty. "I didn't think I'd see you again this soon."

"Same here," Mark replied. "St. John wants me to check out the house and property before anyone goes in."

Gage nodded. "The gates are usually left open during the day when the work crew is here, but it appears as if they're gone now."

"I called a couple of my men, and as soon as they get here we'll make certain the place is secure. Do you have keys to the house?"

"No. But I'll get them from Tonya." He approached her vehicle and tapped on the driver's-side window. She opened the door and he extended his hand to help her out. His arms circled her waist, pulling her close to his body. "How are you?"

Tilting her chin, Tonya smiled up at him. "I'm okay. I didn't expect you to get here so quickly."

He flashed a sheepish grin. "I must admit that I did a little speeding."

"Only a little?" she asked.

"Okay. I did a lot of speeding, because all I could think of was some sick idiot lurking around the property." He glanced over her at the imposing two-story structure at the end of the curving path. "Is the house always left dark at night now that Paige and LeAnn are staying with St. John?"

"Yes. Why?"

"Anyone passing by would assume it's unoccupied, and that will only invite trouble."

"The porch lights are solar-powered, so they come on at dusk and go off at sunrise."

"That's still not enough. Hannah should install timers so lamps can come on and go off at different intervals." The sound of approaching cars caught Gage's attention. "That must be Mark's men. I need the key to the main house so they can go through all of the rooms."

Reaching into her tote, Tonya handed Gage a set of keys to the main house. "I'll also give you the key to the guesthouses."

Gage kissed her forehead. "I'll be right back." He returned to where Mark stood with two men holding military-style flashlights. Overhead light from a street-lamp revealed both men had automatic handguns tucked in holsters at the small of their backs.

The three men made their way up the path leading to DuPont House. At the same time another vehicle arrived, and Gage recognized the car as Hannah's vintage Mercedes-Benz. St. John was driving, and within seconds of the sedan coming to a stop, Hannah was out and running toward him.

"Is she all right?"

"Who are you talking about?"

"Tonya."

He smiled. "Of course she's all right."

Hannah looked over her shoulder at her husband. "St.

John said something like Tonya was afraid to go inside the house because she thought someone was there."

St. John strolled over and angled his head at Hannah. "Stop it, sweetheart. You're just being melodramatic."

She rounded on him. "But didn't you say she didn't want to go into the house?"

He met Gage's eyes. "I said Gage didn't want her to go into the house until it was checked out. That's why I called Mark."

His explanation appeared to satisfy Hannah, as she blew out her breath. "I'm going over to talk to Tonya."

Waiting until Hannah was out of earshot, Gage rested a hand on St. John's shoulder. "I need to talk to you."

"What do you want to say that you don't want Hannah to hear?"

"Damn, *kezen*, I didn't know you could read minds."

St. John laughed. "I can't. It's just that I believe I know you better than you know yourself. After all, I did watch you grow up."

"That's bullshit and you know it, *kezen*. You're thirteen years older than me, and that only makes you an older brother."

"Okay, but as your older brother, *cousin*, I can see that Tonya has your nose so wide open that you can drive a tractor trailer up it."

Gage froze. "You know?" he asked after a pregnant silence.

"Come on, Gage. Only someone who's visually impaired wouldn't see how you look at the woman. Before I married Hannah you got on me about not going out with women after I broke up with Lorna. I could say the same about you, because you haven't brought a woman around to any of the family functions since you and Winnie split up."

"Do me a favor, St. John."

"What?"

"Please don't ever mention her name to me again."

"She can't be the reason you're turned off on women."

Gage paused. "She's part of it. What's the expression about the wife or the husband being the last to know? It was a hard pill to swallow when I found out my wife had been turning tricks to save enough money to live in a big house."

St. John patted his cousin's shoulder in a comforting gesture. "That's water under the bridge now. How serious is this thing between you and Tonya?"

"We're very good friends. I don't know what it is about her, but whenever we're together I can be myself. I can say whatever comes to mind without her catching an attitude or looking at me sideways."

"That's called respect, Gage. She respects your opinions, and hopefully you can respect hers."

"Oh, I do," he said quickly. "And she's not shy about speaking her mind."

St. John smiled. "There you go. It looks as if you've found your soulmate. Don't turn around. The ladies are heading our way."

Gage thought about what St. John said as to his staring at Tonya. He had no idea he had been that obvious. He smiled down at Tonya when she slipped her hand in his. "It will be over soon."

Hannah curved her arm around St. John's waist. "I used my remote to close the gate and it wouldn't move, so it must have malfunctioned. Even if it hadn't, I don't feel comfortable with Tonya living here alone now that my cousins are staying with us."

Tonya shook her head. "I'm okay as long as the gates are closed at night."

"Hannah's right," St. John said. "We have an extra bed-room if you're willing to move in with us until the inn's ready."

Tonya shook her head again. "I can't. You already have a full house."

"I have two extra bedrooms if you don't mind staying with me," Gage suggested.

Tonya pulled her lower lip between her teeth as she seemingly pondered his offer. "I'll stay, but only until the gates are functioning. After that I'm coming back."

Gage looked at Hannah and then St. John. Even if Tonya lived with him until the gates were repaired, it would lessen some of his angst as to her safety. "Okay," he conceded. He felt as if he had won a small victory. "As soon as Mark and his men give us the all-clear signal, I'll go with you to pack a bag for a few days."

"Do you want St. John and me to wait with you?" Hannah asked Gage.

"No. You guys can go on back home."

"Tell Mark to call me when he's finished," St. John said as he led Hannah back to their car.

Gage stood with Tonya, watching as the taillights of the sedan disappeared from view, and then led her to his vehicle. They sat together, held hands, and stared out the windshield. No words were necessary. They were about to become temporary roommates.

Chapter 17

Tonya watched Gage set her bags on the floor next to the closet in the bedroom across the hall from his. The security team had conducted an extensive sweep of the entire property, including the gardens, and found no evidence of an intrusion. Mark told Gage he planned to call St. John to inform him that he would have a two-man team remain on the property until the work crew arrived the following morning.

When she'd sat in Hannah's sunroom what now seemed eons ago, Tonya could not have predicted that hours later she would sleep in a bedroom under the roof of the man with whom she found herself falling in love.

"Have you had dinner?" he asked her.

She turned to look at him. "No, but I don't want to eat anything that's too heavy."

"I can offer you a choice of an asparagus, artichoke, and lobster salad or salmon salade Niçoise."

"I'll have the salmon."

He smiled. "I was hoping you'd say that."

Tonya returned his smile. "Do you need a sous chef? I could make the vinaigrette," she said when he hesitated.

"Sure. Give me a few minutes to change into something more comfortable, and I'll join you in the kitchen."

She nodded. "While you're changing, I'll unpack my bags and put my stuff away."

Tonya, standing next to Gage and cutting red and green peppers into julienne strips, felt that being with him was as natural as breathing. Even if they hadn't agreed on the pace or the direction their relationship would take, there was no doubt they were completely in sync when it came to cooking together.

Gage had put on a playlist featuring blues and jazz songs by Billie Holiday, Sarah Vaughan, and Etta James. "You're really feeling the girls tonight."

"I'm trying to determine which songs I'm going to use for the school's spring concert."

"What about Roberta Flack? I remember my mother telling me that she and my dad drove to Hampton University just to see her in concert. Daddy played her 'Compared to What' so much that I was tempted to scratch the record. But I knew how much he coveted his record collection, so I decided earplugs were a better solution. It was only when I grew older that I came to love her voice."

Lowering his head, Gage kissed her hair. "Thank you for reminding me about Roberta."

"Tell me about your concert." Gage revealed the concert committee's plans for a journey of music and dance beginning with the human voice on the continent of Africa and ending with emergence of music's latest genres: rap and hip-hop.

"We plan to showcase dances from all over the world."

"That sounds daunting."

"Not really. We're planning acts lasting three minutes, which translates into twenty acts per hour. The concert usually runs for two hours, but this year the committee decided to extend it by a half hour. There will be a brief intermission after ninety minutes to give the audience a chance to catch their breath."

Tonya was totally transfixed as Gage outlined the dances from the different countries that would showcase their culture. He talked about the relationship between Irish step dancing and American tap, scatting and rap, and Negro spirituals and blues.

She pointed to the tattooed notes on his right arm. "What are those notes?"

"They're from Handel's 'Messiah,' which I personally believe is the most magnificent piece of music ever written."

The conversation segued from music to dance, and Tonya was amazed as to his breadth of musical knowledge until he boasted proudly that he had graduated from one of the world's preeminent performing arts conservatories.

"Bragging, darling?"

"Hell, yeah, babe."

"Do you have any students that stand out from the others?"

"That's a difficult question to answer, because most

are extremely talented. And if any of them want to audition for Julliard, I wouldn't hesitate to write a letter of recommendation. What's so amazing is that many of my students didn't begin playing an instrument until middle school, and what I'm trying to do is boost their confidence. Since substituting for the orchestra teacher, I've established a practice where I arbitrarily call on a student to come up and play a solo in front of the class."

Tonya halted slicing shallots. "Isn't that intimidating?"

"It's no more intimidating than if they had to audition to get into a college for the performing arts. And if they were taking private lessons at a music school, they would have to play for recitals."

"Is that what you had to do?"

"Yes. The aunt who taught St. John piano also taught me. Our recitals were any time the family got together for a holiday or big event. One Sunday, my aunt put on a musical program at our house, and I was on program to play several hymns. The devil must have gotten into me when I rocked out Little Richard's 'Long Tall Sally,' and Jerry Lee Lewis's 'Great Balls of Fire.' It was so quiet in the place you could hear a rat piss on cotton. I took a bow, threw kisses to the ladies, and then walked out."

Tonya laughed so hard her sides hurt. "How old were you?"

"Thirteen. My aunt said I must have gone temporarily insane and lost my mind, while my parents said if I was on something, that would explain what I did, but if I wasn't, then they were going to help me find it."

"What did they do?"

"I was grounded for the entire summer. When other kids were playing ball or going swimming, I had to get up early and work in the restaurant with Pop."

"I bet that *learned* you," Tonya joked.

"It did. And the days when the restaurant was closed, I wasn't allowed to leave my room except to eat."

"How did you pass the time?"

"I read every book in my mother's bookcase. She didn't like going to the movies, so she'd read books that were turned into films. Her favorite was Ian Fleming's James Bond. Even now she devours anything written by James Patterson, Nicholas Sparks, and Dan Brown. I noticed you have a lot of books and magazines when I slept over at your place."

"I read while listening to music." She sat on a stool and watched Gage almost simultaneously drain a pot of boiled potatoes and plunge them into a bowl of ice water to stop the cooking process. He repeated the motion with a saucepan of green beans, followed by rinsing two hard-boiled eggs under cold water.

"I can drop you off in the morning and pick you up in the afternoon, so you don't have to move your car."

"I have to use my car," Tonya insisted, "because I leave earlier than you do." She'd followed Gage back to his house and parked her SUV alongside his in an indoor lot that offered discount prices for those living in the Lower French Quarter.

"What time do you have to get up in the morning?"

"Five fifteen."

He gave her a questioning look. "Why so early?"

"I have to get ready to be at the restaurant by six."

"You go in at six every day?" She nodded. "Did Eustace tell you to come in at that time?"

"No. I have to be there early on Monday, Wednesday, and Friday when he's at the gym, so coming in the same time on Tuesday and Thursday doesn't present a problem for me."

Reaching into the back pocket of his jeans, Gage removed his cell phone and entered his passcode. "Well, it's a problem for me, because you're putting in too many hours."

Tonya bristled at his tone. How many hours she worked was not his concern or his business. "Don't interfere," she warned.

"What's up, bro?" He'd ignored her; she heard Eustace's voice through the speaker.

"Do you need Tonya to come in early on Tuesdays and Thursdays?"

"No. Why are you asking?"

"She's staying with me until the gates at DuPont House are working again. Hannah doesn't want her to stay there with the property unprotected. I'm asking about those days because I can drop her off and pick her up. That is if you don't mind her coming in at seven-thirty rather than six."

"That's not a problem, Gage. I keep telling Tonya that she's doing too much but she, like every other woman I deal with, ignores the hell out of me."

"I can hear you," Tonya shouted.

"Damn, bro. Why didn't you tell me you had me on speaker?"

Gage winked at Tonya. "Because we're very candid with each other, I didn't want her to think I was snitching on her."

"I hear you, Gage. You know what they say about snitches?"

"They get stitches. And we've both seen her handle a knife."

Tonya struggled not to laugh. "Keep talking about me like I'm not here and somebody *will* get cut."

"Enough talk about knives and stitches," Eustace said. "What's wrong with the gates at DuPont House, Tonya?"

"They won't close."

"Hannah's right about not wanting you to stay there alone. There's no such thing as a crime-free neighborhood. It can happen to you. Where you have people you'll find crazies. You better take good care of my apprentice or you'll hear it from me."

Gage smiled. "Not to worry, big brother. She's safe with me."

Tonya stared at Gage and slowly counted to ten before going off on him. She didn't need him to monitor her hours or intercede where it concerned her and Eustace. He was doing exactly what she'd talked to Hannah about—a man attempting to control her life.

He ended the call, set the phone on the countertop, and eased her off the stool and cradled her to his chest. "I worry about you, Tonya. You were so exhausted yesterday that you couldn't stay to watch the entire game. You can't keep up the same pace and then hit the ground running when it's time for you to open your place. And please don't tell me that you'll have other people in the kitchen helping you. I don't care if you have fifty or a hundred working, all of the responsibility for the restaurant's success or failure is still on your shoulders." He tightened his hold on her waist. "I don't want you to think I'm trying to run your life, because that's the last thing I want to do. Not only do I care about you, but I also care what happens to you."

A knot rose in Tonya's throat when she realized she

had been wrong to compare Gage to her ex. At every turn Samuel attempted to tell her what to do and how to do it. He'd claimed it was concern when she knew it was control.

Her hands came up and she cradled his face. "What is it you want from me?" Her voice was barely a whisper.

Gage closed his eyes. "All I ask is for you to let me take care of you." He opened his eyes; the intensity in the luminous orbs frightened her.

"That's it?"

"That's enough for me."

Going on tiptoe, Tonya brushed her mouth over his. "If that's all you're asking, then I'm more than honored to let you take care of me." She could feel his heart thudding against hers when she moved even closer. "Now it's my turn. What do you want me to give you?"

Gage trailed light kisses along the column of her neck. "I don't think you're ready to give me what I want."

"Try me. I've been known to be a genie on occasion and grant a few wishes."

"Are you sure you want to hear it?"

She nodded. "I'm very sure."

"Don't leave."

Tonya blinked once. "Don't leave?"

"Yes. I want you to stay; move in with me."

Now she was certain he could feel the runaway pumping of her heart against his chest. It was as if everything around them faded, leaving only the tall, incredibly masculine man whose nearness electrified all of her senses.

"Why, Gage?"

"Because it's been a long time since I've felt this connected to a woman."

There was a longing in his voice that told Tonya that Gage was lonely, and she remembered him stating that he didn't like strangers in his house. He was multitalented and owned a beautiful condo; yet when he came home and locked the door there was no one there to talk to, to sleep or wake up with.

She also wasn't a stranger to loneliness, but she wasn't looking for someone to share her life. She loved her career and now looked forward to controlling her own destiny. Right now Tonya likened her life to a beautifully decorated cake with different layers of delicious fillings. And if she took Gage up on his offer to live with him, then he would become the topper on the cake.

She boldly met his eyes. "Do you want a friend or do you want a lover?"

"Right now I'd like a roommate. After that I'm willing to accept whatever you're offering."

Tonya was momentarily surprised by his response. Moving in with Gage definitely had its advantages. She wouldn't have to concern herself with living alone on an estate behind massive iron gates that protected the property from intruders. And more important, she would have a man's protection.

"Okay, Gage. I'll stay."

He picked her up and joined their mouths in a searing kiss that sucked the breath from her lungs. Tonya held onto his neck, her lips parting as she felt the need to get even closer. Her breathing deepened in a slow, measured rhythm, betraying the rush of desire racing throughout her body as the realization washed over her that she wanted Gage to make love to her.

"You can't kiss me like this and then expect me not to be your lover."

"Is that what you want?"

"Yes," she whispered.

"Yes what?" he asked in her ear.

"I want to be your lover."

Gage knew he was lost. The desire he had fought from the instant he saw Tonya exploded uncontrollably until he was shaking from the passion struggling to erupt and embarrass him. Their incomplete dinner forgotten, he swept Tonya up in his arms. Taking long strides, he took the stairs two at a time. Fate had intervened when the gates to the mansion malfunctioned, and now the woman who seemingly understood him better than any other would not only share his bed but also his life.

Tonya had no idea how long he had waited for someone like her—a mature, confident woman not afraid to speak her mind. A woman so unaware of her sensuality he found it enthralling and refreshing.

Gage walked into his bedroom and placed Tonya on the bed, his body following hers down onto the mattress. Table lamps turned to the lowest settings cloaked the room in soft gold light. "Do you want me to use protection?" He didn't have an STD, and even though she couldn't have any more children, he wanted her to feel comfortable making love with him.

"Yes."

He kissed her again and then left the bed. Gage kicked off his running shoes and slowly removed his t-shirt, jeans, and briefs. He managed to dampen his passions so that he was back in control and his penis semi-erect. Opening a drawer in the bedside table, he removed a condom and slipped it under the pillow where he could reach it.

Tonya closed her eyes when Gage returned to the bed, the heat of his muscled physique enveloping her when he relieved her of blouse and jeans. Her bra was next, then the delicate scrap of silk of her panties, leaving her naked and vulnerable. She hadn't realized she had been holding her breath until he pulled her into a tender embrace where her nakedness touched his, making her aware of how different their bodies were.

"I love the way you smell." He ran his fingertips over her throat, shoulders, and along the length of her arm. "Your skin feels like spun silk."

Tonya bared her neck as the heat from his mouth swept from her own to her core. Waves of passion rolled over her until she could not stop her legs from shaking. Gage suckled her breasts, worshipping them, and the moans she sought to suppress escaped her parted lips.

His tongue circled the nipples, leaving them hard, erect, and throbbing. His teeth tightened on the turgid tips, and she felt a violent spasm grip her womb. Her fingers were entwined in the cotton sheets, tightening and ripping them from their fastenings at the same time she arched up off the mattress.

"Gage!" His name exploded from her as he inched down her body, holding her hips to still their thrashing. "Stop! Please!"

But he did not stop. His hot breath seared the tangled curls between her thighs, and Tonya went limp, unable to protest or think of anything except the pleasure her lover offered her. She registered a series of breathless sighs, not realizing they were her own moans of physical satisfaction. Eyes closed, head thrown back, lips parted, back arched, she reveled in the sensations that took her beyond herself, unable to believe she had had to wait until she was fifty to experience the exquisite pleasure Gage wrung from her. Then it began, rippling little tremors increasing and shaking her uncontrollably, which became more volatile when they sought a route of escape.

Gage heard Tonya's breathing come in long, surrendering moans, and he quickly moved up her trembling limbs and reached for the condom. His hand was steady when he tore open the packet and rolled the latex sheath down the length of his erection and eased his sex into her body. He was met with a slight resistance he hadn't expected, and drew back, and with a strong, sure thrust of his hips buried his hardness in the hot, moist, tight flesh pulsing around his own. Her legs circled his waist at the same time he cupped her hips, lifting her higher and permitting him deeper penetration.

Her lover's heat, hardness, and carnal sensuality had awakened the dormant sexuality of her body, and Tonya responded to his passion as hers rose high and higher until it exploded in an awesome, vibrating liquid fire that scorched her mind and left her convulsing in ecstasy. She hadn't quite returned from her own free-fall flight when she heard Gage's groan of satisfaction as he quickened his movements and then collapsed heavily on her sated form. There was only the sound of their labored breathing in the stillness of the bedroom as they lay motionless, enjoying the aftermath of a shared, sweet fulfillment.

Gage reversed their positions, bringing her with him

until she lay sprawled over his body, her legs resting between his. "Did I hurt you, babe?"

"No," she drawled, placing tiny kisses on his throat and over his shoulder. "I'm all right."

"Are you sure?"

She laughed softly. "Very sure."

Gage's right hand moved over her bare hip, caressing the silken flesh. Tonya had no idea how sensuous her voice sounded in the dimly lit room. He drew in a deep breath, luxuriating in the intoxicating fragrance of her perfume. He could not believe the passion she had aroused in him; if possible, he had wanted to make love to her all through the night. Inhaling her scent, tasting her flesh, caressing her silken body had tested the limits of his control. He smiled, knowing there would be many more nights that he would make love to Tonya.

"I thought we were making dinner."

"We were until you compromised me."

"I compromised you?" Gage asked. "You were the one who seduced me."

Tonya ran the tip of her tongue around his ear. "When I decide to seduce you, you'll know that you've been seduced."

"I can't wait."

"Be careful what you ask for, darling."

"I'll want more, more and more until I'm gorged." He inhaled an audible breath. "I don't believe I'll ever tire of you."

"Not even when I'm old and wrinkled and unable to open my legs for you."

"I'll be old, wrinkled, and unable to get it up, right along with you. Even now I'm grayer than you are."

"Your gray hair makes you even more attractive," she countered.

Gage sensed the change in her mood when she grew tense. It was funny how he was able to gauge her moods now that they were intimate. "What's wrong?"

"What makes you think something's wrong?"

"You're tense, Tonya."

"I was trying to imagine what people will say when they find out we're living together."

An angry frown marred Gage's handsome features. "Whatever they say will not change how I feel about you. I'm too old, had to put up with too much shit to concern myself with what people say about me."

"What about your mother, Gage?"

"What about her?"

"Do you think if I ever meet her she will welcome me with open arms once she discovers I moved in with her son after knowing him exactly one month?"

"That's where you're wrong. I met you for the first time right after St. John and Hannah's wedding. And that makes four months instead of one. My mother stopped meddling in my life a long time ago. The only thing she asks is if I've found someone to make me happy."

"What did you tell her?"

"I told her I'd met someone who makes me very, very happy."

Gage wasn't certain what he expected Tonya to say, but it wasn't the silence that followed his pronouncement that she made him happy. Happy and fulfilled.

"Please let me get up, Gage."

"Why?"

"I need to take a shower." Leaning over, Tonya reached

for Gage's t-shirt at the foot of the bed and slipped it over her head. She smiled at him over her shoulder. "I'm going to my bedroom. I'll be down as soon as I'm washed and dressed."

Sitting up and resting his back against a mound of pillows, Gage stared at the door through which Tonya had disappeared. He knew she was concerned about how quickly their relationship had progressed, and he had shocked himself when in a moment of madness he had asked her to live with him. And what surprised him more than his own impulsiveness was her acceptance.

Gage had to acknowledge at forty-six and fifty, respectively, he and Tonya did not have to answer to anyone for their actions or lifestyle, yet she had voiced her concern about how their friends and acquaintances would think of them living together. Hannah, St. John, and now Eustace knew she was living under his roof, and he knew it was only a matter of time before those in New Orleans also became aware of their living arrangements.

Gage swung his legs over the side of the bed and made his way to the en suite bath. Gage discarded the condom, turned on the water in the shower, and stepped under the lukewarm spray, loathing having to wash away the scent of Tonya's perfume. He showered and dressed in record time, and when he reentered the kitchen he found Tonya making the vinaigrette.

He rested his hand at the small of her back as she whisked balsamic vinegar and olive oil in a small bowl. Dipping his head, he pressed a kiss to her bare shoulder. "Love you."

Tonya nodded. "Thank you."

Gage's heart felt like a rock in his chest. He'd just admitted to Tonya that he loved her, and she thanked him as if he had just handed her a cup of coffee and the morning paper. *Act in haste and repent in leisure.* His mother's prophetic warning nagged at him. It was what she had said to him when he told her he had to marry because he had gotten a woman pregnant.

Marriage and living together were life-changing events, and he wondered if perhaps he was doomed to be unlucky in love. His volatile relationship with his ex-wife had been one-sided; he had done all of the compromising while she refused to accept the consequences for her actions.

Gage felt in his heart of hearts that Tonya was the woman he wanted in his life, but he had to make certain to allow her to make her own decisions, or what they would have was a rerun of her marriage.

"I mentioned before I'm not working this weekend. Let me know what you'd like to do or see, and we can plan it together."

She flashed her dimpled smile. "I'll try and come up with something we both like."

"That sounds good."

Chapter 18

Gage opened the gate and walked into the courtyard Friday afternoon to find it ablaze with candles on every level surface. His concern about their living together was offset when Hannah had called to let him know the electrical components for the gates were defective and had to be replaced, which meant Tonya would have to stay with him for an extended period of time. He told his cousin's wife that he would relay the information to Tonya and reassured Hannah that he did not have a problem with Tonya living with him.

He and Tonya had settled into a comfortable routine of alternating cooking for each other. She would surprise him with exotic dishes from Thailand and China. He had raved so much about her *gai pajd bal ga-paw*—a spicy basil chicken with pepper, onion, and chili paste—that she showed him step-by-step how to make the dish. In less than a week he had grown so used to coming home to find her that he couldn't remember when she hadn't been there. She shared his bed, and on occasion his shower. She loved sitting on the roof at night, because it had become her time to unwind and exhale.

Gage noticed there were times when she wasn't very talkative, and he gave her the space she needed to be alone with her thoughts. They hadn't made love since the first night, and again he decided not to pressure her, hoping whenever she was receptive she would let him know.

His gaze swept around the courtyard until he saw her sitting at a table set for two. She stood up, and his jaw dropped when he noticed her outfit. Black strappy stilettos, and a matching barely-there dress ending mid-thigh with a plunging neckline hugged her curvy body like a second skin.

He couldn't stop staring at her slender legs in the heels as she came closer. There was enough light from the candles to illuminate her face. Aptly applied makeup accentuated her large eyes and lush mouth. She leaned into him, and he felt himself succumbing to the hypnotic scent of her perfume. Gage knew he would be able to pick her out in a dark room from among at least fifty other women.

"Welcome home, darling."

Gage ran his tongue over his lower lip. "Thank you, my love."

She stared up at him through her lashes. "I know we talked about going out this weekend, but would it bother you if we spent the entire weekend at home?"

"No . . . no . . . of course not." He didn't know why he was stuttering other than he was becoming more aroused with each passing minute.

"Since the weather is so nice, I thought we would

begin with dinner under the stars. After that we can go inside for after-dinner drinks and dancing."

Gage was so still he could've been a statue. "What are we doing after that?"

Tonya ran her tongue over her lips, bringing his gaze to linger on them. "Would you be opposed to sharing a bath?"

"No."

She smiled. "After the bath we can go to bed and I'll make love to you and then you can make love to me, and if we are not too exhausted we can sleep for a while and go for seconds. How does that sound to you?"

Gage nodded like a bobble-head doll. "I agree to all of the above."

She took his hand. "Come inside and wash up. As soon as you're ready I'll bring out dinner."

Gage didn't know what brought on the change in her, but he wasn't going to question it. He knew something had to have been bothering her when she shut down and shut him out. He walked into the house and was met with a variety of mouthwatering aromas. A wide grin split his face as he anticipated a night filled with seduction and romance. Turning back the cuffs of his shirt, he washed his hands in the bathroom off the kitchen.

"Can I help bring out anything?" There were a number of covered dishes lining the countertop.

Tonya pointed to an aluminum pan with a matching lid. "You can take that one."

After two trips they were finally able to sit and eat. She removed all the lids to the dishes to reveal the Caribbean dishes she had promised him. Tonya pointed to each plate. "There's roast chicken with a garlic rub, rice and pigeon peas, fried plantains with a dipping sauce, and the little turnovers are beef empanadas. And in keeping with the Spanish theme I decided sangría is an appropriate wine. Will you please pour the wine?"

Gage filled two red wineglasses and handed one to Tonya. He could not believe she had put the dinner together so quickly, unless she had left the restaurant early to come home and cook. "What are we toasting?"

"Love."

He sat back in his chair. "Love?"

"Yes. Do you have any idea what this weekend is?"

Realization dawned when he smiled. "Of course. It's Valentine's Day weekend."

Tonya inclined her head. "I couldn't think of anything to buy you, so I decided to make a special dinner."

"I don't need anything, because everything I need is sitting across the table from me. However, I did buy something for you."

Her eyelids fluttered wildly. "You didn't have to get me anything."

"Why don't you let me be the judge of that," he stated emphatically. "I'll give it to you after dinner."

Gage bit into a flaky empanada, and the Latin spices in the beef filling tantalized his palate. He didn't know how she did it, but Tonya was able to cook for two and not have any leftovers, prompting him to refer to her as the queen of tapas. Each dish was more spectacular than the last, and he found himself drinking more wine than usual.

"We came up with a final listing of songs and dances for the concert," he said after draining his glass.

"When do you begin rehearsing?"

"We won't start rehearsing until late March. Auditions begin next week and continue for the next two weeks."

"What about the kids in the drama club? Do they get first choice?"

Gage nodded. "They're already in, but we always try and give other students who haven't joined a club the opportunity to become involved. And because some of the songs and dances are international, we're trying to engage those students from the particular racial or ethnic groups."

Tonya touched a napkin to the corners of her mouth. "When do you rehearse?"

"It's always after classes. I'll be coming home late at least three days a week. And the closer we get to performing, it may be five days and perhaps one weekend for a full dress rehearsal."

"It sounds exciting."

"It is for the students."

"Please, Gage, don't be modest. It has to be exciting for you, too."

"I suppose so, because this is my first time chairing the concert, and my last year teaching."

"What are you going to do once your residency ends?"

"Work at the restaurant so Eustace can take some time off. And don't forget I still play at Jazzes."

"So you're not retiring?"

"I still have a few more years to work a nine-to-five before I kick back and put my feet up."

Tonya touched the stud in her ear. "I sometimes think of what I'd do if I retired. I doubt if I'd travel as much as Paige and LeAnn. Hopefully, I'll have at least one grandbaby to spoil by that time."

"Is your daughter dating anyone?"

"I don't know. Something keeps nagging at me that she is. I suppose she'll tell me when the time comes, because I don't want to be one of those nosy mothers who can't stay out of their children's lives."

Gage smiled. "That means you won't be a meddling mother-in-law."

"Hopefully, I won't."

Resting an arm over the back of his chair, he studied her face in the lengthening shadows. "Mardi Gras is coming up in another three weeks, and the city will turn into one big bacchanal."

"It's not already?"

"No," he said, shaking his head. "You have to experience Mardi Gras firsthand to get the full effect of folks acting like they've lost their minds." Gage pushed back his chair and stood up. "Dinner was incredible." He came around the table and pulled back her chair. "I'll clear the table and bring everything inside. Go on, babe," he urged when she didn't move.

He stood motionlessly, watching the seductive sway of her hips and legs in the sexy heels. It was obvious Tonya was more than comfortable with her sexuality with the overt display of flesh in the revealing dress. He shook his head as if coming out of a trance and stacked plates and flatware to take inside.

Working quickly, Tonya rinsed and stacked pots and dishes in the dishwasher, and by the time Gage brought in the last plate she had finished cleaning up the kitchen. He had tuned the radio to a station playing romantic ballads. He extended his hand when she walked into the living room.

"May I have this dance?"

Smiling, she moved into his embrace. "But of course."

Her heels gave her a height advantage so that she didn't have to lean back to stare up at Gage. "I love dancing with you," she whispered against his warm throat.

"Maybe we should take ballroom dancing this summer with Hannah and St. John."

"I don't think I'm ready for that." Tonya was able to follow Gage when he spun her around and around.

"Very nice," he crooned.

"I have a wonderful leader."

After a while, she lost herself in the music and in the man. Tonya knew she had been in a funk because it was the anniversary of her brother's death, and she kept imagining that he was still alive and had made her an auntie. Ian had so much potential that she still couldn't understand what made him choose the life that was destined to end tragically either by spending countless years in jail or by other dealers looking to take over his territory—or by an early death.

Dusk had descended on the city, and by the time they turned off the music and climbed the stairs to the second story, stars lit up the nighttime sky. Tonya walked into the bathroom, lit a half dozen votive candles, turned off the light, and then turned on the water in the Jacuzzi. A bottle of cognac and two aperitif glasses on a silver tray sat on the window ledge next to the tub.

She returned to the bedroom to find Gage shedding his clothes. And it wasn't for the first time that she marveled at the perfection of his lean, muscled physique. Their eyes met when she slipped out of her shoes and shimmied out of the dress. She recognized lust in his gaze when she stood there wearing nothing but a pair of black bikini panties. Hooking her thumbs in the waistband, she slid them down her thighs and legs without bending her knees, and stepped out of them.

Turning on her heel, she strolled into the bathroom, giving him an unobstructed view of her naked body. She smiled hearing his intake of breath.

She stepped into the warm water and sat down, sighing as the pulsing jets massaged her body. Minutes later Gage joined her, his thick, heavy sex swaying between his thighs. *Sit down!* the silent voice in her head screamed. Him standing over her, semi-erect, was so erotic she feared she'd reach over and caress him.

Gage finally settled in the tub and filled the tiny glasses with the amber liquid. He touched his glass to hers. "Happy Valentine's Day."

"Happy Valentine's Day," she repeated. She sipped the liquor, staring at Gage over the rim as heat warmed her throat and settled in her chest.

He took both glasses and set them on the ledge, and then reached for her and settled her over his thighs. An audible gasp echoed in the bathroom when she felt his erection filling every inch of her vagina. Curving her arms around his neck for support, Tonya began moving over his penis. It began with a slow up-and-down motion, and then increased to frenzied rocking, and Gage's upward thrusting splashed water over the sides of the tub and onto the terracotta floor.

Without warning, he reversed their positions, supporting her body, and his lower body pumped with the velocity of a piston as he wordlessly communicated his masculine dominance over her.

"Marry me," he gasped, his breath hot and heavy in her ear.

Shaking her head, Tonya swallowed to relieve the dryness in her throat from breathing through her mouth. "No, Gage. I can't."

"Marry me!" he repeated.

"No!"

"Please marry me," he intoned, the supplication becoming a litany, which rang in her ear like a chant.

"I can't," she cried out at the same time she felt the walls of her vagina contract. There was one contraction, and then another, and they kept coming as her moans of erotic pleasure became unrestrained screams of ecstasy as she stiffened with the explosive rush of orgasmic fulfillment sweeping through her. The screams subsided to surrendering moans of physical satiation as she closed her eyes and registered the rush of Gage's release bathing her throbbing flesh.

Tears leaked from under her lids. Gage Toussaint possessed the power to assuage her physical need for him, but unknowingly he also had the power to tear her soul apart. She prayed he would not ask her to marry him again, because at that very moment she would have consented. Tonya loved Gage with all of her heart, but not enough to marry him. One marriage in her lifetime was enough.

She refused to look at him when she reached for a cloth from a stack on the ledge and drew it over her body and between her legs. She climbed out of the tub and picked up a towel off the low stool and wrapped it around her body. Walking on bare feet, Tonya entered the bedroom and slipped into bed. She was falling asleep when she felt the warmth of Gage's body as he pressed his chest to her back.

"I'm sorry, Gage."

He kissed the nape of her neck. "It's okay, babe. I should be the one apologizing for pressuring you to live with me and for wanting to marry you."

She turned to face him but couldn't make out his features in the darkened room. "I do love you, but I'm not ready. And I don't know when I'll be ready."

"Hush, sweets. I'm not going anywhere, so whenever you're ready let me know. I promise not to ask you again."

Tonya placed her fingers over his mouth before her mouth replaced her fingers. "I love you. Why I don't know. The list is so long I wouldn't be able to come up with enough words to describe how you make me feel."

He nuzzled her ear. "Knowing you love me is enough."

"For how long, Gage?"

"Until forever."

She repeated the two words in her head until she fell asleep. And when she woke the next morning to rain pelting the windows, she was alone in bed and there was a square gaily wrapped box on the pillow next to hers. Pushing into sitting position, she carefully removed the paper to reveal a navy blue velvet case. Instinct indicated it was a piece of jewelry—but what?

She finally opened the top and gasped. Resting on a bed of white silk was a diamond bangle. The blue-white stones shimmered like stars. After two attempts, Tonya managed to open the double safety catch and slip it on her left wrist. The weight indicated it was more than gold. Perhaps even platinum.

Scrambling out of bed, she raced into the bathroom to brush her teeth and wash her face. Removing the kimono from a wall hook, she slipped it over her head. She entered the bedroom at the same time Gage strolled in carrying two trays.

"I'd hoped to surprise you with breakfast in bed."

"You have," she said, smiling. "With breakfast and with the bracelet." Tonya held up her left arm. "Thank you. It's beautiful."

"You're welcome. Now get back into bed so we can eat together."

She smoothed down the sheet and climbed back into bed, taking the tray from Gage and placing it across her lap. He had prepared a light, fluffy omelet, home fries, toast, and a cup of fresh fruit. "This smells wonderful."

He got into bed next to her. "*Bon appétit.*"

"Thank you." Tonya bit into the omelet filled with green onions and Gruyère. "You're going to spoil me where I'd want breakfast in bed every morning."

Gage ruffled her short hair. "That can be easily arranged."

"Breakfast or spoiling?"

"Both."

"I'm glad you suggested staying in this weekend," Gage said after a comfortable silence. "I know I promised my mother I'd come up to Lafayette to see her, but right now I'm not up to driving more than a hundred fifty miles in the rain."

Tonya's fork stopped in midair when she stared at him. "You canceled seeing your mother to be with me?"

"It's not that."

"What is it, Gage? I don't want your mother angry with me because—"

"Stop it, Tonya. My not seeing my mother has nothing to do with you. I didn't make a firm commitment to see her; otherwise she would've called and read me the riot act."

"I'm sorry I overreacted."

"You're entitled to overreact every once in a while."

"Why, thank you, sir."

He ran a finger down the length of her short nose. "You're welcome, madam."

Tonya sat on the window seat in the garret, staring at the rain sluicing down the glass. She and Gage had shared a shower, splashing each other like little kids before she begged him to stop. She'd retreated to the attic when Gage had to return several phone calls; she didn't want him to think she was eavesdropping on his conversations.

She heard his footsteps coming up the stairs and turned away from the window. The expression on his face was one she would never forget: fear. "What is it?"

"It's Wesley."

Tonya stood up. "What about him?"

"The police just called to say someone found him in an alley beaten so badly he's barely alive."

Tonya was galvanized into action. "I'm coming with you."

She didn't remember putting on her running shoes or grabbing a poncho from the closet. What she did remember was Gage speeding and running red lights to get to the municipal hospital. It appeared that the natural color had drained out of his face, while a muscle twitched nervously in his jaw. As soon as they arrived at the hospital, she took his keys. She wasn't going to allow him to drive like that again and wrap the Audi around a pole.

She felt helpless, impotent—as helpless as she'd felt when she pleaded with her brother to give up selling and using drugs. But all of her pleas had fallen on deaf ears.

Ian had claimed he was in too deep and didn't know how or want to get out.

She sat in the hospital waiting area for family members while Gage spoke to someone at the nurses' station. He was gone for so long Tonya thought he'd forgotten she had come with him.

She popped up when he walked into the room. It was as if he'd aged overnight. "How is he?"

He shook his head. "Not good. Whoever beat him wanted him dead. They've got him hooked up to a machine monitoring his vitals, and they're also trying to flush drugs out of his system. The doctor said he shot up with a lethal cocktail of heroin, crack, and another drug whose name I can't recall."

Tonya rested a hand on his arm. "I thought he lived in Baton Rouge."

"That's what I thought." He ran a hand over his face. "Now that he's here, I can keep an eye on him. I don't know where he got the drugs, but once they release him I'm bringing him home with me—that is if you don't mind him living with us."

Tonya looked at Gage as if he'd lost his mind. "It has nothing to do with whether I mind, Gage. The boy's your son, and it is your responsibility to make sure he gets help and stays clean."

He pulled her into the circle of his arms. "Thank you. That's really a load off my mind."

She wanted to ask him if he really thought she was that callous and would tell him his son couldn't live with them. "How long do they plan to keep him?"

"I don't know. Remember, Tonya, this is not Wesley's first rodeo, but if I have anything to do with it it's going to be his last. There's no way I'm going to send him back to his mother after this." A blood-curdling scream reverberated out in the hall, followed by a woman calling Wesley's name. "Shit! That must be Winifred."

Tonya followed Gage to the hallway, stunned to find a woman clawing at Gage as he tried dislodging himself from her. She had to assume the woman and Gage were around the same age, but his son's mother looked old enough to have been Gage's mother. Her face was sallow and pockmarked, body emaciated, and when she opened her mouth, she was missing several teeth. It didn't take the IQ of a genius to know the woman was abusing meth.

Tonya felt like she was witnessing a brutal assault captured by police or closed circuit cameras when Gage grabbed the woman's upper arms and shook her as if she were a rag doll. Winifred was screaming that he was killing her, and Gage retaliated with, "He can't get clean if you're on the shit, too!"

"Let her go, Gage, before you break her arms," Tonya pleaded as hospital staff and patients came out of their rooms to witness the fracas.

Winifred's cloudy blue-gray eyes filled with tears. "I don't want you anywhere near *my* son. Yes, Gage, *my* son. I told him the truth when he was fifteen when he asked about you; I told him I didn't know who his father was, because I wanted him to hate you just like you hated me for being what you wanted me to be." Spittle had formed at the corners of her mouth.

A member of hospital security arrived, and Gage told him he didn't want Winifred anywhere near his son.

"For the last time, he's not your son!" she screamed.

"I may not have fathered him, but it is my name on his birth certificate, and legally that makes him my son."

Tonya backed away as if they were carrying a communicable disease. She did not want to believe Gage had asked her to marry him, yet did not trust her enough to tell her about his son's paternity, even though he knew the boy wasn't his biological son. Did he believe she would think him a fool for claiming a child belonging to another man? That he'd loved Winifred so much he didn't care if she'd cheated on him with other men?

The questions bombarded her as she left the hospital and sat in his car in the parking lot. What if she had consented to marry him? Would he have hidden the truth from her, or would he have been forthcoming because she said yes?

She punched the start-engine button when he opened the passenger-side door and got in. "How did it go?"

"I don't want to talk about it!"

"You have to talk about, Gage."

"No, I don't, because it's none of your business."

"You're right," she mumbled under her breath. "It is none of my business." As she drove, she acted as if she didn't have a care in the world, while her insides were churning like a whirlpool. Tonya parked the car and went inside the house.

She went into the bedroom, retrieved one of her bags from the closet, and opening and closing drawers, filled the bag with enough clothes to last at least four days.

Gage was sitting on the sofa when she came down the stairs, and she knew she would never forget the haunted look in his eyes. She left the set of keys to the condo on the dining table and walked out of the house.

Gage watched Tonya walk out of the house and out of his life. He wanted to go after her, but his mind was in so much turmoil he wasn't able to form a coherent thought. It had been years since he last saw Winifred, and it only took one glance to know why Wesley wasn't able to stay clean.

At twenty Wesley was no longer a minor, but he was the only father the boy had ever known. And despite Winifred's claim he was not his biological father, Wesley's birth certificate indicated legally he was. He picked up his cell phone and placed a call to his attorney's office, leaving a voice mail message that it was an emergency.

He knew he had treated Tonya unfairly when he told her that what went on between him and his ex was none of her business, but he didn't want to involve her in the ugliness that had begun to plague him within days of exchanging vows with a woman he never should've married.

He tapped Tonya's number, and the call went directly to voice mail. He left a message for her to return his call. Gage knew his life was in crisis: Wesley was in critical condition from a vicious beating, while he'd practically assaulted his ex after her insane display, and the woman he loved beyond description had walked out on him.

Four hours later he called Tonya again, nearly pleading with her to call him. Panicking, Gage called local hotels and motels asking for her, but with no success. He decided to wait until Sunday to contact her again. After a good night's sleep he prayed things would be better.

Chapter 19

Gage alternated pounding on the door and ringing the bell. "Open the damned door!"

He was poised to knock again when the door opened and he came face-to-face with Hannah.

"Have you lost your mind? Come in before you wake up the entire neighborhood."

"I'm sorry I woke you up. I've been calling Tonya and leaving messages, and she hasn't called me back. I thought maybe she was here." He slumped down in an armchair.

"What the hell . . ." St. John walked into the living room in a bathrobe. "Come now, *kezen*, why are you here so early in the morning?"

Gage gave St. John a death stare. "I'm looking for Tonya."

St. John's mouth twisted in a sneer. "If you don't know where your woman is, then I can't help you."

Perched on the arm of the chair, Hannah patted Gage's

head. "She was here last night but left early this morning to go back to the guesthouse. The gates are still open, so you'll be able to get in. Someone from the security company will ask you for ID. I should let you know now that Tonya plans to live at the guesthouse until the workmen tell her she has to leave."

Gage stood up and kissed Hannah's forehead. "Thanks, cousin. I love you."

Hannah shared a glance with her husband. "Your family is crazy."

St. John smiled. "They're your family, too."

Gage felt less anxious when he drove from Marigny to the Garden District. It was an early Sunday morning, and the traffic was light. He maneuvered through the open gates and came to a stop feet from an unmarked dark-colored sedan. A stocky man dressed entirely in black got out and came over to him.

"ID please." Rising slightly, he removed the case with his driver's license from the pocket of his jeans. The man peered closely at his photograph and then returned it. "You can go."

Gage parked near the garages and walked to Tonya's guesthouse. He rang the bell and waited. He was poised to ring it again when he heard Tonya say, "Go away, Gage."

"I can't, Tonya."

"If you don't go away, I'm going to call the police."

"Call them. And right now I don't give a damn. I want you to hear me out, and after that if you don't want to see me, then I'll go away and never bother you again."

The door opened, and Gage's heart turned over when he saw Tonya's face. She'd been crying. He didn't give her the opportunity to react; he just he swept her up in his arms, carried her to the bedroom, and gently placed her on the bed. He lay next to her, making certain they weren't touching.

"I apologize for everything. For you witnessing me at my worst. I had a very confrontational marriage to a woman who raised cuckoldry to an art form. The first time I suspected she was cheating on me I forgave her, but when it happened again I moved out of the bedroom into the one with Wesley. I only stayed because Wesley needed a father. I knew I had to leave when she threw it in my face that Wesley wasn't mine. That she was six weeks pregnant when she slept with me. I thought about going to court to take Wesley away from her, but a paternity test would prove the boy wasn't mine, so I continued to send her money for his support.

"Wesley had just celebrated his fifteenth birthday when his mother told him I wasn't his father. That's when he began drinking and drugging. I didn't see him for years until he was in high school. He told me he wanted to go to college, but his mother wouldn't sign the forms so he could get financial aid. I told him I'd pay his tuition with the proviso he maintain at least a C average. I was the beneficiary of one of my father's insurance policies and my mother was the other. I had invested the proceeds because the money I earned working at the restaurant and playing gigs covered my day-to-day expenses."

"Wesley's mother is a meth head, and the only way he's going to stay clean is if he gets away from her," Tonya stated.

"I know that. I've already called my attorney for his advice. I know I could ask Hannah, but I don't want to involve her in my mess."

"Once he comes out of rehab, he can move in with you. And if he stays clean, I'll hire him to work in the restaurant. He can start as a dishwasher and eventually work up to a busboy."

"Why would you do that for him?"

"Because I had a brother who was strung out on drugs. You're lucky, Gage, because your son is still alive. This past Tuesday would've been my brother's fifty-fourth birthday if he'd lived. He had everything going for him, yet he couldn't resist selling and taking drugs, and in the end it cost him his life."

Gage reached for her hand and laced their fingers together. "Now I know why you were in a funk earlier in the week."

"I'm a lot better than I used to be. I'm sorry I judged you without hearing the whole story."

"I never told anyone about it. Even my mother still believes Wesley's her grandson. I appreciate your offer for Wesley to work in your restaurant, but we Toussaints have a rule that—"

"We won't work at another restaurant unless it's owned by a family member," Tonya said, finishing his statement.

"How do you know that?"

"St. John told me."

"But there's still the possibility that he can work for me. Your son deserves to get his life together before it's too late, and I'm willing to do my part."

Shifting slightly, Gage stared at Tonya. "Are you saying what I think you're saying?"

Her dimples winked at him when she smiled. "I don't know what you're talking about."

"Yes, you do."

Her eyebrows lifted questioningly. "Do I?"

"Do you recall us talking about the word *marry*?"

"I believe I do recall that word."

Gage moved over her body, supporting his greater weight on his elbows. "I think we were moving so quickly we didn't take the time to really get to know each other. It was different for Hannah and St. John because they met each other in high school. I still want to marry you, but I'm willing to wait until you're ready. And if you agree to become a Toussaint, then be prepared to have two Toussaints working for you: me and Wesley."

"You would really come work and with me?"

"Hell, yeah. I'm even willing to work two jobs—one in the kitchen and the other with the band."

Tonya sat up. "Oh, my word! I just came up with the names for the supper club and café."

Gage eased her back down to the mattress. "What are they?"

"Toussaints for the supper club and Martine's for the café."

"How very French," he crooned. "Now, when do you plan to become an official Toussaint?"

"June. I've always wanted to be a June bride."

"Then a June bride you'll be."

"Please let me up, Gage, so I can shower and change. I'm ready to go home so my fiancé can serve me breakfast in bed."

"I'll be in the garden whenever you're ready." He didn't want to tell Tonya that he needed to be alone—alone to pray for his son, to pray for forgiveness, and pray in gratitude that he had met a woman who has restored his faith in love.

Turn the page for
Tonya and Gage's New Orleans cuisine recipes!
Bon appétit!

BEIGNETS

2 cups of self-rising flour
1 Tbsp. Crisco
1 Tbsp. sugar
Vegetable oil for frying
1 cup confectioners' sugar, sifted

1. Combine the flour and Crisco in a bowl with a wire whisk until the mixture resembles coarse cornmeal, with perhaps a few lumps.
2. Warm ¼ cup of water in the microwave oven until barely warm to the touch. Pour the water into a large bowl, add the sugar, and stir until dissolved. Add the flour mixture and blend it with a kitchen fork. Work the dough as little as possible.
3. Turn the dough out on a clean counter and dust with a little flour. Roll it out to a thickness of approximately ¼ inch. Cut into rectangles about 2 x 4 inches. Let sit while oil heats.
4. Pour oil to a depth of 1 inch in a large, deep skillet and heat to 325°. When the beignet dough squares have softened and puffed up a little, drop 4-6 at a time into the hot oil and fry until light brown. Turn once and fry the other side. Drain on paper towels.
5. Dust with confectioners' sugar and serve hot.

Makes 12 to 15 beignets

CREOLE-CAJUN JAMBALAYA

¼ cup vegetable oil

4 lb. chicken-leg quarters—each cut into 4 pieces, bone in

2 lb. andouille or other smoked sausage, cut into ¼-inch-thick slices

2 large yellow onions, coarsely chopped

2 green bell peppers, coarsely chopped

2 ribs celery, coarsely chopped

2 cloves garlic, chopped

2 cups chicken stock

2 Tbsp. Worcestershire sauce

1 Tbsp. Tabasco

1 Tbsp. salt-free Creole seasoning

1 Tbsp. salt

1 bay leaf

1 tsp. dried thyme

½ tsp. dried marjoram

4 cups (uncooked) Uncle Ben's rice, or similar parboiled rice

2 green onions, chopped

3 sprigs flat-leaf parsley, chopped

4 dozen large fresh shrimp

1. Heat the oil in a Dutch oven. Add the chicken and sausage, and brown the chicken all over. Add the onions, peppers, celery, and garlic, and sauté until they wilt. Add the chicken stock and 5 cups of water. Bring to a simmer, stirring to dissolve the browned bits in the pot.

2. Add the Worcestershire sauce, Tabasco, Creole seasoning, bay leaf, thyme, and marjoram. Bring to a
   boil, reduce the heat and simmer for 30 minutes.
   Remove the chicken and set aside. Stir the rice into
   the pot. Cover and simmer for 30 minutes.
3. Meanwhile, remove the chicken meat from the
   bones and set aside. When the rice is cooked, stir in
   the chicken, green onions, parsley, and shrimp. Continue to cook, uncovered, gently stirring occasionally,
   until the rice starts to dry out. Adjust the seasonings
   as needed.

Serves 12 to 15

ROAST BEEF PO'BOYS

Roast Beef and Gravy

4-6 lb. inside round of beef, trimmed
Salt and freshly ground black pepper
4 ribs celery, coarsely chopped
2 medium carrots, coarsely chopped
1 large yellow onion, quartered
1 whole garlic bulb, outer papery skin removed and bulb
    cut in half
2 bay leaves
½ tsp. dried thyme
½ tsp. dried marjoram
¼ tsp. black peppercorns
1-3 Tbsp. flour
1 Tbsp. Worcestershire sauce

Sandwich

3 loaves poor-boy bread or 6 French baguettes, cut
    lengthwise and into sections 6-8 inches long

Garnish

1 head lettuce, shredded coarsely
8 tomatoes, thinly sliced
Mayonnaise
Dill pickle slices

1. Preheat the oven to 350°. Season the beef with salt
    and pepper. Put it in a Dutch oven filled about a

third of the way with water. Add the celery, carrots, onion, garlic, bay leaves, thyme, marjoram, and black peppercorns. Roast uncovered for 4-6 hours, turning the roast and adding water every hour or so. The water level should slowly drop, but don't let it get less than approximately 2 inches deep. The beef is ready when a meat thermometer inserted into the center reads 160°.

2. Remove the roast from the pot and place in a pan that will catch all the juices as it cools.

3. Skim off fat from the stock in the pot. Use a coarse sieve to strain the stock into a bowl, and then return the stock to the pot. Add any juices that come out of the roast as it rests. Bring the stock to a simmer. Skim off any fat that rises to the surface. Cook to a thin gravy consistency.

4. When you're ready to make sandwiches, preheat the oven to 400°. Bring the gravy to a simmer and whisk in the flour (only if the gravy appears to need thickening). Add the Worcestershire sauce and season to taste with salt and pepper.

5. Slice the roast beef as thin as possible. Collect all the crumbs and slivers that fall off and add this to the gravy. Stack as much sliced roast beef as you want on a length of French bread. Garnish with lettuce, tomatoes, mayonnaise, and dill pickles. Spoon on as much gravy as the sandwich can hold. Bake the assembled sandwich for about a minute to toast the bread.

Makes 12-18 po'boys

RED BEANS AND RICE

1 lb. dry kidney beans
¼ cup olive oil
1 large onion, chopped
1 green bell pepper, chopped
2 Tbsp. minced garlic
2 stalks celery, chopped
6 cups water
2 bay leaves
½ tsp. cayenne pepper
1 tsp. dried thyme
¼ tsp. dried sage
1 Tbsp. dried parsley
1 tsp. Cajun seasoning
1 lb. andouille sausage, sliced
4 cups water
2 cups long grain white rice

1. Rinse beans, and then soak in a large pot of water overnight.
2. In a skillet, heat oil over medium heat. Cook onion, bell pepper, garlic, and celery in olive oil for 3 to 4 minutes.
3. Rinse beans, and transfer to a large pot with 6 cups of water. Stir cooked vegetables into beans. Season with bay leaves. Bring to boil, and then reduce heat to medium-low. Simmer for 2-½ hours.
4. Stir sausage into beans and continue to simmer for 30 minutes.
5. Meanwhile, prepare the rice. In a saucepan, bring water and rice to boil. Reduce heat, cover, and simmer for 20 minutes.

Serves 8

GRILLED HONEY CANJUN SHRIMP

1 lb. shrimp, shelled and deveined with tails on
1 Tbsp. melted butter
1½ Tbsp. honey
1 Tbsp. lemon juice
2 dashes Cajun seasoning
Pinch of salt

Dipping Sauce (Optional)

1 Tbsp. olive oil
1 Tbsp. lemon juice
2 cloves garlic, minced
½ Tbsp. chopped parsley

1. Rinse the shrimp, pat dry with paper towels.
2. In a bowl, mix the melted butter, honey, lemon juice, Cajun seasoning, and salt together. Stir to mix well. Prepare the optional Dipping Sauce by mixing all the ingredients together. Set aside.
3. Combine the shrimp and honey mixture together, stir to coat well. Fire up an outdoor grill and grill shrimp with direct fire on both sides until they turn slightly charred and transfer to the top section to cook completely. Transfer to a serving platter and serve with Dipping Sauce.

Serves 3

SPICY GARLIC SHRIMP

Garlic Mayonnaise

½ cup mayonnaise
2 Tbsp. Dijon or Creole mustard
1 Tbsp. red wine vinegar
2 Tbsp. chopped garlic

Shrimp

¼ cup vegetable oil
1 Tbsp. chili powder
½ tsp. salt
¼ tsp. cayenne
1 tsp. chopped garlic
½ lb. small-to-medium shrimp, peeled and deveined
½ medium onion, sliced thinly
Four 2-inch square Jalapeño-Cheese Cornbread
¼ cup garlic mayonnaise

1. To make the garlic mayonnaise: Whisk all of the ingredients together in a bowl. It's better to make this a day ahead of time and refrigerate to let the flavors blend.
2. To prepare the shrimp: Mix the oil, spices, and garlic together in a bowl. Add the shrimp and toss to coat. Cover and let marinate in the refrigerator for 1-2 hours.
3. Heat a medium skillet over medium-high heat. Add the shrimp, the marinade, and the onion, and cook until the shrimp are pink and firm, 4-5 minutes, depending on the size of the shrimp.

4. Split the cornbread square and spread both halves with garlic mayonnaise. Put 2 cornbread halves on each of 4 plates and spoon the shrimp over the bread.

Serves 4

JALAPEÑO-CHEESE CORNBREAD

2 cups self-rising yellow cornmeal
1 cup self-rising flour
1 tsp. salt
4 eggs, beaten
1½ cup buttermilk
1½ cups roughly grated sharp Cheddar cheese
2-3 fresh jalapeños, seeded, membranes removed, and
   chopped
2 Tbsp. vegetable oil

1. Preheat the oven to 400º.
2. Blend the cornmeal, flour, and salt in a bowl. Combine all of the remaining ingredients, except the oil, in a second bowl. Dump the dry ingredients into the wet ingredients and mix completely. If it looks a little stiff, add a little water.
3. Heat the oil in a large cast-iron skillet, tilting the skillet around to coat the entire inner surface. Add the batter to the pan and bang it down on a towel on the countertop. (This evens out the top of the batter.) Place the pan in the oven and bake for about 30 minutes. Check its progress at this point, and continue baking until the top is light brown.
4. Allow cornbread to cool for 5 minutes, and then cut into squares. (Recipe can also be made as muffins or in molds that look like ears of corn.)

FRIED CATFISH

2 lbs. small catfish fillets
1 Tbsp. yellow mustard
2 Tbsp. lemon juice
1 Tbsp. juice from a jar of dill pickles
2 tsp. milder Louisiana hot sauce
1 tsp. Worcestershire sauce
1 cup corn flour (Fish Fry)
1 cup cornmeal
1 Tbsp. salt
½ tsp. granulated garlic
Peanut oil, for frying

1. Wash the catfish and remove the skin and any remaining bones. Cut them on the bias into strips about 1½ inches wide.
2. Blend the mustard, lemon juice, pickle juice, hot sauce, and Worcestershire sauce in a bowl. Put the catfish fillets into the bowl and toss to coat with the marinade. Let marinate for about 30 minutes, refrigerated.
3. Combine the corn flour, cornmeal, salt, and garlic with a fork in a large bowl. Put 4-6 pieces of catfish into the corn-flour mixture and toss to coat the catfish. Repeat with the remaining fish.
4. Pour the oil into a cast-iron skillet or a Dutch oven to a depth of 1 inch and place over medium-high heat until the temperature reaches 375°. Working in batches, fry the catfish until they turn golden brown. Remove with a skimmer or spider utensil. Drain on paper towels.
5. Serve with tartar sauce, pickles, hot sauce, and hush puppies.

HUSH PUPPIES

Vegetable oil, for frying, preferably oil previously used
    for frying fish or chicken
$1\frac{1}{2}$ cups white self-rising cornmeal
$1\frac{1}{2}$ cups self-rising flour
1 tsp. salt
$\frac{1}{2}$ tsp. salt-free Creole seasoning
$\frac{1}{2}$ tsp. sugar
1 cup canned corn, drained
2 green onions, finely chopped
1 small jalapeño pepper, seeded and membrane
    removed, chopped
2 sprigs flat-leaf parsley, chopped
$1\frac{1}{4}$ cups milk
1 egg, beaten

1. Pour the oil into a heavy saucepan to a depth of 1 inch. Heat over medium-high heat until the temperature reaches 350°.
2. Whisk the cornmeal, flour, salt, Creole seasoning, and sugar together in a small bowl. Add the corn, green onions, jalapeño, and parsley, and stir to blend well.
3. In a second, larger bowl beat the milk, egg, and ¼ cup of water together. Add the cornmeal-green onion mixture to the wet ingredients and mix with a whisk until no dry flour is visible. (Add a little more milk to the mixture if necessary. The mixture should be sticky but not runny or grainy.)
4. With a tablespoon, make balls of batter. Fry 4-6 at a time until they're medium brown; they should float

on the oil when they're ready. Remove and drain, and allow the oil temperature to recover before adding more hush puppies.

5. Serve as an appetizer with a mixture of equal parts of mayonnaise, horseradish, and sour cream, or tartar sauce. Or alongside fried seafood or chicken.

Makes about 18 hush puppies

CAJUN SPICE MIX

2 tsp. salt
2 tsp. garlic powder
2½ tsp. paprika
1 tsp. ground black pepper
1 tsp. onion powder
1 tsp. cayenne pepper
1¼ tsp. dried oregano
1¼ tsp. dried thyme
½ tsp. red pepper flakes

Stir together salt, garlic, paprika, black pepper, onion powder, cayenne pepper, oregano, thyme, and red pepper flakes until evenly blended. Store in airtight container.

SALT-FREE CREOLE SEASONING

2 Tbsp. granulated onion
2 Tbsp. freshly ground black pepper
1 Tbsp. paprika
1 tsp. granulated garlic
½ tsp. ground white pepper
¼ tsp. dried thyme
¼ tsp. dried marjoram
⅛ tsp. cayenne
Pinch of dry mustard

Mix all of the ingredients well in a jar with a tight-fitting lid. This will keep for about a year, tightly sealed, in a cool place.

Makes half a cup

SALT-FREE CREOLE SEAFOOD
SEASONING

2 Tbsp. granulated onion
1 Tbsp. freshly ground black pepper
1 Tbsp. paprika
1 tsp. granulated garlic
$\frac{1}{2}$ tsp. ground white pepper
$\frac{1}{4}$ tsp. cayenne
$\frac{1}{4}$ tsp. dried basil
$\frac{1}{4}$ tsp. dried oregano
$\frac{1}{4}$ tsp. dried thyme
Pinch of dry mustard

Mix all of the ingredients well in a jar with a tight-fitting lid. This will keep for about a year, tightly sealed, in a cool place.

Makes half a cup